A Well-Manicured Murder

To my lifelong
heart friend —
Enjoy!
Georgia Adams
aka
Patricia Browning

A Well-Manicured Murder

by

Georgia Adams

Cover design by Diana Black

First edition: September, 2009

ISBN 978-0-9794916-7-2

Georgia Adams is the pen name of Patricia Browning, Joann Dunn and Karen McColgan.

A Well-Manicured Murder

is a

LitChix Murder Mystery

Acknowledgements

Thanks to Chris Roerden, editor extraordinaire, who encouraged us after reading our first effort; attorney Edward T.M. Garland, who patiently answered our questions about Georgia criminal law; author Mary Saxon Wilburn who proofed our last edit for those mistakes that creep into all manuscripts, and Diana Black, author and graphic artist, who gave our book its distinctive cover design. You were all patient teachers and generous with your help.

Chapter 1

Sonny Simmons strode into his party, cowboy boots sparkling with his old football number twenty-five encrusted on the sides with diamonds, and waited to be admired. His baby blue silk-fringed shirt, the color of his eyes, reflected the light from a few too many crystal chandeliers. This was Sonny and wife Andrea's annual Panhandle University Panthers football bash. The guests swarmed beneath black and white streamers. The school's colors reflected the school's racial mix; the student body was white and the football team black. The music pounded, and the scent of barbecue filled the air.

Sonny had a drag queen's love of a drop dead entrance, although he would have decked anyone who suggested he wasn't one hundred percent foursquare American male. Sonny saw himself as the star of his own movie, with six pack abs and a killer smile. Everyone else saw him as an aging flush-faced jock, going to fat around the middle.

"Hey there, Bud." Sonny gave a friendly punch to someone who was nameless to him as were most of the guests. Remembering names was Andrea's job, and she did it well. His wife genuinely liked people; Sonny liked what people could do for him. Apparently they could do quite a lot, if the lavish house was any indication.

Sonny worked his way to one of the food tables. He started heaping barbecue and freshly shucked oysters onto an oversized plate. Ogden Williams, his attorney, sidled up and spoke in a low voice.

"Sonny, what the hell is the matter with you? Your last deal is an engraved invitation to the IRS. I'm not doing it. I want out of this whole shit-pile."

"Ogden, you're such a candy ass. Just do what I tell you. There won't be any trouble. The only way you'll get rid of me is if I die young, and that ain't about to happen." Sonny threw his arm around Ogden's shoulders with a smile that failed to reach his eyes.

"You keep eating like that and you won't make it another day," Ogden said, wiping a handkerchief across his forehead. Sonny slapped him on the back then moved on to the closest bar.

"And what's your name, Honey? You are the most beautiful…"

"Lenora Martin," the bartender interrupted, continuing to make drinks without looking at him.

Sonny looked at her skin, the color of single-malt Scotch, going down smooth and hot at the same time.

"How about jotting your number on a napkin so I can give you a call?" Sonny was a little out of breath. Good barbecue can do that to you.

"How 'bout I do what I'm paid to do and get your favorite, bourbon and Co' Cola?" Lenora looked him in the eye, pulled a glass from under the bar, added ice, and handed it to him.

"Now how'd you know that was my favorite? It's been a long time since I've had one of those. Honey, you have the bluest eyes I've ever seen."

"I know. My momma says I got 'em from my daddy." Lenora handed Sonny the drink wrapped in a cocktail napkin and let her slender dark fingers rest on his for a moment. "Pool 11:30" was jotted on it in ballpoint, right above the gold stamped name of the Simmons home, Chateau Soleil. Sonny glanced at the napkin and shoved it in his back pocket. His smirk betrayed as much pride in his virility as pleasure in a conquest.

Sonny barely had a chance to savor the bourbon and Coke, the drink of his youth, when the front door was flung open with such force that it took a chip out of the wall. There stood Mary Alma Harwick, with her smoky brunette mane and traffic stopping cleavage, dressed in scarlet and screaming her lungs out.

"Where is that son-of-a-bitch Sonny Simmons?" Mary Alma glared at the bar. "I see you over there, you no good bastard, hiding behind that damned barbecue. Come here and face me like a man and tell me why I was not invited."

Sonny downed his drink and hurried to the front door, hoping to move Mary Alma out before any more damage was done. He spoke as softly as possible, "Mary Alma, get yourself on out of here. This is not the time . . ."

Coming up fast behind Sonny, Andrea chimed in, "Get out of here, you whore! And don't ever come into my home again!" Andrea's shouting may not have matched Mary Alma's in volume, but she had home court advantage. Pointing a blood red manicured nail at the door, her fury reflected by the glitter of ten carats of diamonds, Andrea advanced on her enemy.

Sonny's voice had a pleading note as he addressed the two women, "Now ladies, let's be civilized. Surely we can talk quietly." His voice was calm, almost jovial, but there was panic in his eyes. Mary Alma swatted Sonny's plate. It shattered on the black and white marble floor.

"Sonny, I told you not to bring your latest bimbo into my house and I meant it. Get her out of here or you can move into that damn condo with her."

Unaware that Andrea knew of his little arrangement with Mary Alma, Sonny was momentarily unsure of what to do. Getting Mary Alma back outside still seemed like the best course of action. He put his hand under her elbow and tried to guide her back out the door.

Mary Alma stood her ground. "Oh, no you don't, Sonny. You aren't pushing me out of here. You decide right now. It's me or her."

Sonny had heard the "me or her" speech from numerous girlfriends, but he suspected that Mary Alma meant it. Taking her arm more firmly, he propelled her with greater force. Mary Alma struggled free and let out a string of curses. "You bastard! You told me that you were leaving the bitch. I'll see you in hell for this." Mary Alma yanked her arm out of his grasp, stomped out the door, got in her silver Porsche, and shot a rooster tail of gravel behind her as she peeled down the driveway. Swerving hard to the left, laying rubber for a good block, she disappeared into the warm Atlanta night on West Paces Ferry Road.

Chapter 2

Trish Townsend, Andrea's cousin, came in the front door. "Andrea, you look wonderful, but who was that in the driveway? A crazy driver almost hit me."

Andrea dabbed her eyes with a tissue and took a deep breath. "Come on in, Darlin'! Bless your heart. It is so good of you to come to my little party. Let me get you something cold to drink." She threw her arms around Trish and furiously air kissed both cheeks.

"You missed a humiliating spectacle; it's a long story. I'll tell you about it later. Come in the study. I can barely hear you out here." The party crowd filled the front hall, gossiping about the Mary Alma outrage at full volume, loving every minute of it. Andrea took Trish's hand, weaving her way through the throng into the study's relative calm.

"Much better." Andrea brushed her hair back with her fingers. "Between football mania and a juicy new scandal, thanks to Sonny, the noise got unbearable." Trish and Andrea, standing side-by-side, looked more like sisters than cousins. Born minutes apart in the small north Florida town of Lake City, both were tall willowy blondes and their forties had been kind to them. Andrea looked especially glamorous. Her black and white jumpsuit revealed a figure maintained by hours with a personal trainer. Her blond hair fell in waves, nearly covering the Hermes panther print scarf knotted around her throat. She stood on impossibly high Manolo Blahnik zebra-print stilettos.

"So, back to your question. The terrorist that almost hit you was Sonny's latest mistress, Mary Alma Harwick, putting on a show. I know Sonny loves me, but sometimes..." Andrea's eyes began to tear.

Trish hated to see her cousin in such obvious pain.

"Everyone knows you aren't to blame for his behavior. Just ignore it."

Andrea gave a sigh and attempted to smile. She was back on track as the welcoming hostess. "Here you are, Sugah," Andrea lifted a drink from a passing waiter's tray and handed it to Trish, who stared at the pale yellowish concoction over crushed ice in a Martini glass.

"What exactly is this?"

"Why Darlin', that is our drink of the evening. I call it a Panther Piss Martini. It's vodka and a little vermouth-not much of that-and sweet tea with lemon. You'll love it, I know you will."

"Isn't that the same drink you used to make when we were in college? I remember your drinks were famous." Trish attended the larger state university in Tallahassee, but Andrea's parties, even then, pulled in a wide-ranging crowd.

"Well aren't you clever to remember that! It's almost the very same, except in those days I called it the Sorority Sister. Back then it had a cherry on top."

Trish stared at Andrea. "Are you all right Andrea? Really?"

"I'm just fine, Sweetheart. That ugly episode with Mary Alma on top of party jitters, I guess, is enough to make me a little shaky. Actually, I've done very little to prepare for tonight. Claudia has handled almost everything. She is so much more than a personal assistant. I couldn't live without her. Excuse me a minute, Sugah. I see someone I have to bring in here. Don't you go away."

Andrea sailed back into the crush toward the front door. Trish looked around the study. Sonny and Andrea had added some art since she was last in the house. One painting was enormous, almost life-sized, of a handsome chestnut Thoroughbred in the winner's circle, Sonny standing alongside holding the reins with one hand and a silver trophy with the other. Evidence of an expensive hobby with a good excuse for Sonny to be in Palmyra, Virginia with his horses, although his time there was not all spent at the stables.

"Here she is," trilled Andrea, coming up behind Trish. A short serious-looking woman trailed behind her. Trish turned to see Cay Curtis.

"I'm running off again," Andrea said, "but I'll be back. I invited an interesting man I want Cay to meet." With a broad wink, Andrea headed in the direction of the dining room.

"I wish Andrea wouldn't do that." Cay said. "I'm happy single and I want to stay single. I have no desire to be a nurse or a purse." She glanced around the room. "If I ever did find another man, I can guarantee you he wouldn't be at this party."

"Good to see you, too, Cay." Trish laughed, hugged Cay and brought her out of her bad mood. "I thought you weren't going to come tonight. I see you're wearing black and white sox with your Birks to match the Panthers' school colors."

"An accident, I assure you. I wasn't coming tonight. I told Andrea not to expect me. I was tired and out of sorts, but then I thought, why not go. It's better to be with the LitChix, even in a hullabaloo like this, than home alone. Wait, what am I saying? I have a P.D. James waiting for me."

"Well, I'm glad you picked the Chix. P.D. will wait."

"I've never been to Sonny and Andrea's house before," Cay said. "Do you think this place is Andrea's taste, or is it Sonny's?" Cay scrutinized a Leroy Neiman painting on an easel.

"Oh, this is definitely Sonny's taste." Trish said. "Andrea's flashy, but she's the same good ol' girl from Lake City she's always been. Sonny likes to dazzle people with his wealth."

"It does inspire a kind of awe. The outside is a mess with those columns and balconies, and those nudes holding up the *porte cochere.* The house screams tacky, but it must have cost a fortune."

"Sonny has a fortune to spend," Trish said. "He can turn just about anything into money. Andrea told me he vowed he'd show everyone that Sonny Simmons wasn't just some hick from Possum Pocket, West Virginia. He could live in Buckhead with the Turners and the Coxes and have as good as they had. Maybe better. Chateau Soliel is his way of proving it."

Trish sipped of her drink and made a face. "I think all of this is just Sonny being Sonny. He likes to stand out, even in the way he dresses."

Cay scanned the people around her. "Have you seen Jordan?"

"I was about to suggest we go look for her. I'd love to get her Jersey take on this party. Find food and you'll find Jordan." Cay tossed her drink into a plant. The two started toward the open French doors at the far end of the den.

Trish saw Jordan at a carving station in the dining room, piling roast beef on her plate.

"Yoo hoo, Jordan!" Trish waved, hoping to catch Jordan's eye. Trish definitely had the height advantage, while Cay was lost, collar-bone high to everyone else. Plunging ahead, Trish and Cay reached the buffet table just as Jordan finished filling her plate.

Jordan saluted them with her martini glass. "At last! Real people. Trish, stop shaking your head. Nobody heard me. They are all much too drunk. To the LitChix, my mystery sisters. Long may we read," then she drained her drink.

"Mystery sisters?" Cay said. "I love it. Jordan, how did you come up with that? You guys really are my family, you know."

"Jordan, you should wear blue all the time. It really makes your blue eyes stand out." Trish looked around for Jordan's husband. "Is Jim here?" Trish asked.

"What? Are you kidding me? He's training somebody somewhere. The Denver office, I think. I'm left raising our kid alone." Jordan changed the subject. "Look at all this food, would you? And there's more out there," she gestured to the tent beyond the dining room.

"The menu has Sonny written all over it," Trish said as Jordan took another bite. "Ribs, pulled pork, Buffalo chicken wings, oysters, not to mention carving stations for roast beef, smoked ham and who knows what else." She looked over the selections on the linen covered tables. "And barbecue sauce. Lakes of it. If Sonny can't put his signature sauce on food, he doesn't eat it. Since he puts it on everything, that isn't limiting. What a gourmet."

"So, Jordan, were you here for the big hoo-ha?" Trish asked. "Fill us in. I missed the whole thing, although Mary Alma nearly hit me on her way out. I didn't want to ask Andrea too much about it."

"Oh, it hardly bears repeating. But I will." Jordan's eyes twinkled. "One of Sonny's mistresses came in and made a big drunk scene. Actually it was pretty awful. Mary Alma Harwick got into a shouting match with Andrea and then Sonny hustled Mary Alma out while she threatened him. Then she squealed her tires and was gone. That's about all I got out of it. Typical Buckhead party, if you ask me." Jordan looked at Cay. "Now, getting to something I care about, have you seen the upstairs?"

Cay shook her head. Jordan wiped the barbecue sauce from her lips and put her plate down. "Then let's go."

"Do you think we should be doing this?" Cay whispered as she, Jordan, and Trish climbed the stairs. "This carpet is so thick it's like walking in quicksand."

Jordan shook her head. "Of course we should be doing it. You think Sonny built this McMansion and doesn't want people to see it? I'm surprised he isn't giving guided tours. I see an open door; we can kinda casually peek in." Tiptoeing in spite of herself, Jordan led them down a barrel-vaulted hallway lined with paintings of nymphs and naked maidens.

"Do you hear something?" Cay came to a stop, eyes wide. "Someone's in there. We should go back." Cay turned toward the stairs just as they heard Andrea's shrill voice.

"How dare you think you could do that to me and get away with it? Do you think I'm stupid? I know exactly what you're trying to do. I'll see you six feet under before I'll let you pull that on me." There was a slapping sound, and scuffling noises from behind the bedroom door. The LitChix scrambled through the closest door into a bathroom and locked it.

"This is not where I want to be," Cay said. "Too much information."

"Cay, you're such a coward. Maybe we should go in there. What if Andrea needs help?" Jordan made a fist. "Back in Jersey we knew how to take care of creeps like Sonny."

Cay looked at her watch. "Do what you want to, but I am not walking into a domestic dispute. How long do we have to stay in here? It's getting hot. I want to start home by ten-thirty."

Jordan looked at Trish. "And she's a night owl, too. Remind me Cay, why are we friends?"

"Because we're mystery sisters. You said so yourself, smarty pants."

"Right. I forgot. Love ya, sis," and Jordan gave Cay a quick hug.

Trish reached in her purse for a miniature Baby Ruth, tore it open with her teeth, and took a bite. "Okay. Give it a couple more minutes and we'll open the door. If we don't hear anything, we can run for the stairs."

Jordan applied lip gloss while Cay kept track of the time on her watch. When two more minutes were up and there were no new sounds, Jordan peered out. She listened, squared her shoulders, and stepped out as if she were exactly where she intended to be. The little parade headed downstairs where all three picked up another drink from the bar and tried to act casual, while looking around for Andrea.

"Poor Andrea," Trish said. "She should have divorced Sonny a long time ago. He has such an inflated opinion of himself. I'm sure this latest episode is just an example of the stallion expanding his herd, but, really, what a jerk."

"Damn straight," Jordan said, lifting her glass. "He's a man who deserves a 'whuppin,' as you say down here."

"He might deserve it, but guys like him never get it," Trish said.

"You never know," Jordan said. "You just never know."

Chapter 3

One hundred yards behind Chateau Soleil, a slender man, all in black, was stretched out carefully along a magnolia limb. Positioned there since nightfall, steadying his Norwegian Vapensmia on its little bipod, the man known as The Gypsy peered through the night scope toward the unfinished pool. It was too early for any action. He had been told his target would come into view around midnight.

Action of another sort began somewhat earlier below his perch. A gorgeous blonde appeared wearing what looked to be a black bikini and stiletto heels. On closer inspection, the bikini turned out to be lace undies. While The Gypsy was a master of self-discipline, the woman was definitely a distraction. She began speaking to someone she called "Buck baby," encouraging haste because she didn't want anyone at the party to miss her.

The man answering to "Buck baby" came into view, a big blond in boxer shorts, muscles going soft, an aging Brad Pitt look-alike. Always thinking of an avenue of escape, The Gypsy knew he could eliminate this Buck character if necessary. Refocusing his attention on the back of the house, The Gypsy wanted to take his time, go slowly and quietly, and give the excellent service that had gained him an international reputation. Below him, Buck appeared to be using the same MO with the gorgeous blonde. He was taking his time, going slowly and quietly, and giving excellent service.

The area along the far side of the pool was empty, except for a couple of lawn chairs, perilously close to the pool's edge. He saw someone walk briskly across the rear of the house, apparently coming from the party tent and entering a door into the garage. She came out of the garage door with a second person. Probably another woman, but with dark slacks and white shirt, he couldn't be sure.

The Gypsy had been told that his target would be alone, but the scene was quite confusing. Below him, on the chaise under the magnolia, the woman offered encouragement, Buck grunted and she praised him lavishly.

Now a dark-haired woman in a red dress appeared by the chairs at the far end of the pool. Where had she come from? It was just a little after 11:30; what were all these people doing? The Gypsy had to admit in spite of his professional experience, he had been distracted briefly by the goings-on below.

Soon, a man fitting the description of Sonny Simmons came around the side of the house and staggered in the general direction of the lawn chairs. The Gypsy cursed under his breath. Sonny was supposed to be alone, yet a whole army was out there with him. The Gypsy understood this to be a clean, straightforward hit. In the course of his career, he had done messy jobs, but this one had been represented as quick and easy. He should have charged more.

One of the women put her hands on Sonny's chest and shoved him into a chair. She was speaking to him, shaking her finger in his face. The Gypsy couldn't hear what she was saying because of the music and the party noise coming from the house, but the delivery did not look friendly.

The woman in the red dress stepped forward. She wound something around Sonny's neck and leaned back, using all her strength to pull it tight. Sonny moved in slow motion as he grabbed at his throat and clawed the air. The third tormentor wore dark pants. Her white blouse was all that really showed, the rest of her blended into the night. She swung and hit Sonny on the head with something obviously heavy, like a statue, but small and dark.

The Gypsy hated disorganization. No one told him amateurs would show up and steal his thunder. This was turning into one of those Chevy Chase vacation movies. He wanted to do the job he was paid to do and leave.

Directly below him once again he heard a disturbance. Buck, tripped on a tree root while dressing, fell hard and let out an expletive, which the blonde promptly shushed. "Do you know what it would mean for both of us if we were caught?" She let out a little giggle and added, "That's probably one reason this is so much fun."

The Gypsy heard the scraping of the heavy back gate as a half dressed Buck eased it open and squeezed through. Concentrating on the view through his scope, the Gypsy saw Sonny trying to stand but wobbling back and forth. The Gypsy realized he was going to have to take his shot whether the women moved away or remained where they were. He had been on this job long enough and wasn't coming back another day.

As Sonny teetered on the edge of the pool, The Gypsy smoothly squeezed off a single shot. It pierced its target just above the collar button. Sonny fell with a sickening thunk, landing twelve feet below on the empty concrete bottom. The sound was covered by a salsa beat coming from the speakers in the buffet tent. The Gypsy was grateful his Vapensmia had a silencer, one of the few military rifles so equipped. The blonde getting dressed below him didn't even notice.

Still watching through his scope, The Gypsy saw one of the women pick up a large silver-colored pot and toss the contents on Sonny's crumpled form. The air filled with the smell of barbecue sauce.

The blonde, now dressed, headed toward the main house, and the three women disappeared into the door at the rear of the garage. The Gypsy slid out of the tree as sinuously as a snake. A small tear in the sleeve of his favorite black turtleneck annoyed him. He moved quickly, breaking down his gun and putting it in the tennis bag he left in the shrubs near the gate. As he pulled the gate open just far enough to slip through, he heard a scream from the back of the house. Sonny had been found.

Chapter 4

"Was that a scream? I hate it when somebody screams. It's never good." Cay jumped out of her chair.

"Where's everybody going?" Jordan asked, looking toward the back door. "Probably some drunk fell in the pool. I say we stay right here until we find out what happened. Besides, it's my job to keep Cay from having a panic attack."

They heard a man in the entry hall say, "Please, stay calm. Someone has been hurt. Dr. Munro is out there to help. I've called 911, so be patient."

"Who's talking?" Cay asked standing on tiptoe. "I can't see who it is."

"I don't know who's speaking," Trish said. "Some short middle aged man."

"Well that sets him apart," Jordan said. "They are in such scarce supply around here."

"Where's Andrea? And Sonny? Do they know what's going on?" Trish wondered aloud.

Lacking further information, the guests settled down, most of them getting fresh drinks and finding a place to sit and gossip. The unexplained scream offered the most interesting topic of the evening, more so even than the dramatic arrival and equally dramatic departure of Sonny's mistress, Mary Alma Harwick. The party definitely felt over. Trish, Jordan, and Cay followed a number of other guests into the study.

"Where do you think the scream came from?" Cay asked.

Trish was now really worried, since neither Andrea nor Sonny had shown up. "I'm certain it came from outside. My guess is it came from behind the house. The scream sounded like a woman. Omigosh, you don't think Andrea is hurt, do you?"

"My impression of Andrea is she's a girl who can take care of herself," Jordan said. "Of course I don't know her as well as you do, Trish."

Trish nodded. "Never underestimate Andrea. Because she is so glamorous, a lot of people dismiss her too quickly. Blonde jokes don't apply to her. She's actually very smart and perceptive."

Cay looked around. "Seems to me lot of people have already left. A whole pack of fortyish bottle blondes are gone. Probably a good thing. Their expressions of concern would definitely be limited by their Botox treatments."

Trish asked. "Do either of you see Ogden, Sonny's attorney? If he were here, we'd know it, because he would be managing everything."

"If Ogden is who I think he is, I saw him sitting right over there about a half hour ago with a piece of pecan pie. That man can eat," Cay said, with a certain admiration in her voice.

Jordan suddenly elbowed Cay and Trish and jerked her head to the right.

"Ow!" Cay said loudly. "What . . . ?"

Jordan gave her a stern look, held her finger to her lips while jerking her head again.

A man was speaking in a low voice to two others who were leaning in closely. "I overheard someone say his neck was broken, but there was something funny about it."

"What do you mean, 'funny'?" one of them asked.

"Like maybe that wasn't what killed him. There was other evidence...."

"If that was Frank Munro you overheard, he's no cop," the third member of the group said. "Hell, he's barely a doctor. How does he know what's evidence?"

"Something about a black panther statue. I know Frank was comforting Andrea back there, but I couldn't hear any more. The police came and pushed us back inside."

Jordan's eyes grew huge. The unmistakable flash of blue and white lights reflected through the arched windows from every direction.

A woman stepped into the front hall and raised her voice. "I'm Detective Morrow with the Atlanta Police Department. We need to take statements from each of you before you leave, so get comfortable and expect to be here for a while."

"Did you hear that? There's no doubt about it," Trish's voice took on a frantic note. "A crime has been committed, maybe murder, and those men said *his* neck, so it's a man who's dead. We've got to find Andrea right now." Trish forged ahead toward the kitchen. "Follow me," she called over her shoulder. "Someone back here may have seen her."

Trish pushed through the heavy door into the kitchen. "Excuse me, I'm looking for Mrs. Simmons. Has anyone seen her? Oh, Mrs. Berry, it's good to see you. Have you seen Mrs. Simmons?"

Mrs. Berry, the caterer, spoke up. "Mrs. Townsend, I'm so glad to see you. I haven't seen you since I catered your poor husband's funeral. I'm so worried I'm 'bout to have a heart attack." Mrs. Berry was breathing heavily. "There has been such a commotion out back, and someone told us to all stay inside, don't nobody leave."

"I'm worried, too. If I could just talk to Mrs. Simmons maybe I could get some answers for both of us."

Mrs. Berry rubbed her hands together. "I think she's in the breakfast room with a big, rude man. They came through here a second ago. That man didn't even take off his hat in the house." Mrs. Berry raised her voice. "Keep on cleaning up, everybody. As soon as the police say we can go, I want to leave this place. I don't like to be anywhere near a dead person if I can help it."

"A dead person and a man with a hat?" Cay hissed. "She said he was wearing a hat!"

"What is that supposed to mean?" Jordan asked.

"It means he is with the Hat Squad-the homicide cops. They wear these forties-style fedoras. What we overheard must be true. Some man must have been murdered! Could it be Sonny?"

"We can only hope," Jordan quipped. Trish frowned at her.

Mrs. Berry was still talking to Trish. "I gotta let my people go home. Somebody needs to get in here and tell us what's going on and when we can go."

"I couldn't agree more," Trish said. "When I find someone in charge, I'll make sure they talk to you."

"I'd appreciate that, yes I would," Mrs. Berry said.

Trish nearly stumbled over Cay and Jordan as she turned back into the hall. "Let's check in the breakfast room."

Cay grabbed Trish's arm. "Trish, the man who came in was with the Hat Squad. That's homicide...."

"Hurry up. We've got to find Andrea," Trish said, picking up the pace.

She tapped on the breakfast room door. A man's voice answered. "Yes?"

The Chix looked at each other. "Is Mrs. Simmons in there? This is Trish Townsend, her cousin." Trish was attempting to sound as calm and as authoritative as possible.

The dark-haired policewoman, Helen Morrow, opened the door. "Yes?" she asked.

Trish looked over Morrow's shoulder, "I'm Mrs. Simmons' cousin, and I'm looking for her."

"Oh, Trish!" Andrea fairly shouted. "Darlin', I'm fine. There has been an accident, a terrible accident, and as

soon as I know what's happened, I'll let you know."
Andrea, who had been sitting in a yellow plaid armchair,
stood, looking a great deal less than fine. "Sweetheart, I'm
mortified to have everyone put out this way. I hope it won't
be much longer."

Andrea's assistant Claudia was also in the room,
standing next to Andrea's chair. Claudia placed her hand
on her employer's arm and whispered something quietly to
her. Trish noticed Andrea was barefoot, covered with
blood, and reeking of barbecue sauce. Turning to the
policeman, Trish said, "And you are?"

"Detective Bongiovanni. We'll be talking with the
rest of you shortly. For now we need to speak to Mrs.
Simmons privately." The Chix looked for the man's hat,
trying not to be obvious. Jordan spied it on a side table and
nudged Cay, who crossly nudged her back.

Trish stood up straighter. "The kitchen staff needs
to know how long you need them here, and so do the
guests. It's quite late. Surely you don't need everyone to
stay,"

"I'm afraid right now we do, Ma'am," Detective
Bongiovanni said firmly. "And this investigation will go
faster if you all just wait in the other room."

"Andrea, do you need for me to stay with you? I'd
be happy to," Trish said, giving a harsh look to the
detective. As gracious as Trish was, she was not going to
be patronized or treated dismissively. Jordan and Cay
watched, feeling Trish was doing better on her own than
with a couple of tongue-tied sidekicks.

"Trish dear, I'll talk to you shortly. I promise. I'm
just finding out some things myself." Andrea was starting
to shake.

Trish was now visibly upset. "Look at Mrs.
Simmons! She's in shock! Certainly you can see that. She
needs to lie down and she needs a doctor!"

Claudia spoke up. "Mrs. Simmons, why don't you sit down." Looking at Trish, Claudia said, "This is a great strain for Mrs. Simmons, but as soon as the detectives are finished with us, we'll go upstairs and she can see you all there, isn't that right, Mrs. Simmons?"

"Yes, that's right, dear. Trish, I'll see you, Cay and Jordan, upstairs." Andrea sat back on the yellow chair. Frowning, Detective Bongiovanni firmly shut the door.

"Well, I never," Cay said. "Who does he think he is? And as for that woman detective..."

"Did you see it? Did you see his hat?" Jordan was clearly excited. "You don't think that they think that Andrea . . .? Oy, this is just like *Law and Order*. That Detective Bongiovanni is for sure from Jersey. I'd know that accent anywhere."

"I don't feel good about this at all," Trish said, as they went back into the study. "With all the police here, something really bad has happened. That means Andrea is in there with two detectives all by herself. I have to call Ogden, right now. He's not a criminal attorney, but Andrea needs a lawyer with her." Trish reached in her purse for her cell phone. Whispering and stuttering a bit from the nervousness that was beginning to overtake her, she told Ogden in no uncertain terms that he was needed back at the Simmons' residence immediately.

"I'll be there in twenty minutes, tops," Ogden said.

* * *

At about the time Ogden was rushing up West Paces Ferry to Andrea's aid, the bartender, Lenora Martin, was guiding her gray Toyota sedan south on I-75, past the industrial area south of Atlanta on her way to McDonough. Lenora had told her mother she would be late coming to her house, but would go to church with her in the morning. Lenora took a short detour through a gas station to drop three pairs of paper shoe covers and latex gloves into a trash can.

Mary Alma was at home wearing her slippers and bathrobe, curled up with a Patricia Sprinkle mystery and a martini. Although dressed suitably to greet unexpected guests, she was obviously in for the night, playing the role of the woman scorned.

After helping Andrea upstairs, Claudia was excused by the detectives and brushed past Ogden at the sitting room doorway. She slipped noiselessly down the staircase, wondering who had called Ogden and chiding herself for not thinking to call him herself. She admired her recently manicured hand resting on the curving banister. Andrea advised her to always wear disposable gloves for any chore that might chip a nail or soil her hands. Claudia was beginning to appreciate the wisdom of that advice.

The young man at the bottom of the stairs guided her to an evidence tech taking fingernail scrapings.

"Your hands, Ma'am," he said, holding a little metal tool and a plastic evidence bag.

"Of course," she said, smiling at him. "It would be my pleasure."

Chapter 5

"Trish, can y'all come up here?" Andrea called from the top of the stairs. The last of the police and partygoers had left. Even the caterers had gone. It was nearly three in the morning. "Y'all are such dear friends to stay all this time. Come on up right now, please."

When the three reached the top of the stairs, they each hugged Andrea.

Trish studied Andrea's face. "Andrea, are you all right? Shouldn't you be going to bed?"

"I couldn't sleep right now, Trish. I'm so keyed up, and I won't take the sleeping pills Frank Munro left for me. I don't want them."

Andrea wore a black silk negligee with matching slippers. "The police took the clothes I had on tonight. Even my favorite shoes. I'll probably never see them again. They were Manolo Blahniks from Neiman's, you know, not some cheap Chinese knock-offs. Such a waste."

"Let's go back into your sitting room, dear," Trish said, taking Andrea by the arm. "Do you want some decaf or a diet coke without caffeine?"

"No thanks. But, I really need to talk."

The three LitChix followed Andrea into the cream and blue sitting room, where she headed to a delicately carved settee. She picked up her white Maltipoo, Mr. Chanel, and hugged him close.

Cay said, "Can you tell us what is going on? Or if it's too painful, don't worry, we'll understand."

Andrea sighed. "Cay, that's so kind of you. I don't even understand what's going on myself. I was out by the back gate, and when I started back to the house. I saw something in the pool."

"I thought the pool was a construction area," Jordan said.

"It is and we did have it blocked off. I'll explain why I was in the back in a minute. Maybe I heard a noise, I'm not sure, but I walked over by the pool. When I looked down into the pool, I saw…" She started to cry. Trish handed her cousin a box of tissues and gradually she regained her composure.

"There was Sonny, just lying in the empty pool on the cold concrete. I climbed down into the pool and put my arms around him. Then Frank Munro got in the pool and pulled me off Sonny. He told me he'd called an ambulance. Sonny was all sprawled out, with his head at a funny angle. I think I asked Frank if Sonny was dead, I'm not sure. Pretty soon the ambulance people were all over the place, and someone helped me out of the pool. It's like a horrible dream." Andrea dabbed her eyes. "My panther scarf was around Sonny's neck. I remember taking the scarf off earlier because I got hot, but I can't remember where I left it. There was blood and barbecue sauce all over Sonny. The sauce got all over my jumpsuit, and I guess that is why the police took it. Did anyone tell y'all what happened? I really don't know any of the details yet."

Trish shook her head. "No one has told us a thing, dear. The police just took our names, phone numbers, statements, fingerprints, and scraped under our fingernails. They said they might need to question everyone again later. This is the first we're hearing of any of this. We got no details from the investigators." She patted Andrea's shoulder. "You have to be exhausted, Andrea. Don't you think you should try to sleep now?"

"I have to confess something or I will never be able to rest."

Trish, Jordan, and Cay looked at one other with undisguised alarm.

"Maybe you shouldn't tell us anything, Andrea. It might be better to just talk to your lawyer right now."

Trish could imagine one of them being called at a trial to give damning testimony against her cousin.

"I have to talk to someone about this, and I trust y'all completely. Mama always said that confession is good for the soul."

Cay resisted the urge to put her fingers in her ears.

"I was behind the pool tonight with another man."

This is not what Trish had been expecting to hear.

"Oh, Andrea, you don't have to explain anything to us."

"Don't stop her now." Jordan's remark drew glares from the other Chix, so she sat up on the edge of her chair and said, "What? Confession is good for the soul, right?"

"I was entertaining a gentleman caller."

"A 'gentleman caller?' Like a lover? You were having an affair?" Trish was having a hard time absorbing Andrea's remarks.

"I guess you could call it that," Andrea said. "Buck and I have had this little thing going, and it's hard to find time to get together during football season."

"Did I miss something? What does football season have to do with it?" Cay was no football fan, but she knew enough to know a *non sequitur* when she heard it.

Andrea's words were muffled as she buried her face into Mr. Chanel's fur. "Buck's an assistant football coach for Lovett. Fall is a very busy time for him."

Trish nearly fell off her chair. "Dear God, Andrea! That is treason. How could you possibly?"

"I know. That's why it's so hard to tell anyone about it. For the mother of a Westminster Wildcat, let alone the quarterback's mother, to be dallying with a Lovett football coach, well, it's unthinkable. I know. That's why I didn't say anything to the police. I knew Buck would lose his job, and I would be thrown out of the Catbackers." Andrea hung her head and the tears flowed.

In Andrea's circle, there were forgivable circumstances for killing one's husband, but there was never a forgivable reason for canoodling with the enemy.

"When and where exactly did this, ahh, event take place?" Jordan was now fully involved in the scenario that Andrea was describing.

"Under a magnolia, at the far end of the pool. It's almost impossible to see under those low branches, and it's close enough to the back gate so Buck could meet me without being seen. He left before I spotted Sonny. Oh, that image of Sonny splayed out there, with his beautiful blue silk shirt soaked in barbecue sauce - I can't get it out of my mind." Andrea pulled another handful of tissues from the box.

"You can see why I didn't tell the police. I'm sure they wouldn't leave Buck out of it. No, I told them I thought I heard a noise, and I was checking to make sure no guests had wandered into the pool area by mistake."

"Bless your heart." Trish moved to the settee to hug her cousin. "I am so sorry. This is such a mess. I know you are terribly confused and upset right now. It's amazing you're so composed."

Cay had all she could handle for one evening. "Andrea, I don't want to leave you alone tonight, or rather this morning. But I have to get home now, and I'm sure that Jordan and Trish do too."

"Don't you worry a bit. Y'all go on home. Claudia will stay with me. I'll be fine now that I've talked things out. I'll be in touch tomorrow. Maybe by then some of the horror will be easier to handle."

Each of the Chix hugged Andrea again, telling her they were available for her night or day. They opened the sitting room door to leave. Claudia appeared and held the door for them. She looked as fresh in her gray silk pants and shirt as she had at the beginning of the evening. She smiled and thanked them for being with Andrea. Then she entered the sitting room and firmly closed the door behind her.

As the three approached the front door, Trish asked, "What do y'all think of Claudia?"

"She gives me the creeps." Cay shivered.

"A refugee from the Addams Family," Jordan said, and the others agreed.

Chapter 6

Claudia opened the massive front door to Chateau Soleil. Trish brushed by her with a curt "I'm here to see my cousin."

"She's in her sitting room upstairs," Claudia said.

Trish hurried up the stairs, then knocked on Andrea's bedroom door.

"Trish, is that you? Come on in. Oh, I'm so happy you came over. Darlin', I need a shoulder to cry on." Andrea jumped up from her sitting room settee and hugged Trish. "I know I've been hard to reach, Darlin', Claudia is very protective. She's been a real watchdog. I'm sorry you were worried."

"Worried? When I couldn't even talk to you, I decided to come on over. I wasn't about to let Claudia keep me away.

"Sweetheart, I couldn't believe it when Claudia told me you were at the police station this morning. Tell me all about it," said Trish, taking a seat on one of the blue toile slipper chairs.

"It was awful." Andrea sat back down pulling Mr. Chanel into her lap. "Ogden went with me to police headquarters. Today! Sunday, if you can imagine. I lost a whole day in that hideous place."

"Start from the beginning and don't leave anything out," said Trish.

"Well, first Ogden called me early this morning and said the police wanted me to answer a lot of questions, and it would be better for me to cooperate. I shouldn't say much at all, just answer their questions and not volunteer anything they didn't ask. Oh, and Ogden told me to dress down, as if I wouldn't know what to wear. I was so groggy, but then I remembered Sonny at the bottom of the pool, and of course the children and I couldn't stop crying."

"Do the children know what is going on?" asked Trish.

"Telling them about it was horrible. EJ and Mary Marshall were staying overnight with friends, so Claudia got them early this morning and brought them back home. I had to tell them their father was dead. I was so afraid they would hear the news from someone else before I could tell them.

"Poor Mary Marshall just cried. She didn't say a word; she cried and went in her room. She wouldn't talk to Claudia or to me. EJ was really serious. He wanted to know what happened, and of course I still don't know exactly. He's brooding, staring at sports on TV. I called Missy in Texas and couldn't get her. I left a message on her machine to call Mama, but I didn't say anything about her Daddy. I guess she'll call me back later, or maybe I'll call her again.

"And, omigod, Sonny's parents and his brothers! How could I have not called them first thing? Oh, Trish . . " and she started to cry.

"Bless your heart. You can't think of everything. This has been a terrible ordeal for you," said Trish. She went to the dresser and brought some tissues for Andrea.

"I do need to calm down. Where was I? Oh, yes, Ogden told me to dress down. That really did annoy me. I'm not flashy, am I?"

Trish hesitated, choosing her words carefully. "What did you wear?"

"I wore my black Donna Karan knit pants and the matching sweater-coat thing, oh, and low-heel black shoes. If Donna Karan isn't dressed down, then I don't know what is. I wore the small wedding ring Sonny gave me when we first married. The other rings he bought me later seemed too flashy for a meeting with the police. I wore my pearls." Andrea put Mr. Chanel on his cheetah covered bed.

"Anyway, Ogden drove me to the police station downtown. What an awful place. You wouldn't believe the terrible shade of institutional green they've painted the walls. To think we taxpayers foot the bill for something so ugly. The same two detectives, Bongiovanni and Morrow, were there, and a bunch of others. Everybody was looking at me like I'm some kind of criminal. They put Ogden and me in this bare room, just a table and chairs, and the detectives wanted to know what happened, so I told them. I'd already told Ogden and he said it was okay as long as I didn't elaborate on anything, so I was very careful. I just told them that I was out near the back gate and I heard something so I walked over by the pool. There was Sonny all crumpled on the bottom. I screamed and that's all I remember." Andrea stood up and began to pace..

"Ogden may not be a criminal lawyer, but you can trust his advice." Trish was relieved to hear Andrea had been careful with what she told the police. Andrea was given to a certain effusiveness that could get her in trouble.

"Of course, they asked me why I was by the pool in the first place, and I told them I was just checking to make sure no one was back there, since the pool wasn't finished. I told them the same thing when they took my shoes last night. My zebra-striped Manolos with the little chain ankle straps. They were so cute, but I did ruin them with the mud from the construction dirt. Anyway, off they went to the crime lab. I suppose they won't be wearable after this.

"When they understood I wasn't going to say anything else, they showed me a bunch of pictures. They said they were evidence. Trish, I think those detectives are trying to blame me for Sonny's death!" Andrea stopped to blow her nose.

"Blame you? That's sheer nonsense," Trish said. "After all, what real evidence could they have?"

"For one thing, the two detectives showed a picture of Sonny lying in the pool with my beautiful panther scarf wrapped around his neck. So much blood on it! It's ruined forever. And they have one of my acrylic nails in a baggie. They said it was caught in the fringe of Sonny's shirt. Later I figured out how that happened. He and I had a little altercation earlier in the evening. I slapped him and broke my nail, so it probably got stuck then. But I didn't want to say anything, because if they knew we'd had a fight, who knows what else they would have thought." Andrea poured herself a glass of water, offering some to Trish.

Trish shook her head. "Andrea, I need to confess something to you, too. Jordan, Cay, and I were touring the upstairs during the party and overheard you and Sonny fighting. We hid in a bathroom until we thought you all returned to the party. We didn't say anything about it to the police, either, for the same reason you didn't. Sorry, Sweet Pea."

Andrea gave her cousin a quick hug. "Don't fret, Trish. I appreciate y'all caring so much. Where was I? Well, then there was the panther statue from his desk. It was in the pool too. They think he was hit on the head with it. I've got no idea what to think of that. Do you? They said the lab techs were looking at the blood and sauce on my jumpsuit."

"I know it's hard, but go on. I need to hear everything." Trish patted Andrea's knee.

"Oh, yeah, they had these notes." Andrea heard Trish gasp and asked, "Are you okay? Sure you don't want some water?"

Changing her mind, Trish got up and poured herself a glass.

"Any way, Sonny had two notes on him, and they found a third back by the pool house. He had a cocktail napkin in his back pocket that had something like '11:30 Pool' on it, and a gushy note on pink scented paper from some 'Mystery Woman' who said she had the hots for him and would give him a 'present he'd never forget' if he met her at the pool at midnight. Then there was my note."

"Your note? You wrote a note to Sonny?" Trish tried to remain calm.

"Yes, I wrote a note, too, but I didn't tell the police it was mine. I didn't have to. It was on my blue monogrammed paper and it said 'meet me at the pool *house*, 11:00 . *Pool house*, mind you, not *pool*, and blah blah blah, but I didn't write it to Sonny. It was for Buck. He must have dropped it when he took off his clothes."

Trish felt as if she needed to come up for air. People have been sent to the chair on less evidence. "Heavens to Betsy, Andrea, do you realize you lied to the police? All right, maybe you didn't exactly lie, but you said you didn't tell them you wrote one of the notes. You're going to have to tell the police about Buck. There was a note on your paper, in your handwriting, about meeting someone at the pool house. The police must think you wrote it to Sonny, maybe to lure him to the pool and murder him. What did Ogden say? You did tell him, didn't you?"

"Wel-l-l, sorta."

"Andrea, what do you mean 'well sort of;' you need a *criminal* attorney. Be sure you tell him about Buck. I need something stronger than water. Let's go downstairs to the bar."

Chapter 8

Helen threw an empty paper coffee cup from the night before into the trashcan by her desk at police headquarters. "Well, that was quite a performance Mrs. Simmons gave yesterday. What do you make of her story?" Helen Morrow raised her eyebrows.

Jerry Bongiovanni remembered the scent of Andrea's Shalimar which had temporarily masked the disinfectant odor of the police headquarters. "Wow, I wouldn't be human if I didn't say Mrs. Simmons, ah, Andrea, is something." He cleared his throat a little too loudly. "However, I think she better come back with more ammo than that corporate lawyer had in his arsenal. There are too many holes in her story and too much evidence against her."

Jerry rose from his scarred desk. "Let's go in and talk this case over with the Chief."

The two detectives made their way through the maze of desks to the office of Chief Miller Cantrell. They waited outside the glass window to his office, while Cantrell finished a heated telephone conversation. He slammed down the receiver and motioned to the two detectives while reaching into his bottom desk drawer for a roll of Tums.

"I don't need to tell you that we are on the hot seat with this Simmons' murder. I just got off the phone with the Mayor and she says give this case top priority. It isn't everyday that someone with his money and connections gets whacked on West Paces Ferry Road, and at his own party, for Chrissake. Damn, there had to be over a hundred of Atlanta's major players present. I need results fast." He chewed a couple of Tums. "Okay, bring me up to date."

Jerry and Helen glanced quickly at each other, and Helen started telling about their investigation. "Based on the reports of the partygoers, Andrea Simmons publicly threatened her husband at their party when his mistress, Mary Alma Harwick, appeared. We understand this wasn't the first violent argument they'd had over his extramarital affairs. Granted, Mary Alma and the missus weren't the only people there who had a serious grievance with the deceased, but . . . ." Her voice trailed off.

"All right, how about hard evidence? What did the investigative team come up with when they finished their examination?"

Jerry answered, "The mud on Mrs. Simmons shoes matched the construction area around the pool. Her jumpsuit was covered with Mr. Simmons' blood and with barbecue sauce. The scarf Mrs. Simmons was seen wearing earlier in the evening was wrapped around his neck. A black panther statue from his den was in the pool with his blood on it." Jerry cleared his throat. "We also found one of Mrs. Simmons' fake fingernails embedded in the fringe of the deceased's shirt which could have come off during a struggle. If that's not enough, Mr. Simmons was poisoned."

"Good God! Is that what killed the poor bastard?" Cantrell asked.

"No, the amount of poison was just enough to disorient him, probably to offset the advantage of his strength and size."

Helen added, "Plus Mrs. Simmons was found at the bottom of the pool with him. A note in her handwriting on her personal stationery, inviting him to join her at 11:00 was found under the magnolia at the opposite end of the pool."

Jerry continued. "Two more notes were found, each in a different handwriting. One was on the back of a cocktail napkin. It said, 'Pool at 11:30'. Another was on scented pink paper, inviting him to the pool area at midnight. This guy was busier than an adolescent in heat."

Miller stared at the roll of Tums. He appeared to be reading the directions on the label.

Jerry rubbed his forehead and said, "I can't figure out whether the wife planted those other notes to confuse us and muddy the waters or . . . well, there is the overkill factor. This guy was poisoned, strangled, and hit over the head with his own panther statue. But none of those things was the cause of death. The ME said the fall into the pool broke his neck, but Mr. Simmons, Sonny, was probably dead when he hit the concrete. He was shot in the throat with a high-powered rifle, probably just before he fell. The bullet in Sonny was a type used in some military rifles, probably one with a silencer. That's clearly the mark of a professional shooter, an assassin. We deliberately kept that last piece of information out of the press and from our interview with the missus. We wanted to see if she would trip herself up. She didn't."

Helen continued, "Examination of the property in the back of the house showed considerable activity. Several footprints were there around a chaise lounge. Two sets most likely were male and one matched the stiletto heels that the wife wore to the party. She could have been with a male accomplice.

"There are also a set of footprints of a man's bare feet, but they seem to match up in size with one of the two sets of male shoe prints. Clearly there were two men. There is no way to tell if they were made at the same time or not. It rained two days ago, so the ground was still soft."

Jerry began to pace in front of the chief's desk. "Man, it's a mess," he said. "There's too much evidence. She doesn't seem dumb enough to leave so many damning clues around, but, it's possible."

"Seems to me this is too much for one person to pull off." The Chief frowned. "Interpol sent us information earlier this week just days before the Simmons murder. The Gypsy arrived in Miami. You've heard of him, I'm sure.

He's tied to some very big hits internationally." The chief put a handful of Tums in his mouth. "It is possible he came to Atlanta, but he isn't cheap. It would take someone with considerable means to hire him. First thing Monday, check Mrs. Simmons' bank account for any interesting withdrawals. Also, find out about Simmons' insurance, and take a look at his will as soon as it's filed. Find out if anybody gets rich all of a sudden."

"We've already checked her bank accounts this morning," Jerry said. "She has a monthly withdrawal of $1,000.00 we can't pin down. That's not enough to buy her a hit man, if that's what we're looking for."

Helen said, "For a woman like her, it's probably tips for take-out food. That's pocket change, Jerry."

The chief pounded his chest. "What about other suspects? Talk again to some of the guests at the party; find out more about the mistress who made such a big scene. Who are Sonny's enemies? Talk to some of the movers and shakers that did business with Sonny. I saw Mag Cramer on the guest list; ask him about Sonny's activities. Get me a suspect quick before I have to run out of my heart burn medicine."

"Okay," said Helen. "We'll get started right now. Someone must have hated Simmons enough to kill him or know someone who did. Who would profit the most by Simmons' death besides his widow? Who would be that afraid of him or hate him that much?"

Jerry stared at his notes. "There is the female bartender who several partygoers mentioned as staring at Sonny, followed by a brief conversation between them. Probably nothing, but you never know. We didn't get a chance to talk to her last night. Let's start with Mag Cramer and the mistress, then move on to the bartender."

Helen put her hands on her hips. "We might as well take on the Chamber of Commerce as Mag Cramer.

He practically remade downtown Atlanta. You've been in Atlanta long enough to hear about him, right?"

"In Jersey, that's where we look first," said Jerry. "Follow the money. I don't think the South is much different. Money talks; could just as easily be, money kills. Besides, he may have some insights. Let's go and pay Mr. Cramer a visit."

Chapter 9

"I love the Midtown part of Atlanta," Detective Morrow said. "If I were younger, no kids, I would definitely live here. This is the real city."

Morrow and Bongiovanni were driving north on Peachtree Street, where Ponce de Leon intersects and the Fox Theater anchors blocks of coffee shops filled with the young, executive, and artsy heaped together. Heading off the surface streets onto a short section of highway, Bongiovanni circled around to a new power building, One Cramer Plaza, a high-rise that housed Cramer International on the top ten floors. It followed a popular development motif in Atlanta: give a building a name that could not identify its location, and scrap the names of the old historic streets that were bulldozed for its birth. Thus, One Atlantic Plaza, One Financial Center, giving newcomers and cab drivers fits, since mapmakers could not keep up with the commercial building boom.

The rule with cops is to leave the police cruiser at the curb, ready to move out. But One Cramer Plaza rose far from the curb, buried in the center of a large, heavily landscaped park, and the street in front, such as it was, was more of an entrance to the highway. It took some driving around for the two detectives to figure out how one actually got into the place.

"If this isn't the damnedest thing," Bongiovanni said through clenched teeth. "One more try and I'm going to drive over the curb, through his pansies and right up to the front door."

"Go ahead." Morrow chuckled. "I'd like to see it." She was disappointed when Bongiovanni found a lane that turned into the park and eventually wound its way toward the building.

"So this Cramer guy is a real estate developer, is he? Damned worst way to get into a building I've ever seen," Bongiovanni muttered.

One Cramer Plaza was an impressive glass pyramid. Above the thirty-second floor, each additional floor was a little smaller than the last, so the top of the building narrowed to a pinnacle that almost disappeared into the clouds. Mag Cramer's office occupied the very top of the pinnacle, and the symbolism was not lost on the public.

According to the marble directory in the lobby, Cramer International started on the forty-seventh floor. Although Bongiovanni would have preferred to come unannounced, he knew better than to assume Mag Cramer would be in, so he had made an appointment.

Getting off the elevator at forty-seven, Morrow and Bongiovanni stepped onto a mushroom colored carpet so deep they felt off balance. In the distance, a perfectly groomed young woman sat at an oval table. There were no papers, no phone, nothing to indicate she had anything to do but sit and look exquisite. Only a single white orchid, growing from a pale celadon pot, interrupted the immaculate rosewood surface. The walls featured eclectic modern works of art, reflecting Mag Cramer's obsession with the new and innovative.

"I'm Detective Bongiovanni. This is Detective Morrow. We have an appointment with Mr. Cramer."

The young woman, whose features were an ambiguous combination of Asian, Native American, and perhaps, but not necessarily, Caucasian, gave them a glowing smile. Detective Morrow knew without even looking that she would have a flawless French manicure.

"Welcome," she said in a near whisper. "Will you have a seat please? Mr. Cramer will be right with you." She stood and escorted them to a cluster of luxuriously cushioned chairs. "May I get you something? Coffee? Tea?"

"No thank you," Morrow said. There was no sign that the elegant receptionist had called Mr. Cramer or buzzed him or whatever she did. She simply returned to her desk and sat in an attentive but calm pose.

Within minutes, a door in the paneling slid open and Mag Cramer stepped out. The receptionist rose and smiled with an expression of total devotion on her face. "Mr. Cramer, the Atlanta Police Detectives are here to speak with you."

Big and solid, with a full head of silver hair, Mag looked like the oil roustabout he had been when he started business. Now he wore a suit, but an ordinary off-the-rack brand, and a tie without a pedigree. The little development business Mag began had grown exponentially and eventually became a conglomerate specializing in the renewal of vast city areas. On scraped-clean ground, not just in Atlanta but around the world, rose Mag Cramer developments: homes, offices, shops, sports arenas - in fact, whole new cities to which tenants flocked. Those who were displaced, well, they weren't the sort who had real clout.

With only a nod to Helen, he extended his hand to Bongiovanni first. Then in a gesture both patronizing and imperious, he put both of his beefy hands around Helen's, acting as if he had called the police, not the other way around. Cramer said, "Thank you so much for coming. It's a pleasure to see Atlanta's finest. Come up to my office and let's talk." He led them to a door almost hidden in the paneling. Inside the small elevator, Mozart played quietly, and a slight, scented breeze blew. A small bench was placed against the rear wall, in case the trip proved too exhausting. Detective Bongiovanni didn't see any buttons or feel any movement. A moment later, the door opened into Mag's office.

Cramer's office was smaller than expected, but the wall of glass looking southeast over the city made it seem infinite. To the right of the elevator stood a glass and chrome conference table covered with blueprints and renderings.

"This is a new office for me," Mag said. "Up until a few months ago, I had an office looking northwest. I like to see my developments, and that was where we had four or five major projects going up. Those are mostly finished now, and *that* is the future." He waved his hand toward the windows. "Don't see anything, do ya? Just some trees and some low industrial buildings, some shitty little neighborhoods. Oh, pardon me, ma'am. I don't like to swear in front of a lady. Anyway, all that," and he waved at the window again, "is about to change. Mag Cramer is moving in. Lofts, condos, top line stores, offices, and theaters will soon sprout up, leading the way to quality growth. Schools will follow, the whole income profile will shoot up, meaning more tax revenues for the city and there you have it, a new productive part of this great city is born. Makes me feel like a kid, creating cities with Legos." He grinned boyishly. "Could I give you officers a tour of our place up here? Everything's state of the art."

"Thank you, Mr. Cramer," Morrow said, "but we should probably get down to business."

"Oh ho, I like the way the lady thinks," Mag said. His tone was always condescending when speaking to women. "Well, let's get down to business, then. What can I do for you?"

Bongiovanni began. "You can tell us what you know about the night of the murder at the Simmons' party."

Mag sat down behind his desk. "That was a horrible, horrible tragedy, wasn't it? I'm still in shock. What is the world coming to? Murdered at his own home no less. I was no fan of Sonny's, but he was a young guy on the move and was a big player on the Atlanta scene. What killed him, exactly?"

"We're not ready to disclose that information," Bongiovanni explained as he started taking notes. "If you weren't a fan of Mr. Simmons, as you say, why were you at his party?"

"That was my wife's doing. Melanie volunteers at the High Museum with Sonny's wife, and she said we'd be there, but Melanie sprained her ankle and couldn't go, so she asked me to drop by on my way home from the office, around eight p.m.."

"You were coming home from the office at eight p.m. on a Saturday night?" Bongiovanni made an entry in his notebook.

Mag gave him a weary smile. "That was an early night. Deals don't get made on a nine-to-five schedule, Detective. I am here until close to midnight many nights, and that includes Saturdays. My one rule is I don't work Sundays."

Detective Morrow said. "So, you were saying that you didn't particularly like Mr. Simmons. Could you elaborate on that?"

"Oh, I liked Sonny, all right, as a person. I wasn't a fan of the way he did business. Making deals, a man's word is everything. We have all the lawyers and accountants to put it on paper, but the deal maker has to have everybody's trust or he ain't got jack shit. Pardon me again, *ma'am*. I'm gonna have to watch my mouth."

"Think nothing of it, Mr. Cramer," Morrow said. "I've heard considerably worse."

"Yes, well, the point is, you couldn't always trust Sonny, business-wise. He was a wily cuss, and he'd try to get out of a deal with you if something better came in through the back door in the meantime. No one would've faulted him for it if he had been upfront, but he was always sort of sneakin' around, if you get my drift. You never knew where you stood with Sonny. He could be your best friend while he was tryin' to cut you out of a deal behind your back. That's a real good way to make enemies."

"Were you an enemy?" Morrow asked.

"Me? No ma'am. Sonny didn't bother me. I was in the business a long time before he was, and I've watched him and others come and go. You see, Sonny thought he was a lot bigger and more powerful than he really was. He thought he could get away with anything. But there are much bigger players out there, and not just in the development game, either."

"What game would you be talking about?" Bongiovanni asked.

"Financing, lending for starters. There are the legitimate sources, banks, S and L's, that sort of thing." Mag hesitated carefully choosing his words. "There is the under-the-table-stuff, unfriendlies, as we would say."

"Unfriendlies? You mean governments?" Helen looked puzzled.

"That, and factions, international interests looking for a place to put money, work their way in, finance their own projects. Hell, I don't know specifics. I stay out of that stuff, but there are rumors, and some of them are probably true. Sonny was spread out all over. He had those damn horses in Virginia, and an offshore oil rig I heard was going under in more ways than one." Mag rearranged some pictures on his desk. "He was spread way too thin, is my guess, and he didn't always do business with patient-type people in three-piece suits, if you get my drift."

"Can you tell us anyone else who knows about these rumors? Anyone we could talk to?"

"Probably anyone at Sonny's party who's in the development business. His attorney, Ogden Williams, is known as one of Atlanta's most highly connected. He'd be a good place to start finding out about Sonny's enemies and activities. I stay far away from those questionable transactions. I can't afford to have any smell of that stuff clinging to me. I deal with municipalities, and there isn't a one that wants to have a scandal. Sooner or later, there would have been a scandal attached to Sonny. That's for sure. My sainted mama used to tell me, lie down with dogs, get up with fleas."

Detectives Morrow and Bongiovanni asked questions for another ten minutes, until it was obvious that no specifics were coming from Mag Cramer. They thanked him for his time and left business cards in case he should think of something. Mag walked them to the elevator and the door opened without the press of a button.

Once they were out of the building, Morrow said, "Well, that was interesting. I think he's a sexist pig. Aside from that, what do you think?"

"Me? I think he's got a crush on you," Jerry teased.

"Oh, yes, let me touch up my make-up. Oops, I don't wear any. Gag."

"I bet all that mysterious hinting about foreign governments and dirty deals is just a lot of noise. We should look closer to home. It is very strange that he never mentioned doing business with Sonny when other people have told us Cramer was in several ventures with him." Bongiovanni added, "Don't scratch through his name, yet. We may need to question him again later, if you get *my* drift."

They got into the car and headed north on Peachtree toward Mary Alma's apartment.

Chapter 10

Mary Alma turned on her intercom. "Yes?"

The condo doorman said, "Ms. Harwick? A lady and a gentleman are here to see you. From the police department."

Mary Alma paused for just a second. She had been expecting this. "Send them up. Thank you." Now the entire building would be buzzing. The lobby could be empty when someone arrived, but within the hour it seemed as if everyone knew who was visiting whom.

Mary Alma quickly put Vick's salve in her eyes. It went to work immediately, irritating her eyes making them red and watery. She started dabbing her eyes with a monogrammed lace hankie. Mary Alma answered the door with the caution she always used. She looked out the peep hole, then opened the door a crack with the chain lock still in place to examine their credentials before permitting Detectives Bongiovanni and Morrow to enter.

"Good morning. I'm Mary Alma Harwick. How may I help you?" She ushered them into her burgundy and navy living room, with its wide expanse of glass looking south toward the city. Mary Alma knew why they were here, of course, and she hoped she also knew just how to help them. She was glad she picked the outfit she wore. A beige silk blouse and matching Ellen Tracy silk shantung slacks, which spoke of a conservative dignity that her situation lacked. Everything about the room and her clothes were chosen deliberately to emphasize her brunette beauty. She was the main attraction and she wanted to leave no doubt about that.

Mary Alma motioned them to two comfortable chairs. Sonny had been adamant that this not be a "girlie" apartment with decorative but uncomfortable furniture. The club chairs were upholstered in a Scalamandre burgundy plaid. "May I get you coffee or sweet tea? Both are already made," she offered with a shaky smile.

"No, thank you," Morrow said. "We have a few questions about the night Mr. Simmons was killed. Are you familiar with what I'm talking about?"

"Of course. I was there for a while, as I'm sure you know. And I saw the awful news on the TV ." She dabbed at her teary eyes. *Take the initiative,* she thought. *Be disarmingly forthcoming. Be appropriately sad.* "Mr. Simmons and I had . . . had an . . . arrangement for quite some time, and I'd decided it was time for it to change. I was a bit indiscreet, I regret to say, and made something of a scene at the party."

"Do you know what time you arrived at the Simmons' house?" Bongiovanni asked.

"No, not exactly. Around nine, maybe a little later."

"And how long were you there?"

"Not long at all." Mary Alma gave a nervous laugh. "It turned into a shouting match with Mrs. Simmons. It was truly awful. I really don't know why I picked that night to confront Sonny. One too many apple martinis, I guess. I was back here before ten. I know that, because I watched the Fox evening news, then went to bed. Oh, I did make one stop on the way home. I went to the Publix up on Peachtree and bought aspirin and a salad. Then I came home."

"Did anyone see you there?" Detective Morrow asked, "Someone who might verify the time?"

"I didn't see anyone I knew, if that's what you mean. I probably have the receipt still in my bag, if you want it. Besides, wouldn't Publix have a video security camera that would back up my story?" Mary Alma wasn't sure why she threw in this last remark. She had to be careful. There was a danger in saying too much, either out of nervousness or increasing confidence.

"Are you sure you didn't go out again for any reason?" Morrow asked.

"Go out again? Where would I've gone? I am not a party girl, if that's what you are suggesting. I don't go to bars or play around. My relationship with Mr. Simmons was complicated. It wasn't shabby, though. I wanted him to decide between me and his wife." Mary Alma thought that her last line might not have been the best thing to say, but it was too late now. She really was going to have to slow down and think. She wanted this to be her first and last police interview. She daintily pressed her hankie to her nose and sniffed.

"How did you feel about Mrs. Simmons?" Bongiovanni asked.

Mary Alma registered a little surprise. "Andrea? At first I envied her, I guess, but once I knew Sonny was only concerned with his business interests, before his family, before me, before everyone, well, then I guess I felt sort of sorry for her. I could move on but she had children."

Helen asked, "Did you have a reason to think that Mrs. Simmons wanted to move on?"

"No, we didn't really associate. But I never had the impression she wanted out of the marriage, if that's what you mean." She used her hankie again wishing she had used less Vick's.

Changing the subject, Jerry asked, "Is this your condominium, Ms. Harwick? Do you hold the title?"

Mary Alma turned her full attention to Jerry, staring at him with her intense green eyes. "No, no this condo is – was - Mr. Simmons'. He said he bought it as an investment."

As Mary Alma answered the detectives' questions she was appraising their appearance. The woman looked tired, with shadowy circles under her eyes. All in all, for not wearing make-up, she was quite pretty. Her short dark hair curled and waved artistically, although with very little professional attention. *A better haircut and some highlights would help her appearance a lot*, thought Mary Alma. She noticed that Helen's hands were badly in need of a manicure. Short, ragged nails and untended cuticles. Mary Alma shuddered.

Bongiovanni, in contrast, had carefully groomed hands, smooth with even perfectly trimmed nails. *I'll bet he gets a manicure and doesn't tell anyone*, Mary Alma thought. His hair was cut very short. He reminded her of an actor she liked. *What was his name? Slender, dark, hooded eyes . . . I know,* she thought, *Stanley Tucci. He looks like a younger and taller Stanley Tucci.*

"Does that mean you will be moving, then?"

"What? I'm sorry, Detective Bongiovanni. I lost my train of thought for a second. Could you repeat the question?" Mary Alma knew she needed to focus on the matter at hand.

"Will you be moving?" he asked again.

"Well, I do have a lease here, just a little thing Sonny drew up to make sure that I had my rights, but the answer is yes, I will be moving. In fact, I've taken a small place in a high-rise farther up Peachtree." Mary Alma was looking forward to the move, because she would be closer to Phipps Plaza, where she liked to shop, and she could furnish her new place according to her own taste.

Morrow handed her a notepad and said, "If you have that address handy, we'd appreciate it if you'd jot it down for us."

Mary Alma took the pad with a perfectly manicured hand. Sonny had given her plenty of jewelry, most encrusted with large colored stones, but Mary Alma chose to wear, on her right hand, her great grandmother's wedding ring, a smallish emerald with a few diamonds on either side, set in rose gold, in the style late in the eighteen hundreds.

Detective Bongiovanni watched her write. Mary Alma had a sparkle about her that set her apart. Maybe it was her eyes; he wasn't sure. Mary Alma was vivacious and full of life just sitting still, and he could see her appeal to a man like Sonny, or in fact to any man. *She must have looked hot the night of Sonny's party. Everyone who had seen her storming into the house in a scarlet dress could describe her perfectly. Yeah, she definitely made an impression.*

"Tell us about your car, Ms. Harwick," Detective Morrow said. "The car you were driving the night of the party."

"I was driving my sweet old silver Porsche. And it is old. I bought it myself, with trust fund money I got when I turned twenty-five, and it's all mine. Mr. Simmons had nothing to do with it."

"Do you park it in the building garage?"

"Yes. My space is number forty-one, if you're looking for it. There's a security camera at the elevators and at the garage exit, which will help you confirm when I left and returned." Mary Alma flashed an innocent smile.

"We know all about those, but thank you, ma'am," Bongiovanni said. "Should we need them, we will go through procedure with building management."

Helen leaned forward. "Ms. Harwick, do you know if Sonny had enemies, or someone who hated him enough to want him dead?"

Mary Alma had anticipated this question. "Not really. Sonny made a lot of people angry, but I don't know of anyone who would risk actually killing him." She paused to give the impression she was thinking about her answer. "Sonny left a lot of furious people in his wake, but none of them were the kind to resort to violence. Lawsuits, in a heartbeat, but murder, no. Daddy washed his hands of Sonny and told me that he would never supply cement to him again. Sonny was too hard to deal with and didn't always pay his bills on time."

Helen leaned forward. "Oh, is your father's business Harwick Cement? I'm just making the connection."

Mary Alma smiled. "Yes, that's right. Daddy owns the largest cement company in the Southeast." She quickly looked serious again. "To be perfectly honest, Sonny never talked about his business to me. The only things I know are common gossip I've picked up being around my daddy and his friends."

Helen nodded.

Mary Alma resisted the temptation to ask the detectives anything about Sonny's death or whether they had a suspect, thinking she might open a can of worms for which she was unprepared. The detectives asked what she wore to the party and if they could see the dress. When she told them it was at the dry cleaners because she had spilled a drink on herself that evening, they seemed to lose interest in her clothes. Eventually they stood up to leave, everyone shook hands, and Mary Alma promised to keep herself available. The interview seemed undramatic and inconclusive, not what Mary Alma anticipated from the television programs she watched.

Although she hadn't smoked in some time and Sonny would have pitched a fit if he had known she was going to smoke in the condo, Mary Alma rummaged through some old handbags and found a few cigarettes in a crumpled package. She put one between her lips and went back in the living room to find matches. The first thing she found was the large, wand-shaped fireplace starter, and she lit up, nearly singeing her eyebrows in the process. Hands shaking, Mary Alma poured some vodka into a glass at the bar, threw in a couple of cubes from the ice maker, and sat facing the view.

Take a deep breath, she told herself. *You did fine. Relax, you have nothing to worry about. Don't forget to return Mother's Beemer.* She kept the mantra going in her head while she drank and smoked and stared out the window.

* * *

"So, what about *Miss* Mary Alma?" Morrow asked, once they got in the elevator. "With her lace hankie and antique ring, I got the picture - she's old Southern royalty. Her daddy is the second generation in the cement business. The King of Concrete." She gave a little snort.

Jerry raised his eyebrows. "Do I think she's guilty? No, that's not my first instinct, although it's too early to rule anyone out. She sure is moving into a new place pretty fast.

"Yes, she probably had motive; security cameras, and Publix receipts aside, but she doesn't look strong enough to have done Sonny much bodily harm, but where I come from, innocent people don't have such verifiable alibis. And as for..."

"Wait a second." Morrow answered her cell phone and gave reassuring instructions to one of her children, then said to Bongiovanni, "I don't think she really had opportunity, at least not from what I heard and saw today. Of course, she could be hiding plenty. She seemed pretty level headed, at least as level headed as one could be in her situation. The rich really aren't like you and me, are they, Jerry?"

"That's for sure." They exited the building and headed toward their white Crown Vic parked at the curb. "Here, you drive," and he flipped the keys to her. "Next stop, the bartender's. Lenora Martin's apartment is farther north on Peachtree. Drive till you get to Piedmont, then go right. She's in an apartment where Piedmont and Roswell join, near Old Ivy."

Detective Morrow turned a tire-squealing U in the middle of Peachtree and headed up the road.

Chapter 11

Lenora Martin lived in an older brick two story building with an inner courtyard. The place looked well maintained but less expensive than most of the apartments and condos nearby.

Detectives Morrow and Bongiovanni climbed the stairs to the second floor. Lenora's apartment was at the end of the hall. Their knock was answered by a voice from deep inside.

"Hold on. Just wait, okay?" A full two minutes later, the voice was closer. "Who is it?"

"It's Detectives Morrow and Bongiovanni from Atlanta Homicide. May we speak with you, please?" Detective Morrow was always careful to be polite, especially with women. It encouraged trust.

"Yes, of course. I just washed my hair. Give me a minute."

Jerry and Helen waited for a few more minutes. Then Lenora opened the door.

"Come in, officers. Sorry to keep you waiting." It was obvious she was telling the truth about washing her hair, because it hung in loose wet ringlets and dripped onto her shoulders. Even without makeup, Lenora was startlingly good looking. Her brilliant blue eyes and the perfect coffee-colored skin were a combination that made people stare whether they wanted to or not.

"It's 'Detectives,' not 'officers,' but that's all right," Bongiovanni said.

"Oh. Sorry. Would you like to sit down?" She led them into a small living room furnished in IKEA modern, with blond oak and blue and white canvas cushions on the sofa and club chair. Lenora pulled out a computer chair for herself, and Morrow sat on the sofa. Bongiovanni walked around and looked out of the window at her view of additional parking places and a narrow strip of woods.

"Lived here long?" he asked.

"No. I recently moved from my mother's home in McDonough." Her voice was steady. "May I ask why you're here?"

Jerry turned around to face Lenora. "You must have heard about the incident at the Simmons' residence. It has been on all the TV channels and the front page of the Sunday Constitution. I understand you were there. Is that right?"

Think carefully, take your time, be accurate she told herself. "Yes, I was there working for my Aunt Berry. She was the caterer. I work part-time with her to supplement the commission I get from a boutique in Buckhead on Paces Place."

Jerry continued. "What do you know about the incident concerning Mr. Simmons?"

"Well, I know that Mr. Simmons is dead, and he fell into his empty pool. The only thing I know is what I hear on TV, I don't take the Atlanta paper."

Helen spoke up. "Did you see Mr. Simmons the night of his party?"

"Yes, I did. Mr. Simmons came up to the bar and asked me for a drink."

"How did he appear to you Saturday night?"

"What do you mean?" Lenora asked.

"Was he angry? Agitated?

"He seemed in good spirits. In my opinion he had too much to drink. He was pretty red in the face and was flirting with all of the women."

"Did he flirt with you?"

"Of course. I mean, men always flirt with women bartenders. Just harmless stuff."

Jerry interrupted. "What did you think about that, his flirting with you?"

"Sir, excuse me, but if a little flirting upset me I could never be a bartender, could I?"

Jerry continued the questioning. "While you were working, did a Ms. Harwick come in?"

"The lady who caused the big scene? I'll say so. She was a whole lot drunk. She wasn't there more than a few minutes and then she took off in her car and laid rubber all the way up the road. It was something."

"What time did you leave?" Morrow asked.

"Not too long after that lady. Before ten, I'd say. I was getting a headache and Aunt Berry had plenty of help so she didn't mind my leaving."

"Did you come to your apartment after that?"

"No. I drove all the way down to my mama's home in McDonough. I promised to go to church with her on Sunday, and I didn't want to get up before dawn, so I headed down there and arrived around midnight. Mama was expecting me later, because I had told her I was working that night."

"Can we get in touch with your mother if we need to verify the time you got there?"

"Sure. Just don't scare her, please. She works so hard. I don't want her to think I'm in some kind of trouble. Do you want her number?"

"We'll call you if we need it," Morrow said. Verification by a loving mother was seldom valuable. "Is there anything you think we should know? Any observations you may have made, people who stood out for some reason?"

After hesitating for a moment, Lenora said, "I can't think of anything more to tell you. As I said, I wasn't there for the whole party. I'll call you if I remember anything."
She took the card Bongiovanni offered.

Leaving Lenora's apartment, Morrow thought of, but didn't mention, Lenora's perfectly manicured hands. She wondered, *does the whole world get a manicure but me?*

"So, what's your take on Lenora Martin?" Bongiovanni asked.

"Huh? Oh, I don't know. I'll have to think about her for a while and review my notes. Her story seemed to make sense, but it seemed so tidy somehow."

"You drive again?" he asked.

"Now I know how you get out of the office before I do," Morrow said, as she got into the car. "You do your paperwork on the move."

* * *

"Mama, I want you to do something for me," Lenora said. "Are you listening? Well, Saturday night I bartended for Aunt Berry before I drove down to see you. Do you remember that? If anybody asks you, I got to your house around midnight, all right? Yes, I know it was closer to two, but this is important. I want you to tell anyone who asks that it was around midnight. Now this is a secret talk you and I are having, okay? There was some trouble at the party after I left, and I don't want anyone to think I was still there. Does this make sense to you? I just don't want any trouble. Okay, Mama. I love you too. I'll be back to see you soon. Take your pills, Mama. Be good."

Lenora felt terribly alone, but she knew she could not contact Mary Alma or Claudia. She would have to wait until the following Saturday at ten when they all had appointments for manicures at Spa a Trois in Buckhead. Since their fortuitous meeting at Spa a Trois, where talk had turned to Sonny Simmons and a kind of frontier justice, they had made it their meeting place.

Lenora seldom drank, because she saw up close what it did to others, but she had some red wine on the sideboard, a gift from a dinner guest. After a couple of glasses, she was somewhat calmer and much sleepier. Lenora was glad tomorrow was her day off, because she would never make it in to work at the boutique.

I wonder if they will call the owner, she thought. *Damn, I hope not.* They dressed a lot of high profile women. *Any hint of scandal could get me fired.*

She needed to determine if she handled the detectives' questions well. It all went so smoothly, she didn't want any problems now. The only thing the three women had not planned on was Sonny falling into the pool. What had caused him to lose his balance at that moment? It still puzzled her.

Chapter 12

The procession of cars turned off Peachtree Street and pulled into the Second Ponce de Leon Baptist Church parking lot. Robert E. Lee Simmons, Bobby Lee to nearly everyone, bounced over the curb in his Humvee. His daughter, Tyler Louise and his wife Serena were used to a rough ride, but bouncing up and down as if they were on a trampoline was annoying when they were trying to look dignified.

"I'm glad we didn't bring anybody with us," Tyler Louise grumbled. "This car's embarrassing." At thirteen, Tyler Louise was embarrassed by just about everything her parents did, said, wore, or owned. But more than many thirteen-year-olds, she had issues. These were dealt with on a weekly basis by a therapist, but they remained persistent.

"Tyler Louise, you stay with me," Serena commanded. Tyler Louise rolled her eyes and slouched as much as possible. Irritation was beginning to show in Serena's voice. "Let's get into the church and sit down. We're here to mourn your Uncle Sonny, and we are going to show everyone he had a civilized family." They moved with a sizable group walking up a slight hill to the front of the church. Another clutch of mourners was gathered outside the front doors, having a last cigarette or exchanging gossip.

Second Ponce de Leon Baptist Church, an upscale Southern Baptist church, was located on the corner of Peachtree Street and West Wesley Road. It inhabits a section of town known as Jesus Junction. Across the side street to the south is the Catholic Cathedral of Christ the King and on the third corner to the north is the impressive

Gothic-styled St. Philip's Episcopal Cathedral. Without a doubt, Sonny was being eulogized in one of the holiest places in Buckhead.

Quietly and with as much dignity as possible, the mourners competed for an aisle seat to get the better view. Sonny's open ebonized mahogany coffin was displayed in the front of the sanctuary, blanketed with a spray of white calla lilies, baby's breath, and dozens upon dozens of white roses. Other floral arrangements sent by friends honored Andrea's request that all the flowers be white and the ribbons black.

One spray from the Virginia Racing Commission was in the shape of a horseshoe with a banner across it reading, "He ain't nothing but a winner!" This was one of Sonny's favorite quotes from Alabama football coach Paul "Bear" Bryant. Another particularly large arrangement was from the Panhandle University Alumni Board, honoring all the years that Sonny contributed heavily to its athletic fund. A satin ribbon proclaimed "Number 25 has crossed the goal line for the last time."

Most of the mourners were dressed in the latest fashions. Fortunately for the fashionistas, the new color for the season was black. Ladies glanced subtly at newcomers to assess the choice of designers. Were they wearing Chanel, St. John's knits, or Ellen Tracy? Carrying Vuitton, Hermes, or Fendi? Walking on Blahnik's or Ferragamo's? Designer clothing was *de rigueur*, and there were no acceptable substitutes.

Isabelle O'Brien, Sonny's secretary, sat discreetly in the back of the church. Totally unaware of any fashion standards or trends, her hair, black streaked with gray, was rolled into a style that had died with the fifties, about the time she was born.

She carried a rosary, and as soon as she sat down, she started silently mouthing her prayer, "Hail Mary, full of grace . . . ." Isabelle had been Sonny's right hand from the day he opened an Atlanta office off Chattahoochee Avenue in a primarily industrial area. Isabelle was discreet, efficient, and, most importantly, devoted to Sonny. She was one of the few present with red-rimmed eyes who seemed genuinely sorry about his death.

Isabelle shared a little house not far from the Amtrak station with her perpetually demanding mother. Sonny's office was a place of respite for her. She had no personal life to speak of, and labored uncomplaining most weekends and holidays, never taking a vacation. Those who knew both Isabelle and Sonny agreed that she was a saint.

The crowd softly mumbled speculating about the cause of Sonny's death. Everyone was still shocked over the latest news that his death was not an accident but a homicide. Sonny offended a lot of people in his life, but no one could imagine who would actually kill him or why. This sort of thing just did not happen in Buckhead.

The first rows of pews were reserved for Sonny's relatives from Possum Pocket, West Virginia, and Andrea's relatives from Florida. When the family filed in, the organ music swelled and the congregation rose.

Andrea came in wearing a sedate black Armani suit and a vintage Chanel hat with a veil. The women in the sanctuary nodded their approval. Her three strands of pearls and the diamond bow pin on her lapel completed the look of a tastefully dressed widow. She walked with her three children, Missy, EJ, and Mary Marshall, to the front row, accompanied by her parents.

"There's Mary Marshall," Serena pointed out to Tyler Louise. Mary Marshall was wearing a dark blue Betsey Johnson dress. She sat with eyes cast down, the picture of a bereaved daughter. In reality, she was text-messaging a friend about plans for later, but she was skillful at tucking her tiny phone where no one could see.

"You two spent some time together back at the house. Do you like her?" Serena asked. "Mary Marshall seems like a nice girl - uh, young lady."

"She's a cheerleader, Mom. What do you want? I asked her if I could touch her pom-poms."

"Were you rude, Tyler Louise?" Serena snapped. "You could learn a thing or two from her."

Trish and her family came in after the Simmons. Her deep turquoise Prada suit raised a few eyebrows, but it looked sedate enough to be acceptable.

Breaking with protocol, Andrea invited the two other LitChix to be part of the family processional and to sit with them on the front pews. Cay and Jordan were glad to honor Andrea's friendship by being included. As they took their seats, Cay whispered to Jordan. "Is that what I think it is? I can't look. Is it Sonny?"

"If you mean is it an open coffin, yes it is. Surely you've been to an open coffin funeral before."

"Yes, but I've never had a front row seat at one in the Baptist church. I don't have to go up there, do I?"

"Oy, Cay, stop being such a baby. No, you don't have to go up there. Just look the other way."

Cay concentrated on her hands, the funeral program, the crystal chandelier, and anything else but the sight of Sonny laid to rest in the polished black coffin lined with white satin.

"I don't know if I'm going to make it through this," Cay muttered.

The minister stood and walked slowly to the podium to begin the service. To Sonny's kin from Possum Pocket, this service did not have the emotional tug of a real country "home going." There was no outright weeping, no one was "moved by the spirit" to cry out Sonny's name, and the minister was never going to work up to a fever pitch at the unemotional rate he was going. Cay and Jordan tried to feel sad, but both thought Andrea was better off without Sonny. A large number of people checking their watches evidently felt the same way. Sonny's mother Miss Adeline and Isabelle were the only two crying audibly as the minister spoke.

"Today we bid goodbye to Elliot Earle Simmons, Senior, known to us all as Sonny. We shall see him again resting in the bosom of his Lord and Savior . . . " and so forth. Just plug in a different name and the minister's words could be for anyone. It was obvious he did not really know Sonny.

Turning to Jordan, Cay whispered, "Who's that?" She motioned to a beautiful bi-racial young woman sitting on the left side of the church.

"You mean that African-American girl? Or I should say 'woman,'" Jordan said. "Anyone who looks like that is no girl. She bartended the night of Sonny's party. Lenora Martin, that's her name. She works a lot of Buckhead parties. Why would she be here? Think maybe she was more than a bartender?"

The minister paused and nodded to Sonny's brother Big. "Jefferson Davis Simmons, brother of the deceased, will now say a few words."

Big was an imposing man. It was easier to imagine him in hunting camouflage than in the conservative dark suit he was wearing. Andrea had lent him one of Sonny's Ralph Lauren silk ties, in a vain attempt to upgrade his image for the critical audience he faced. Big and his twin brother Bobby Lee were pillars of their church back home, but were more than a little ill at ease in Second Ponce.

Big cleared his throat and tapped the microphone. "Hello there, folks. It wouldn't be right to bury my brother Sonny without saying some good words about him. From the time Sonny first held a shotgun, when he was just a little feller, he was a good hunter. Sonny could shoot straight in the fields and shoot straight with you in life. He was a man who spoke his mind. You knew right where you stood with Sonny, and it's true that some people didn't like that. We had a saying about him: 'He might punch you in the gut, but he would never knife you in the back.'

"I used to love to watch him play football. When Sonny had the ball, everyone had to scatter or he would run right over 'em." Big pulled at his tie to loosen it. "Sonny, I reckon you're in the biggest stakes game ever right now. We're countin' on you to catch one of them long passes from St. Peter, and he'll say, 'Why, it's Sonny Simmons. Make way everybody!' And St. Pete will open those pearly gates for you and you'll tell him your brothers Bobby Lee and Big and all the rest of the Simmonses are comin' right behind you. Sonny, one day up there with the Lord we'll have the biggest barbecue ever, with everyone who has already passed over. We'll all be reunited, and it'll be one hell of a party. Amen." The last was said as a shout.

As Big took his seat, the audience sat perfectly still. In an attempt to restore dignity, the minister stood, cleared his throat, and asked the congregation to rise and say the Lord's Prayer. Ogden Williams, Sonny's attorney, read a few Bible verses followed by the congregation singing one of Sonny's favorite hymns, *Just as I Am*. Then the organ music grew louder and the family made its exit out the side door, while the mourners, shaking their heads, moved toward the front exit. There was murmuring, never loud enough to be impolite, punctuated with "No, I never," "unbelievable," and sometimes "bizarre."

"That Big. He could say things better than anybody, couldn't he now," said Miss Adeline blowing her nose. "I didn't know my boy had such beautiful words in him."

"You done good, Son" said Vergy Senior and he thumped Big on his back.

"Where to now?" Cay asked no one in particular.

"On to the cemetery," Jordan said. "Did you see where Sonny is going to be buried?"

"Where?" Cay asked. "Who will have him?"

Joining her friends, Trish replied, "Apparently the oldest, most famous cemetery in Atlanta, that's all."

"Oakland? He's being buried at Oakland? That's so far away." Cay heaved a sigh as she fell back into the padded leather upholstery of the limo provided by the funeral home. "It will take us an hour to get there with the traffic."

Famous for its Civil War section, grand mausoleums, and the graves of many of Atlanta's most powerful and famous, Oakland took new "residents" at the rate of about one a month. The white limousines carrying the family led the funeral processional.

Cay rubbed her sore feet. "Why I thought wearing heels was a good idea, I'll never know. No one looked at my feet anyway. It's already been a long day and it isn't over yet. After the cemetery, we have to go back to Andrea's and offer our condolences. As soon as that's over, I am headed home. I'm suffering from sensory overload." Little did Cay know that the day was far from ending.

Chapter 13

It had been a long time since Cay had felt a car glide. Her practical beige Volvo wagon was inching toward the quarter million mile mark, an example of regular upkeep and earnest prayer. It ran dependably, but it didn't glide. The luxurious white limousine she shared with Trish and Jordan felt as if it were headed into deep space: quiet, frictionless, dark.

"Let's see what's in the bar," Jordan said, opening a burled walnut panel next to her seat. "No liquor!" she exclaimed. "Just Coke, sparkling water, and apple juice. Apple juice?" The cut crystal old fashioned glasses sparkled against the mirrored backing of the niche.

"It would be nice to have this all the time, wouldn't it?" Trish sighed.

"You couldn't get another car in your driveway," Jordan said.

"Oh, I'd settle for a smaller car. I wouldn't need a limo. A Rolls or a Bentley would do. Even a Mercedes. As long as it was beautifully upholstered and came with a driver."

"And dark inside," added Cay.

"You just want to take a nap," Jordan said.

"Yes, I do. And I may fall asleep before we get to the cemetery."

The limo headed south on Peachtree, past the condo tower famous as Elton John's Atlanta residence, then started the multiple turns leading to the interstate.

"Andrea's holding up well," Trish said. "I was proud of her and the children. They presented a dignified front for the funeral crowd."

"No offence to you or your family, Trish, but do you think Andrea killed Sonny? She could be fried," said Jordan.

"Jordan, that's so tacky," Cay said.

"Just asking," responded Jordan.

Trish crossed her legs and leaned back, unwrapping a miniature Snickers bar. "She certainly had provocation and opportunity. I would have left Sonny long ago if I'd been married to him. But Andrea is more practical than I am. She had a big financial investment in her marriage. I don't mean to suggest that she's a gold-digger, because she's most definitely not, but the insurance company will pay her millions with Sonny's death. Ogden told Andrea long ago Sonny was worth more to her dead than alive. And frankly, she told me if she got divorced she didn't trust the courts to be fair to women any more."

Jordan nodded.

Cay asked," Does anyone know how Sonny actually died? I know he was found at the bottom of the pool, but I've heard everything being gossiped, from strangling, to a blow to the head, to poison darts."

"I think it was just poison, not poison darts," Jordan said.

"I like the darts angle," Cay said. "I'm sticking with that until proven wrong."

* * *

Similar speculation was taking place in most of the cars and limousines in the funeral procession. Sonny had his fingers in many pies, and a majority of them were not what you would call the wholesome apple kind mother used to make.

The procession turned off I-75 onto Martin Luther King Drive, a sign the cemetery would not be that much farther. As they rode past the Georgia State Capitol, Trish said, "This part of town always makes me sad. Old Atlanta is disappearing. Now it's all concrete and ugly, not a hint of the beauty that used to be here."

"Face it, Trish," Cay said. "The real old Atlanta vanished with Sherman when he passed through on his way to Savannah."

Just then a cement truck backed out in front of their limo, bringing the procession to a halt. "Ah, progress at its finest," Trish said, gazing out her window.

"I want his job," Cay said, pointing to a hard-hatted worker snoozing on a little patch of grass. "Honestly, Atlanta traffic gets worse daily. Turn around and look at all the cars in the procession behind us. There must be close to one hundred. We look like a circus parade."

"If you ask me, this whole funeral crowd is one big circus," Jordan said tugging her skirt down.

Cay scrunched her face. "Yeah, and with that slit in your skirt up to your belly button, you're flying without a net. Do you want a safety pin?"

"The slit is not that high! I'm just short. When I stand up it'll be fine."

The limo turned past the gates of Oakland. A sign warned that vehicles of oversized length or excessive width, except for hearses, were to park in a nearby lot.

"These are the original paths," said Trish, "one hundred fifty years old, some of them, with tight twists and turns."

"Does that mean we have to walk?" Cay asked. "I hate to put my shoes back on."

"You'll make it Cay," said Jordan. "Hang in there a little longer."

Trish took out a mirror and a brush from her purse and did some touch-ups to her hair. Jordan put on some lip gloss. Cay stared at both women. "Primping for the dead?"

"Good thing I love you Cay." Trish said. "Let's get out and follow the crowd. Everyone ready?" They slid across the seat.

Exiting the car, Cay mumbled, "This must be like being born. I want to stay in the car where it's dark and comfy."

Jordan stopped walking. "What the hell . . .? Tell me I'm seeing things."

"Well, if you think it's Bobby Lee's Humvee, you'd be right," Cay said.

"But how . . .?" Trish asked. Bobby Lee was grinning from ear to ear wiping the sweat from his forehead with a navy blue bandana.

"I always carry one of these things in my back pocket," Bobby Lee said. "Sweat like a damn pig."

"And that's not the only porcine thing about him," Trish said.

"How did ya get this Hummer up here?" A mourner Trish didn't recognize was lovingly caressing its massive bumper.

"Off road!" Bobby Lee shouted. "That's what them's things are made for."

"But the graves," Trish said, in spite of herself.

"Don't you worry none, little lady. Didn't hurt none of them. That's the beauty of this baby - built like a tank but can roll over almost anything and hardly squash it at all. A miracle of modern engineering. Can't do better'n the army is what I always say."

Jordan and Cay each took Trish by an arm and briskly moved away. Trish appeared to be strangling on her own suppressed words, and in a minute or two the result would not be pretty.

"Forget about Bobby Lee," Cay said. "We are here for Andrea. Let's stand right over there." She gestured to an empty space on the grass a few feet behind where Andrea was standing. "Oh, dear God in heaven." Cay put her hand to her lips.

"What is it? Cay, what's the matter?" Jordan followed Cay's gaze.

Just below the rise, on the other side of the hill, stood a new mausoleum, startling by any standard. Oakland's grand mausoleums are justifiably famous, but none could approach this one for jaw-dropping hubris. From the two torches blazing with eternal flames, held aloft by marble weeping goddesses, to the iron gates emblazoned with the sunburst and large 'S' that matched the gates at Chateau Soleil, the mausoleum could only belong to Sonny Simmons.

Sonny's final resting place was already attracting a steady stream of tourists. A few were even taking photos while the mourners gathered.

"When could he have done this?" Jordan asked. "Andrea wouldn't have built it!"

"I agree. This edifice isn't Andrea's work; I'm sure of that," Trish said. "Sonny probably made a deal with the builders of his house. Put the leftovers, plus a few more things, over here. Two bad taste monuments for the price of one."

"Should we go down closer to Andrea?" Jordan whispered. Andrea had teetered down the hill, hanging onto EJ and Big. Bobby Lee found himself holding up his parents, Vergy Senior and Miss Adeline, both of whom looked wan and frail.

"No, I like this vantage point," Cay said. "You can see some interesting things from up here. Plus I'm not moving these feet one more inch."

The casket was in place and the service was about to begin. Jordan, Cay, and Trish spotted the figure just opposite them at the same time. Lenora Martin, who had tended bar at Sonny's party, stood rigid, glaring at the mausoleum.

"How did she get up here? She must have come around another way." said Jordan. Lenora's hair was pulled back in a tight bun, and the black trench coat gave no hint of the friendly, charming girl that Jordan remembered.

"She seems to be alone," Cay observed. "Why don't we speak to her after the service?"

"To be nice or to be nosy?" Trish asked.

"What do you think," Cay said with a little smile. "My mother always told me to include those who stayed off to themselves. Maybe she is just shy."

"I don't think shy is exactly it," Jordan commented. "And when did you ever do what your mother told you? Look, what is Lenora doing?"

Lenora's left hand was in her coat pocket, but her right arm was raised. Her right hand pointed toward Sonny's casket, her second and fourth fingers extended.

"She's sending out roots," Jordan hissed. "I can't believe it. They do it that way in only one place. She has to be a McDonough girl. That gives her away."

"What are you talking about?" Cay squeezed in closer. "What is roots? I mean, what are roots, whatever?"

Jordan turned away from the mausoleum so they wouldn't be overheard. "I'll tell you more later, but basically, it's a curse like voodoo, but it's a special kind. McDonough has sayings and customs that exist nowhere else. Apparently Lenora decided it's never too late for a curse."

"Are you making that up?" Trish asked.

"No, I mean it," Jordan said. "I studied this at Emory when I got my masters in linguistics. There are these little islands of customs and language here and there, and McDonough is one of them."

"Well, I declare," Trish said. "You learn something new every day. It takes a Jersey girl to educate me about my own backyard."

"Why is she doing it? A curse seems pretty harsh, since Sonny's already dead." Cay found herself rubbing her arms and shivering a little.

* * *

Dead wasn't good enough for Lenora Martin. She wanted Sonny Simmons roasting in a full-bore Baptist hell for the misery he had given to her Mama and all the other women he had wronged. Before Sonny's casket was fully in its mausoleum resting place, Lenora turned and hurried away, heading down hill to her gray Toyota sedan, and driving quickly into the busy city streets.

"We won't be talking to her now," Jordan said, watching Lenora drive away. "Damn. I'd like to know more about her."

"So would I, but she didn't look like the chatty type," Trish said.

"She scares me," Cay said.

"You don't believe in that voodoo stuff, do you?" Jordan asked. "You are too rational."

"Of course I believe in it," Cay said. "I believe in everything. Everything works: prayers, curses, ghosts, UFOs. It's all in what you believe to be true. It's irrational to *not* believe in things just because you can't see or touch them."

Jordan grinned. "Oh, like gas."

"I don't think I'll try to figure that one out," Trish said. "It looks like the service is over, and we managed to talk through the whole thing. I hope nobody noticed. Let's head back to the limo. We'll talk to Andrea at the house. She should have a few minutes alone with Sonny."

As the three passed a granite mausoleum a few yards from Sonny's, Trish was startled to see several pairs of legs sticking out, as if people were sitting on the ground. She peered around the side and saw exactly that: Tyler Louise, Mary Marshall, and EJ sitting on a mossy stretch close to the wall, smoking marijuana. She pretended she hadn't seen a thing and kept going.

While Andrea stood silently staring into the open doors of the mausoleum, Isabelle slipped her arms around her and gave her a sympathetic hug. Behind them, Claudia Bannon stood stone-faced. She stepped forward, thanked Isabelle with a small, tight smile, and gently led Andrea back toward the limousine, a protective arm around her shoulder.

"It's interesting how they group together, isn't it?" Morrow said to Bongiovanni. "For instance, those three women were together at the party. They'll support the wife, no matter what. But why would Lenora Martin be here? She didn't say anything about knowing Simmons well enough to attend his funeral."

Jerry shook his head. "Boy, she is a piece of work. Did you see what she was doing? That *figa* thing was straight out of a B movie. I didn't think voodoo was practiced in Atlanta."

"It may look silly to you, Jerry, but Lenora must believe in it or she wouldn't have done it, and that's what counts."

Jerry frowned. "Do you think Voodoo comes with secret potions . . . like poison?"

"Ummm, could be," she said, enjoying Jerry's discomfort. She eased their unmarked car down the road below the mausoleum, missing one of the most interesting moments so far that day.

* * *

"Somebody call nine-one-one!" said a voice, and cell phones popped out of almost every pocket and purse.

"He dropped down, stiff as a board," Serena squealed, staring at Vergy Senior, who lay quivering on the ground.

Miss Adeline stopped them. "Vergy don't need no nine-one-one. He's got the 'sight!' He's talkin' to White Bull. Give 'im air."

"More like Fulla Bull," Jordan whispered. Catching a look from Cay, she asked, "What? It's better to laugh than cry, isn't it?"

Cay hissed, "Jordan, is silence never an option with you?"

Vergy eventually flopped into a heap on the grass. Miss Adeline knelt down and patted his hand. "What's it this time?" She shouted, just inches from his face. Vergy Senior was a little hard of hearing. "What did White Bull say?"

"Couldn't hardly make it out," Vergy croaked, his voice as raspy as a bullfrog. "It sounded like he said 'more than one will be accused.' But it could have been 'the wrong one will be accused.' Hell, I don't know. It's not like the damn Indian calls me on the phone. He's talkin' from the other side, you know." Vergy shook his head as if to clear his thoughts. He got up with the assistance of Big and Bobby Lee.

Cay and Jordan exchanged wide-eyed looks. Trish stared without blinking.

Serena, spotting Tyler Louise and her pot smoking cousins, let out a bellow, "Tyler Louise, you get over here, right now!"

"What a buzz-kill," giggled Tyler Louise from her marijuana cloud. Some of the mourners gave Serena side-long glances as they passed. She was certainly tacky. Of course Sonny was tacky, too, but the size of his bank account and West Paces Ferry address allowed a lot of bad taste to be overlooked.

Chapter 14

"My feet hurt worse now," Cay said getting out of her car. "I should have worn my Birks."

"That's what you get for wearing Birkenstocks all the time," Trish said. "Your feet expand and then you can't wear normal shoes anymore. Although you could add some glitter and turquoise to them and . . . no, even that wouldn't make them more stylish."

Jordan asked, "Do you have black funeral socks with little caskets on them for the next funeral?"

Cay ignored her and walked faster up the long cobblestone driveway to Andrea's house. Suppressing laughter, Jordan and Trish tried to catch up with her.

"I don't think we should stay long, do you?" Jordan asked. "Andrea's probably exhausted and ready for a nap."

"We'll say our hellos and then we can leave," Trish said. "I'm ready for a nap, too. Sonny's funeral was exhausting."

"Funerals are always exhausting." Cay stopped and massaged her feet.

"This one was unusually long, I thought," Jordan added. "Didn't you all think it was long?"

Trish answered, "Not as long as a lot of them I've been to. You get a country funeral, you can go all day. Here in Atlanta, they move 'em in and move 'em out with a little more speed. City churches can't spend a whole day on one funeral, no matter whose it is."

When they reached the front door, Cay was out of breath. "I have to lose some weight or exercise more," she said, panting. "That driveway almost killed me."

A uniformed butler and maid stood inside the open front door to receive coats, packages, and anything anyone wanted to hand off, such as a smoked ham or zucchini soufflé. From time to time, the butler said to no one in particular, "There's a buffet being served in the dining room."

"I thought the thing about a buffet was that you served yourself," Jordan said under her breath. When the LitChix entered the dining room, they saw this wasn't any ordinary spread. Enormous silver trays filled with sliced hickory smoked ham and turkey were interspersed with baskets of home baked biscuits. A chef sliced prime rib and served it to the guests. Crystal bowls of lobster salad and boiled shrimp competed with Georgia Sea Island crab. There were tiered compotes of fruit, cheesecakes, and petit fours. The display would have put a lavish wedding reception to shame.

White roses and calla lilies in tall silver epergnes, topped by five-branched candelabra, towered over the food table. One expected to congratulate a happy bride and groom, not shed a tear for the loss of one of the city's bigger wheeler dealers. The guests were not sure if they should be mourning or celebrating, but many were doing the latter.

The Vergy Simmons' clan was unusually silent as they piled their plates high. Accustomed to picnic tables heaped with pot luck at family reunions and funerals, they were more subdued by the sheer glitter of everything than by the quantity. After filling their plates, they exited to the garden to eat, uncomfortable in the formality of the dining room.

A white-gloved waiter handed Jordan a plate. She raised her eyebrows in a signal to the Chix: *I told you so.* The music on the sound system began. Blaring much too loudly from hidden speakers in every room, the unmistakable call to "Let's Get This Party Started" rang out. It was quickly replaced by Mahler's Fourth.

"Mahler," Cay sighed. "That brings back a memory or two."

"You are such an intellectual," Jordan said. "Who would even know that was Mahler, let alone have a memory associated with it."

Clearing her throat to get their attention, Trish said, "Okay, girls, back to reality. We ought to find Andrea and give her our condolences again. Let's walk around a bit and look for her."

They reluctantly left the dining room, having sampled only a few selections.

"I'm coming back," Jordan said. "I haven't tried the roast beef yet."

As Mahler rumbled in the background, the LitChix worked their way into the library. Cay would have liked the opportunity to help Andrea and Sonny assemble a fine custom library, since this was not just her career but her passion. To her regret, Sonny filled the beautiful heart of pine shelves on his own. Many of the books were fascinating, Cay admitted. She saw works on the antebellum South and the War of Northern Aggression, as Sonny called it, and wonderfully illustrated volumes on antique weapons and military paraphernalia.

"I could move in here!" Cay's voice was filled with awe and admiration.

"It really is exquisite, isn't it," Trish replied.

"Wow," Jordan said. "It's hard to believe the person who did this room also designed the outside of the house. I mean, they are so far apart in taste. One is *gavone* and the other is, well, elegant. Maybe Sonny had more depth than we give him credit for."

Cay stared at Jordan and raised her eyebrows.

Jordan explained "*Gavone*! You know, tacky, garish."

Trish said, "This library must have cost more than most houses. I'd never have thought Sonny had such refined taste."

"Actually, he had a really good decorator." Andrea said as she came into the library and slipped into the little conversation group.

"Andrea! I'm so sorry we were gossipy!" Trish said hastily. "Please don't be offended. This library is such an amazing room."

"I'm not offended at all," Andrea said. "Sonny was smart enough to always learn from the best. He even hired one of Atlanta's leading social arbiters, Carolyn Luesing, to give him polish. His goal was to be comfortable in any social situation. Sonny failed to realize there are some things money cannot buy, and class is not for sale."

Jordan blurted out, "I always said that Sonny had such bad taste that even poison would taste good to him." As a horrified look spread over her face she exclaimed, "Oh, Andrea! I cannot believe I just made such a thoughtless remark. Fuck."

Andrea's expression was one of utter surprise, but she recovered quickly enough to say, "I always appreciate your honesty and candor, Jordan." Turning to include the others, Andrea said, "I hope you weren't planning on rushing off. I'd like the four of us to go upstairs later. I need to change out of this funeral suit, and there are some things I'm concerned about and I don't want to talk them over with anyone associated with Sonny. At least not yet."

Trish hugged her cousin. "Andrea, we're here when you need us. Just let us know when you're ready."

"Bless your heart, Trish," Andrea said. She moved back into the entry to receive the condolences of several couples wearing appropriately sad expressions.

Cay said, "I guess its time for me to find a chair. Either that or go barefoot. You two mingle if you want to. I'm going to park myself right over there." She gestured to a comfortable looking club chair. "I saw a waiter with a drink tray just a minute ago. After your *faux pas,* Jordan, I think I will read a little, relax, and catch up with you two later. I'll be fine."

"Come on Jordan, let's mingle and see if we can find some pate of crow for you to spread on crackers." With that, Trish hooked her arm around Jordan's and led her back to the dining room.

Cay helped herself to a glass of sweet tea when the waiter came by. She was afraid that alcohol combined with the stress of the day would put her right to sleep. She wiggled out of her shoes and picked up a copy of *Southern Living* magazine from a small ornately painted French table next to the chair.

"Don't that just beat all," a male voice said behind her right shoulder. "We thought we had him dead to rights, and he managed to weasel out of our reach again."

Another male voice drawled, "Well, you were partly right, you did have him dead." Then both men chuckled. Cay didn't turn her head. The two having the conversation were sitting on a sofa, separated from Cay only by a narrow table. Obviously they thought they couldn't be heard; perhaps they didn't even notice her, a small figure almost swallowed up by the deep chair. She pretended to be deeply engrossed in an article about a huge Jekyll Island beach house, all the while listening intently.

"No chance to get any of it back now," the first man said.

"I don't see why not," the second replied. "The corporation is still going, isn't it?"

"We just don't have the evidence, Mag, and without Sonny, we aren't going to get it."

At the mention of Mag, Cay's head whipped around in spite of herself. Was that Magnusson Cramer? He was pictured regularly in the newspapers, and not just in the *Atlanta Journal Constitution*. He and Melanie Inman Cramer, his wife of twenty-five years, were patrons of the arts, gave to worthy charities and, perhaps as insurance, underwrote the building costs of the neo-Gothic church that everyone was calling Our Lady of Conspicuous Consumption. Mag liked to say that he made it and she spent it. Melanie was an Inman and her pockets were, if anything, deeper than Mag's. On top of that, she was old Atlanta, which trumped money any day.

Cay quickly looked back to her magazine. Her face felt warm. *Did I hear something I wasn't supposed to? Was that just business talk or were they serious about some kind of illegal shenanigans?* She put the magazine down and got up as slowly and casually as possible. Cay tried to slip her feet into her shoes, but they would not go. With all the dignity she could muster, Cay picked up her shoes, put them under her arm, and headed off to look for Jordan and Trish. She found them soon enough, standing next to the staircase.

"Good. I was about to come and get you. Andrea has gone upstairs and we're going up to sit with her for a while," Trish said.

"Wait," Cay said. "I think I overheard something important. It sounded as if, maybe, someone was trying to get the goods on Sonny for some kind of crooked deal. I'm positive one of the people was Mag Cramer. I don't know who the other man was."

"Hon," Jordan said, "everyone was always trying to get the goods on Sonny, but no one ever did. Now they probably never will. He was slippery as an eel."

"But what if it was reason for murder?" Cay asked. "They haven't charged anyone with his death yet, have they? Maybe these men know something."

"Leave it to the police, Cay," Trish said. "This is a high profile case. I'm sure they'll be thorough."

Jordan was half-way up the stairs. "C'mon," she hissed in a loud whisper. "I don't want to spend the rest of the day here. Move it along, Chix."

Trish and Cay followed her. At the top of the stairs Trish took the lead down the hall and into Andrea's bedroom.

Andrea was curled up at the head of the massive canopy bed, against a fortress of lacy monogrammed pillows. She was still wearing the black Armani suit she wore to the funeral, chaste in its simplicity. She cuddled Mr. Chanel while she spoke to an older woman seated on the slipper chair next to her bed. When the three entered, she brightened a little, but didn't change her position.

"Darlin's! Oh, thank y'all for coming up to visit. I do need to talk to you." Andrea's eyes were red-rimmed, and she looked a little pale. "Miss Adeline, you know my cousin, Trish. Well, these are two more of my dearest friends in the world, Jordan McKeehan and Cay Curtis. I don't know what I would do without all three of them."

Turning her attention to Sonny's mama, Jordan started, "Mrs. Simmons, we're so sorry . . ." and the others echoed, "So sorry . . ."

" . . . about Sonny," Jordan finished, not knowing what else to say.

Trish leaned down and kissed Miss Adeline's cheek.

"Girls, call me Miss Adeline like Trish and Andrea do. Thank you for your kindness. It's an awful day, but an old woman like me has had awful days before. I lost another boy before this, you know."

Jordan and Cay shook their heads "no" in unison.

"Oh, yes, my oldest, Vergy Junior." Miss Adeline held Trish's hand in a firm and surprisingly strong grip. "It was almost twenty years ago to the day," Miss Adeline went on. "Ain't that strange? I like to think of Vergy Junior up there with his Lord and Savior, huntin' and shootin' and raisin' hell. It brings a smile to my lips."

"How, how . . . extraordinary," Jordan said with alarm.

"Yes, that's certainly the truth," Andrea agreed, getting anxious to move her mother-in-law along to her own room. "You must be so tired, Miss Adeline. Why don't you go have a rest and I'll have some food sent to your room."

"I think I will rest for a bit. No food, Honey. Couldn't eat a thing." Miss Adeline painfully moved her thin frame from the chair, said, "Nice to meet y'all," and teetered toward her room.

"Miss Adeline's a dear, but she does go on and on. Now we can talk," said Andrea.

Trish sat on the bed and patted Andrea on the knee. "We're here to let you know that anything you need, you tell us. That isn't just a polite remark. Women friends are the best friends."

When Miss Adeline was safely out of earshot Andrea said, "I am gettin' truly worried here. The police have dropped by almost daily, asking the same questions: where was I, who was here, all about the food and the caterers and all of the guests, and on and on. I asked them if I was under suspicion for the murder of my own husband, and they said 'Everyone is under suspicion,' as if that were some clever remark. I told the detectives I'd appreciate it if they would avoid visitin' today because I had to bury my husband, but did you see those vultures at Oakland checking out everyone at the funeral? That was over the top to me. The nerve." Andrea stopped talking. Her diatribe had worn her out.

Trish moved from the bed to the slipper chair, a little shaken. "Do you really think you're the prime suspect in Sonny's murder?"

Andrea looked at Cay and Jordan. "As I'm sure Trish told you, there are a few things that could make me look sort of guilty. Y'all are the only ones who know that I was meeting with a gentleman caller while Sonny was being . . . uh, murdered. Everyone knew Sonny was getting less discreet about his affairs. It wouldn't be too hard for the police to find out his insurance policy made him worth a great deal more to me dead than divorced." Tears shown in her eyes as she spoke.

"Were you planning to get a divorce?" Jordan asked.

"It was what he was planning that could be the problem. If he really was going to divorce me to marry Mary Alma, it would certainly give me a motive, but Sonny threatened things all the time. That's one way he controlled people. I was used to it. I certainly wouldn't *murder* him over it. I still found the old fool damned attractive, and he was the father of my children."

Cay said, "Andrea, before we came up here, I was sitting in the library and I overheard two men talking about some kind of deal Sonny was involved with. They didn't sound too happy. One of the men was Mag Cramer."

"I wouldn't pay any attention, if I were you," Andrea said. "You know these financial types, always moanin' and groanin' about the deal that got away."

Actually Cay did not know those financial types. Andrea and Sonny moved in an entirely different circle. Cay did know, however, when something sounded suspicious, and the overheard conversation still bothered her. She would never underestimate the power of money to inspire greed, or revenge to provide a motive for murder.

Jordan seemed more interested in another aspect of what Cay had to say. "How do you know Mag Cramer?"

"How could anyone miss that mug of his?" Cay replied. "He's either opening another office tower or working with the Atlanta mayor on some urban renewal project. Or showing off his money and his wife at this or that society ball. All his activities are recorded in just about every newspaper and magazine I pick up. He must have a great public relations firm to spin such a positive image of himself. I'd have to be blind, deaf, or dumb not to know who Mag Cramer is."

"Oh my goodness, Cay," Andrea said. "Someone of Mag's stature would never be involved in a murder. He has too much at stake."

"Those are just the types who think they're above the law," Jordan said. "Remember our Jersey governor? Oh, well."

Andrea changed the subject. "Would y'all like a little something? Some sweet tea and sandwiches maybe? I'll call Claudia to bring something up. All of a sudden I'm starved." Andrea pressed the intercom button and made her request. "I think I'll change out of these depressing black clothes while we're waiting. Just make yourselves comfortable." Andrea slid off the bed, handing Mr. Chanel to Trish. "I'll be right back," and she headed into her dressing room.

Trish and Mr. Chanel eyed each other for a moment, then he licked her face and settled comfortably into her lap. The three LitChix, Trish, Cay, and Jordan were quiet, not wanting to seem as if they were gossiping behind Andrea's back. Eventually Jordan broke the silence. "It was a nice funeral. Didn't you think so, Cay?"

"I thought it was one of the most bizarre events I have ever been to."

"Well, no shit, Cay, I was trying to be nice. Okay, forget that. It was just a thought. I've been to more exciting funerals in Jersey."

"How so?"

"Better you not know. If I told you, I'd have to kill you. Just kidding. Don't panic, Cay!"

"Well," said Cay, "all that carrying on seemed pretty undignified to me, but then Sonny was pretty undignified. No reason his funeral should be any different. Sort of Fellini's *Satyricon* meets *The Dukes of Hazzard*."

"I'm back," Andrea announced as she swept into the room. Jordan didn't think of Vera Wang for an after-the-funeral ensemble, but Andrea did look lovely in a long ice blue satin robe with kimono sleeves.

She scooped up Mr. Chanel from Trish's lap. A tap at the door was followed by Claudia walking in, followed by a uniformed butler carrying a silver tray laden with sandwiches, petit fours, and sweet tea in Waterford crystal goblets.

"Oh, good," Andrea said with genuine enthusiasm. "We'll eat at the tea table. Claudia, you're such a dear." Andrea gave her a grateful hug. "I don't know what I'd do without you."

"Thank you, Andrea. This is nothing, really." In a soft voice Claudia asked, "Is there anything else I can do for you?" Her affection for Andrea was obvious.

"This is lovely. Thanks so much for all you've done at this horrible time in my life. I'll call you if we need anything else. Thank you too" she called to the back of the retreating butler. "Now what have we here?" Andrea began picking through the pile of sandwiches with enthusiasm. After selecting one, she took a sip of her sweet tea. "Every time I drink sweet tea I will think of Sonny. I always said that good sweet tea, with just a touch of lemon, tasted the way magnolia blossoms smell. When we first got this property, Sonny laid out where the pool would be, then he planted magnolia trees all across the far end of the property so I would always have my sweet tea aroma in the air. He could really be very thoughtful."

"You're right," Trish said softly. "You always said that Sonny was quite a guy. I hope he appreciated your faith in him, Andrea. Not many women who would work so hard to find the good side of a man like Sonny."

Chapter 15

"Why would I miss the game tonight? It's the most important one of the whole season. Just because we buried Sonny today isn't an excuse for missing the Westminster - Lovett game," said Andrea. "Besides, Sonny would want me to go, and I'd feel closer in spirit to him there."

Cay, Jordan, and Trish exchanged horrified glances. After a moment Trish said, "Okay. It might do you good to go, and I know EJ would want you there. Trey doesn't expect me, but he's always glad when his mama sees him play."

"Jim's out of town, again," added Jordan. "But I always go see Michael play."

"Since I brought my car, I'll go on home," said Cay. "Besides my feet have given out and will no longer fit into my shoes."

"Oh, no you don't, Darlin'," said Andrea. "I need you with me for moral support."

"But I don't know one thing about football, I don't like football, and if those aren't reasons enough, I'm in my nice suit with my only good pair of heels that no longer can be forced onto my aching feet!"

"No problem, Cay. That's something we have in common. We both wear the same size, remember?" Andrea was not about to take "no" for an answer. Even though the game had already started, she wanted to see her son, EJ, play quarterback, and she wanted to be surrounded by her friends tonight. If she went with the LitChix, she wouldn't have to sit with the Simmons bunch, who were equally determined to go to the game. Andrea buzzed the intercom for Claudia with instructions to find Cay some comfortable shoes suitable for the big game.

The game between Westminster and Lovett was the most important one either team played all year. The schools could have a terrible season, not win a single game, yet if they emerged victorious on this night, all was forgiven. On the other hand, if either school won every game *but* this one, Buckhead bragging rights belonged to the other school and they would never hear the end of it!

The windows of every business in the immediate area of the rival schools were filled with signs made by the cheerleaders. Even the I-75 overpass located on the way to each campus became a billboard announcing premature victories. A lot was at stake in this game. Adolescent hormones were pumping overtime and the adults were just as excited.

No one remembered when football morphed from a sport to a religion and then into a cult at Westminster. The team was the heart and soul of the school. It wasn't that the team was particularly good. They hadn't made it to the state finals in the Georgia Dome since 1978. It was just the social and political thing to do.

An entire social structure for parents evolved around the team. There were parties for the boys, coaches, cheerleaders, and parents after the home games, lunches for the mothers at the OK Café before each game. There was even a pecking order to where you sat during the game. The real queens of football's inner circle were the captains' moms. To become a captain of the football team was an honor given to the really rich, to the really politically connected, and, occasionally, to a really good kid. Jordan had a really good kid, Michael, who was elected a team captain, and that is how this Jersey girl ended up as treasurer of the mothers group the same year that Sonny met his maker.

"What better celebration of our brother Sonny's new life in the risen Lord than a little football! Yee Haw!" Bobby Lee Simmons shouted from his Humvee as it wheeled and bounced down Andrea's drive and onto West Paces Ferry Road, heading for the Westminster stadium. Big and Vergy Senior grinned and shouted a rebel yell along with Bobby Lee. The rest of the Simmons clan piled into a white SUV and followed a little more sedately. But not much.

Cay was mortified to find herself on the way to the big game wearing glitter trimmed tennies. She slouched in the car as far down as she could, hoping no one would see her. Maintaining dignity was out of the question; the only solution to her dilemma was to be out of sight. She muttered, "How did I ever get myself talked into this?"

Arriving at the stadium just as the second half started, Cay looked around in amazement and said, "Why are all these otherwise sane people wearing wildcat masks? Is it Halloween already?"

"No, Darlin'," answered Trish, "Westminster's mascot is the wildcat and everyone cheering for them wants to be easily identified. If I'd known I was coming, I would have mine on too."

"I never wear mine," Jordan whispered so only Cay could hear. "Football mania is a little too Southern for me."

During the game Cay turned to Trish and asked, "How many innings do they have left?"

"You're kidding, right?" Trish had her first clue it was going to be a long night. Several of the Westminster parents glared at Cay.

"Come on, Cay," Jordan said. "You and I are going to the concession stand. Can we get anyone a Co' Cola or popcorn?" She had acquired enough Southernese to pronounce Coca Cola without a Jersey accent. Jordan dragged a reluctant Cay behind her while Andrea and Trish sighed with relief.

"We did talk her into coming, right?" asked Trish.

"Yep, guilty as charged!" replied Andrea.

"Don't say that so loudly, Andrea. Some people might not know you're teasing. I think because Cay is from the Midwest she'll never get the importance of football in the South."

As Cay and Jordan stood in line to place their orders, they couldn't help overhearing two women discussing Andrea and Sonny. "I think it is just awful that their children are allowed to stay at Westminster. To think his murder has been spread all over the newspapers and television. That's not the kind of sensationalism we want for the image of our school. Sonny was so tacky. I don't care how much money he gave to the school or how popular his children are, they clearly don't belong here."

Although the temperature was only fifty-seven degrees, one of the women wore a full-length mink coat with an enormous gold Cartier wildcat pendant around her neck. "Don't talk so loudly, Susan. You wouldn't want anyone to think that you're a gossip, would you?"

The two women moved over to another group also talking about Sonny and Andrea. Everyone seemed to enjoy comparing notes on what really happened to Sonny Simmons and whether Andrea was the killer.

Jordan and Cay didn't say a word. They looked at each other, placed their order as calmly as possible, and started walking back to the stands. "Jordan, as much as I hate gossip, those women did have a point. Do you think there's any way Andrea could be involved in Sonny's death?"

"You know, Cay, I love gossip, but I really don't know what to think. I only know Andrea through Trish. Trish got all of us on the board of Art and Soul, and that's been my main contact with Andrea until now. I do know for sure Andrea is a good person. Sonny just sucked all the class out of her, but I don't think she is capable of anything like murder. I think those women have a bad case of Friday Night Slights."

Cay grabbed Jordan's arm, "Omigod, do you see what I see? Is that Andrea?"

"Where?"

"Up there, climbing up the back of the bleachers!"

"Oy, I'd recognize those leopard skin ankle boots anywhere! What the . . . ? She's gonna kill herself! Move it! Let's get the hell over there."

Huffing from the exertion, Cay managed to say, "You grab one foot and I'll get the other. We have to pull her down before she breaks a leg or worse."

Jordan got a firm grip on Andrea's ankle and pulled. "Andrea, what in the world are you thinking? Get down from there right now!"

Andrea tried to shake off Jordan and Cay, but they tightened their grips. She started backing down the bleachers. "What the hell, I have to talk to Buck! He's up in that little building where the line coaches sit. If I'm gonna end our 'thing' as Lanier insists, I need to talk to him. Anything less would be rude."

Jordan threw her hands up in the air. "I swear to God you Southerners are crazy with these 'manners' crap! Rude is the least of your problems, Hon."

Cay put her hand on her heaving chest. "Okay, so you climb up the bleachers where one million people can see you. Anyone looking would recognize your leopard boots anywhere. I think you've got a little crazy going on here. When your head clears, you can give ol' Buck a phone call. I am sure he would prefer it that way."

"Maybe you're right," Andrea said. "There are other coaches in there, and that could be a little awkward."

Cay heaved a sigh of relief. "Thank God. I thought I was going to have to climb up there after you. Suddenly sitting down and watching a little football sounds like a wonderful idea."

As soon as the three were back in their stadium seats, the crowd began thunderously cheering and stomping. Andrea pointed at the field and shouted, "Look, look! It's EJ! He's heading for a touchdown. C'mon, EJ!" She screamed. "Omigod, he made it! We won the game!"

Andrea, Trish, and Jordan hugged and jumped up and down. Cay remained seated and smiled.

The horn sounded, ending the game. Half of the stands emptied and ran onto the field, yelling and congratulating the players, shouting, "We're number one! We're number one!" The goal post swayed as the fans rocked it violently in their excitement. Many of the senior players embraced, realizing this would be their last game against Lovett. Then they turned to shake hands with their biggest rivals.

The Simmons clan was ecstatic! EJ was a hero. He scored the winning touchdown. All they could say was how proud Sonny would have been, and they knew he was cheering up in heaven, or wherever he landed. If he were in a place where he couldn't see football that would be true hell for him.

Chapter 16

Claudia tapped firmly on Andrea's bedroom door. It was early Sunday morning, barely seven, and Andrea was still asleep, but she knew Andrea would want the news right away.

"Andrea? Andrea? I have some tea for you," Claudia said, hoping the tea would soften the blow.

"What? What time is it? It's dark out." Slowly Andrea sat up and pushed the hair out of her face. "Nothing's happened to the children has it? Tell me they're all right."

"They're fine. I woke you early because I knew you would want to see today's paper. You might want to talk to the children first, before they have a chance to read it."

"Oh, no. Omigod, what is it?"

Claudia handed her the business section of the Sunday *Atlanta Journal Constitution*. It looked more like the *Times* Sunday Style section, with color photos of impressive houses and women in dramatic gowns at various charity events. A screamingly large headline read, "Buckhead Biggie Barbecued."

"This is the worst kind of tabloid journalism. Look at this." Claudia pointed to a picture of Sonny's mausoleum, and another of Andrea laughing with the LitChix at the cemetery, as if she weren't grieving over the death of her husband.

"Oh, shit, I can't believe this. It is horrible. But thank you, Claudia. It's better that I know immediately." She sipped her tea and read a sidebar about Sonny's womanizing and rumors of his shady business deals. She threw the paper across the room.

"Omigod! I can't read this trash. I've got to get up and do something. Claudia, when EJ and Mary Marshall wake up tell them I want them . . . tell them the cable is out or something. I don't want them finding out about this until I can talk to them." Andrea frowned. "I want to dash out for a while, but I'll be back in a couple of hours, and they will probably still be asleep. If they wake up though, tell them I want them to stay home today."

She jumped out of bed and headed for the bathroom, trying to think what she needed to do. Call Trish. That was the first thing that popped into her mind. Trish would come up with something.

* * *

Jordan never went to Art and Soul in the Grant Park neighborhood alone and didn't want to do it now, but she was behind in their financial records and had to go. Jordan called Trish hoping she would volunteer to ride along with her.

"Just a minute, Jordan, hold on," Trish said, "Andrea's calling. I better take it. I'll call you back if I lose you." She clicked her phone to pick up the new call.

Listening with increasing consternation, Trish asked, "This is all in the paper today, Andrea? No, I haven't read it yet. Let's go somewhere and talk through this mess. No, I agree that going out in public might be unwise." Trish listened some more, as Andrea confided the police were watching her house and she didn't want them to follow her.

Remembering that Jordan was on hold, Trish asked, "Why don't you meet Jordan and me at Art and Soul? We'd have privacy there. But how will you get rid of the police?"

"I'll think of something." Andrea started to bite her nails. She stopped, realizing she hadn't done that since the seventh grade. "If I don't show up by . . . let's say eight-thirty, you can assume I'm not coming."

"This sounds like a scary mystery novel. Really, Andrea, it gives me the creeps."

* * *

Andrea decided to go out incognito. She rummaged through her closet for a pair of old jeans then tiptoed into EJ's room and carefully removed one of his hooded sweatshirt and a baseball cap. Her plan was to pass for a teenage boy. Putting on her ensemble, she looked in the mirror and decided that, from a distance, she might pass.

Andrea slipped down the back stairs to the garage to drive EJ's 4x4 when she saw Manuel's old truck bounce through the gate at the far end of the yard. She had forgotten the gardener said he would be at the house early on Sunday to be sure everything in the yard was in good shape after the funeral reception. It was Manuel's way of paying condolences, keeping the grounds looking their best out of respect for his late employer.

Running toward the truck, Andrea called, "Manuel, may I borrow your truck for a little errand?"

Manuel's eyes widened at Andrea's changed appearance. "My truck? It rides pretty rough, Ma'am. I don't know if you..."

"I grew up driving trucks, Manuel. I'm from the country and we were driving by twelve. Don't worry about me. I want to pick up some iris a friend dug for me."

"Iris, Ma'am? I don't think it's time to plant iris."

"Or whatever. Some plants. What time do you go home today?"

"Maybe three? But if you want..."

"Three is fine. I'll be back long before that," and she held out her hand for the keys, which Manuel handed over somewhat reluctantly.

Manuel opened the driver's door for her. Once a dark green, the truck was now a mélange of rust, patches of blue, and possibly other colors obscured by dirt.

Andrea climbed in and looked around. A spit cup, half full of brown sediment and foul-smelling juice was jammed between the seats to accommodate Manuel's chewing tobacco habit. There were numerous empty Styrofoam cups, paper scraps, lunch wrappers, and unidentified detritus throughout the small cab. The driver's seat was split cleanly down the middle, making Andrea sink nearly to dashboard level. Gazing at the dashboard, she realized there was no speedometer, only a gaping hole with a few wires sticking out. Andrea gingerly lifted what appeared to be Manuel's lunchbox from the passenger seat and held it out the window for him. She turned the key in the ignition and gave it some gas.

I have to remember that this is a shift, she thought. *Don't forget the clutch.* It had been a long time since she had to think about the sequence of clutch, stick, gas. She jammed it into gear, let out the clutch, and the truck bounced forward with an oily backfire, startling her into slamming on the brakes and stalling the engine. *Stay calm. I don't want to attract attention and alert the cops, the neighbors and everyone else watching the house for entertainment.* She took a deep breath, started again, and this time managed to work the truck out the back gate, around the corner, and out onto West Paces Ferry. "I can't believe this thing doesn't have power steering," she muttered under her breath, hauling the steering wheel around with both hands.

Jerking and lurching along, Andrea crossed Northside Parkway to pick up I-75 South. She checked her rearview mirror frequently, holding it in place to see, since it otherwise swayed back and forth reflecting the nothing. Several times she went off exit ramps to see if anyone was following, and then back onto the interstate, but traffic was relatively light and she seemed to be alone. Beginning to get the hang of driving the truck, Andrea felt free and almost happy for the first time in many days.

* * *

About the time Andrea was looking for the Grant Park exit, Cay was pulling into Art and Soul's narrow driveway. Trish called Cay and told her that she was needed at Art and Soul.

Perhaps Andrea didn't appreciate how close she was to a murder charge against her, but Trish thought things were beginning to look bleak. Maybe if the LitChix put their heads together with Andrea they would find a way to help her. Trish smiled as she saw Cay get out of her car. She remembered their telephone conversation earlier.

"Should I stop for bagels?" Cay asked.

"Yes, I guess so. We'll have to eat something."

"What kind do you want?"

"I don't care. Get a selection."

"How about cream cheese?"

"Cay! Just do it! It doesn't matter."

"Yes it does. You always say that the food makes the difference."

Cay had her there. Trish was very particular about what was served. "Okay. Get plain, poppy seed, and everything bagels. Get plain and veggie cream cheese. There's a coffee pot and plenty of coffee at Art and Soul, so unless you want orange juice, just get bagels and cream cheese."

"What about donuts?"

"Cay!"

"Never mind. See you there," and Cay hung up, smiling.

Trish and Jordan arrived minutes ahead of Cay and parked on the street, violating any number of posted parking restrictions. They didn't see a newspaper in the driveway.

"Maybe they don't take the paper," Jordan said.

"I don't see any papers," Trish said, looking around the neighborhood. "Either everyone here gets up mighty early or the AJC hasn't been delivered yet."

It began to drizzle, making the already gloomy day even more dreary.

Cay came in the back door with a large bag of bagels. The brewing coffee had already scented the little kitchen.

"If there is a better smell, I don't know what it is," Cay said. "What's up?"

"Apparently, you haven't read today's paper either," Trish said gesturing to the paper on the kitchen table.

"No, I haven't. Why?"

Trish went on to explain the coverage slamming Sonny and his entire family, the stories about his mistresses and business deals, and the picture of Andrea with them at the cemetery, making them look like giddy revelers.

"Did I look fat?" Cay asked. "I didn't even see a photographer."

Trish peered over the top of her reading glasses. "It's not about you, Cay. It's not about any of us. Only Andrea. The headline screamed 'murder,' and you know that everyone likes to see the rich and powerful have troubles. It makes them feel better."

"*Schaddenfreud,*" Cay said. "That's what it's called, when you are happy to see something bad happen to someone else."

"Jimmy said that very thing," Jordan said. "Not the Schaddenwhatever, but how people like to see the mighty brought down."

"You didn't tell us Jimmy was back," Trish said.

"Oh, he's still in Denver, assembling the company team, as he puts it, but we do talk every night, and I keep him filled in. He said it would be a real plus for our local-yokel prosecutor to try a rich girl like Andrea - his words, not mine - and get a murder conviction. It would improve his popularity and help him get ahead in the polls. I guess he has political aspirations, and, let's face it, most of his potential constituents probably don't have mansions on West Paces Ferry.

"Let me see that picture of us again." Jordan picked up the paper. "Damn, my butt looks good." She tossed it back down.

Trish glanced out the window at the rickety truck progressing noisily down the street. Slowly, it ground to a halt in front of Art and Soul. "What in the world?" she said.

Cay peeked out the window just as the truck emitted a puff of black smoke from the tail pipe, followed by a large bang.

"Who is it?" Jordan asked.

"I don't know. Maybe someone who doesn't know we're closed today." A thin man slid out of the driver's seat. The sweatshirt hood was pulled all the way up, and his shoulders were hunched against the increasingly heavy rain.

"Bolt the door," Cay said. "These things can turn ugly." She jumped toward the door and turned the deadbolt. The figure was undeniably coming toward them.

"Oh, for heavens sake!" Trish exclaimed. "Open the door, I recognize that poor wretch!" To Cay's horror, Trish unbolted the door and threw it open. Andrea dashed inside and pulled off her rain-spattered sweatshirt.

"I think I aged ten years," Cay said. "That was a pretty good disguise."

Andrea shook raindrops out of her hair. "Dear God, this is a horrible day for me, but seeing y'all and smelling that coffee makes me feel so much better. Claudia is always bringing me hot tea, and damn, I don't even like hot tea." She smiled sadly. "I wish we were meeting to discuss a Lisa Scottilini mystery instead of . . . of . . . you know. Any way, I can face everything a lot better with us all together."

Andrea gestured to the paper on the table. "Look at Sonny's relatives. That photo is just plain cruel. It makes them look like hicks. And look at this unflattering shot of me. In here somewhere they call me a bleached Buckhead blonde! I am most certainly not a bleached blonde. Highlights, maybe, but that's all. I pay too much money to be called a bleached blonde; the reporter makes me sound like a bimbo."

"Let's sit down," Trish said, motioning everyone toward the round oak kitchen table. "Andrea, we are really worried, and we want to know what we can do to help."

"To tell the truth, I'm scared shitless. Trish, if anything happens, you'll take care of my kids, won't you?"

"Andrea, for heavens sake! Of course I'd take your children, but you don't talk like that. You have to fight back. We all have to fight back." Cay and Jordan nodded. "You're innocent and we aren't gonna let the police pin Sonny's murder on you."

"I was just so stupid. I didn't think about creating an alibi for myself. Everything that happened that night makes me look so guilty. Now the press is crucifying me. Everyone has to think I murdered my husband without a second thought."

"Well, you certainly didn't know Sonny was going to be murdered," Jordan said. "Innocent people aren't careful. They don't have to be."

"That's exactly right," said Andrea. "Like that stupid argument I had with Sonny about that awful Mary Alma. I slapped him, and that must be when I lost that acrylic nail. When the police found it, stuck to the fringe on his shirt, they said I lost it when I was trying to choke him or some such ridiculous thing."

"We heard the argument," Trish looking at Cay and Jordan. "Remember I told you. We came upstairs to look around, and we heard something going on, so we jumped in the powder room. We can testify to that fact if we have to."

"It was her idea to check out the upstairs," Cay said, pointing to Jordan.

"That's all right. I don't mind people looking at the house. Any way, Sonny and I argued a lot. Oh, all that stuff the paper wrote about Sonny and shady deals all over the place. That's so rotten. Sonny pushed the envelope, but he wasn't a crook, for God's sake. I hope and pray his Mama doesn't read this." Andrea massaged her temples. "Say, did ya'll tell the police about our argument in the bedroom?"

"No, we didn't," Cay said, and Jordan shook her head.

"We said very little to the police," Trish said, "and nothing about the argument. I knew they would use it against you, and none of us wanted to give them reason to think you might have killed Sonny."

Andrea patted Trish's hand. "The fact that I was down in the pool with Sonny when Dr. Munro found me made the police think I was guilty. I don't even remember that. I think I was in shock. I did get his blood and that awful barbecue sauce on me, and that was good enough for the investigators to point their fingers at me. They confused me saying all this stuff about the panther statue. That's the one that used to be in the library, and my beautiful scarf around his neck, and poison - oh, it's all in here, thank you very much," she said waving toward the paper. "But listen to this," and she traced her finger down the page until she came to the paragraph she was looking for. "The coroner disclosed that Mr. Simmons was killed by a single shot, delivered by a high-powered rifle . . . Then here: blah, blah . . . and the fall into the empty concrete pool broke his neck." Andrea began to cry.

"Now, I ask you, how was one person supposed to do all that? No one could be in two places at once. If someone shot poor Sonny, they must have been hiding a good distance away."

Cay nodded. "You're right, Andrea. How do the police explain that? They must have talked about his being shot when you went down to headquarters."

"They did not, and as much as those detectives have been snooping around my yard, no one has said a word to me about a shooting. I'm Sonny's wife. They let me find out in the newspaper!" Andrea reached for the cup of coffee Trish put on the table next to her.

Jordan patted Andrea on the back. "This whole mess is plain awful. Just awful. Everyone knows reporters aren't the standard for accuracy. Most of the time they have no idea what they are talking about, but they write it any way."

"I hate to put it this way, but maybe that's good news. That he was shot, I mean." Everyone looked at Cay. "If the shot is what killed him, it should be pretty obvious you didn't do it. They would have found evidence like gunpowder on your hands. They always do on TV. Plus, you would have had to be a very good shot, not to mention a fast runner. You would have had to shoot him from someplace, probably across the pool, then run around to the other end before the bullet got there."

"Well, unfortunately, they have my shoe prints and Buck's at the far end of the pool under the magnolias."

"Do you think anyone has any aspirin?" Cay asked. "I am getting a really bad headache."

"Have a bagel," Jordan said. "I have a feeling we are going to be here for a while."

Chapter 17

"Wait a minute. Let me make sure I understand what you're saying. Cay, you think there were two killers?" Trish leaned in closer.

"At least two," said Cay, taking a sip of her coffee. "Or at least two who wanted to kill Sonny. One shot him, and that was successful. Another one tried to choke him, hit him over the head, and poison him."

"Don't forget the barbecue sauce," Jordan added. "It says right here in the paper that he had a whole lot of barbecue sauce poured over him. Holy shit, what did Vergy say when he had his fit at the cemetery? Didn't he say that more than one would be accused or something like that? Is it possible that ol' Fulla Bull knew what he was talking about? Too weird."

"I don't know about Vergy's vision but it does sound like more than two people to me," Cay said. "Pass the bagels, please. If just one person was hitting him, strangling him, poisoning, pouring - well, it would be impossible! The evidence definitely says that there were more than two. Andrea, what did the police say about all of that when they questioned you?"

Andrea shrugged. "They mostly showed me pictures and said that all the evidence pointed to me. Maybe they thought I'd confess or something."

Trish's hand began to tremble a little on her coffee cup and it wasn't from the caffeine. "If they didn't even say anything about the bullet wound, maybe they thought you would say something to give yourself away. Oh, Andrea, you are a suspect, all right."

"I think what we have here is definitely a hit man, or a hit woman," Jordan said, picking up a bagel with poppy seeds.

"A hit man? How do you come up with that?" Andrea asked. "I've been thinking it was somebody Sonny screwed in business. I don't for a minute think he did every bad thing the paper says he did, but he did make people angry sometimes. Maybe he made the wrong guy upset, one who was a really good shot."

"Sonny moved with big players," Jordan said. "In that crowd, they don't do their own dirty work. Yes, he probably did make some other powerful guy upset, as you put it, but then Mr. Mogul would see the problem was taken care of, without dirtying his own hands. Do I have any poppy seeds in my teeth?"

Ignoring Jordan's question Cay asked. "Is that how it's done in Jersey?"

"That's how it's done everywhere," Jordan said taking out her mirror to look at her teeth.

"And where was this hit, ah, *person*?" Andrea asked. "And no, you don't have any poppy seeds in your teeth."

Jordan got up to refill her coffee cup. "You have a lot of trees and shrubs. That shouldn't be too hard to figure out. The cops have probably tramped over every square inch already, looking for clues."

"Well, if I was back near the pool house, and there was a hit person shooting at Sonny across the pool, then the hit person must have been near me. Oooh, that's disgusting to even think about. Do you think he saw me, with Buck? Do you think he watched us? Now I'll have the willies all day."

"*This* is what you're worrying about?" asked Jordan. She calmly placed her palms down on the table. "Okay, let's start from the top. Do you know what all Sonny was involved in that might make someone want him dead?"

Andrea took a bite of her bagel then spread more cream cheese on it. "I've thought about that, and there were a lot of things, I guess. Like when that offshore oil rig he was invested in sank, and all those poor people died. That wasn't Sonny's fault, but you know how people want to place blame, and Sonny was an obvious target.

"And then there were all of those race horses. They never seemed to win, but it didn't really bother Sonny. He just liked being around the stables up in Virginia. It broke his heart when that barn burned and all those magnificent animals were lost. One of the trainers died trying to get the horses out." Andrea reached for another half bagel, reconsidered and put it back.

"And he got some horrible threats, right here in Atlanta, after that huge office tower over in Taiwan or Singapore or some such place collapsed while it was being built. He couldn't help it. Some contractor cheated on the materials, but you know who people blamed. Sonny had a run of bad luck, but he had a lot more successes. People just don't talk about those."

"Good grief, the man was a walking target!" Cay said. "The question is who *didn't* want him dead."

They turned their attention back to the newspaper. Andrea read the rest of the article aloud. She was more angry than hurt now, which Trish thought was positive.

"That's right, Sweet Pea," Trish said. "You aren't a victim. You're much stronger and smarter than Sonny led you to believe. You have to take charge, Andrea, and defend yourself."

"I am taking charge of my defense. I met with Lanier Poole, the criminal lawyer Ogden got for me. He's supposed to be dynamite in the court room, maybe even the best there is in the Southeast. Well, I went to his office, and at first I wasn't impressed. It didn't look all that successful, if you know what I mean. I had to wait for thirty minutes. I was just about to leave when this absolutely charming man opens his office door and tells me how sorry he is about the unfortunate event. I was completely…."

"Turned on," Cay muttered, rolling her eyes.

Trish thought of the Lanier Poole she had seen on the TV news, all silver hair and perfect teeth. Everyone said hiring Lanier Poole was as good as confessing your guilt, but it was more dangerous not to hire him. Nearly all his clients got off, and those who didn't probably couldn't have been successfully defended by Johnny Cochran himself. Ogden must think it looked pretty bad for Andrea for him to turn her defense over to Lanier.

"I told Lanier all about how I loved Sonny when he was poor and strugglin' and well, I also told him about Buck. There are some potential problems with my affair."

Cay loved Andrea's phrasing. *Potential problems such as last meals and appeals to the governor for clemency?*

"Lanier said firmly that I had to get rid of Buck, and I've done that." Seeing Jordan gulp, Andrea added, "I don't mean 'get rid' of in the Jersey sense, Jordan. When I couldn't get to him during the football game, I called him up and told him it was over between us.

"Lanier also told me to dress down in public from now on. No designer suits, no flashy jewelry or designer handbags. Only two-inch heels or less, darken my hair a few shades and go with a French twist. Oh, and wear natural looking makeup and no red lipstick. I guess I have to trust him."

"So, for one thousand bucks an hour, you got great makeover tips," said Jordan.

Andrea stood up and went to put her coffee cup in the kitchen sink.

"That's pretty," she said, pointing to a little watercolor on the windowsill. "Did one of the Art and Soul ladies paint this?"

"Yes," Trish said. "A young woman named Maggie. She was such a pathetic thing when she first started coming here. But little by little, she got some confidence. That's part of the reason the board wanted to start this gallery. Sales from arts and crafts have given money to so many needy people and also helped their self-esteem." The painting was very simple, just a porch on a rundown-looking house, but with a huge pot of geraniums on a lopsided table, blazing red in a spot of sun.

"Has she sold anything?" Andrea asked.

"Not yet, but she will."

"Well, she has now. I want it. It cheers me up somehow and maybe if I buy it, it'll cheer her up, too."

Andrea checked the price tag, took fifty dollars out of her wallet and handed it to Jordan. "I don't have the right change, but keep it. You can put the extra money to good use around here."

Jordan went to get the cash box. "Are you sure you don't want change? That's about four times the cost of the painting."

"Sonny always said I would be rich on his life insurance when he died. I guess I'll find out about that tomorrow when I meet with Ogden for the reading of his will, so let's hope I can afford to be generous."

"Okay, Chix," said Trish, "I told Andrea we wanted to help her, so, we need some sort of a plan. What can we actually do?"

"We could sleuth," Jordan said.

"And what exactly would that be, *sleuthing*?" asked Cay.

"Well, for one thing," said Jordan. "We could look around the magnolias in the back. I know the cops and the crime lab people have been there, but that doesn't mean we can't look too."

"Can we just walk in there?" Cay asked. "Isn't it a crime scene?"

"Not anymore." Andrea said. "Do you really think there was a hit man out there that night?" Andrea shivered. "I didn't know Buck and I were on stage."

"Maybe that's where we should start." Trish said. "We should try to figure out where the hit man would have been hiding. It's as good a plan as any."

"You're welcome to come over anytime and start sleuthing," Andrea said. "I have to go home. I want to be there when the children wake up. I'll have to tell them about the newspaper, but I want to take the sting out of it, as much as I can. Oh, I'll have to call Sonny's relatives, and my parents, and of course Missy, my oldest."

"At least she probably won't see the paper," Trish said.

"Don't bet on it," Jordan replied. "Thanks to CNN, news travels fast and gossip travels faster."

Andrea picked up Manuel's huge keychain from the kitchen counter. It was made from a carabiner strung with keys, a child's photo, tags of various sorts, and topped off with a three-inch Our Lady of Guadeloupe statuette.

"What a cute little girl," Trish said, looking at the tiny photo in its battered frame. A gap-toothed girl of six or seven grinned through the yellowed plastic.

Andrea realized that she didn't know whether the child was Manuel's daughter or a granddaughter. She had no idea how old Manuel was. She saw him nearly every day, yet where he lived, his family - if he had one - had never been of any interest to her before. "Yes, she is cute. I should ask Manuel about her sometime." Something about the key chain, a man's life in a bundle of keys, made her sad for a moment.

"Well, I've got to go," said Andrea. "I see the paper is here. I'll toss it to y'all on my way out." She headed down the sidewalk, threw the heavy-plastic wrapped newspaper back toward Art and Soul, missing her mark by quite a distance, then noisily revved the old truck's engine before taking off with a bang, literally.

Cay said, "That's one thing we don't have to worry about. If she shoots like she throws, she wouldn't have nailed Sonny in a million years. Some waiter would have been dead in the tent fifty feet away."

"Cay, that's not nice!" Jordan said, laughing. "You don't think she did it, do you?"

"No, but all those little personal, feminine touches surrounding the murder are puzzling, don't you think?"

"Such as?"

"Well, would a man pour barbecue sauce on Sonny? He would not. That was a woman making a statement, such as, 'Sonny's a pig,' or 'I'm sick of you putting barbecue sauce on every durn piece of food that goes in your mouth.'"

"The scarf was definitely a feminine touch," Jordan said.

"But," said Trish, "would Andrea have used her favorite scarf? She was really upset about it being ruined. I'm just giving a what-if. I don't think for a minute she did it."

"Then that raises the question of what woman *did* do it? Maybe a woman who disliked Andrea as well as Sonny. Using Andrea's favorite scarf, would implicate Andrea and give her a good jab at the same time." Jordan was warming to her subject. "She'd have to be pretty gutsy. The paper says Sonny was apparently hit over the head with a heavy panther statue. I don't think many women would care to bash someone's head in, or is that just sexist thinking?"

"Don't forget the poison." Cay said. "Now *that* is a woman's weapon. Clean, distanced from the result. Someone had to slip him a small dose - the paper said there wasn't enough in his system to kill him. Almost anyone could have done that. Even the pretty bartender we saw at the funeral giving him the finger."

"It's not the finger, for heaven sake," Jordan insisted. "It's *roots*, and it's an old cultural tradition of some of the people with Creole heritage. But I know who you mean. It was Lenora Martin who did that and she was tending bar at the party. Still, we shouldn't necessarily pin the poison on her. What could she have against Sonny? Anyone could have handed him a poisoned drink, even Andrea."

Trish said, "I'd put my money on the lady in red, Mary Alma Harwick. She was furious, boozed up, and out for blood."

Jordan frowned. "Do you think she did the whole thing, or do you mean just the poison? I don't think she did the shooting. I think that's another story, and we have to look at that very carefully. But it wouldn't surprise me if she did some or all of the other things."

"Unless she was a juggler," Cay said, "she couldn't do it alone. Think how busy the poor woman would have been. 'Here, Sonny, have a poisoned drink. Wait a minute let me bash you over the head with this handy statue. Hang on, I have a scarf right here I want to choke you with. And for good measure, here is a gallon of barbecue sauce in this vat sitting right here. I'll just pour it on you for that extra-special touch.'"

"You do have a point." Trish laughed rinsing out the coffee mugs. "That would have been a lot for one person to pull off."

"So we must be looking at a conspiracy," Jordan said. "Goody. There is nothing I like more than a juicy conspiracy."

Trish turned around and put her hands behind her. "We have to focus on proving Andrea is innocent. So I guess we need to find the real killers. I suggest that we check out Mary Alma first. Who's with me?" Both Cay and Jordan raised their hands.

"Cay, could you go this afternoon?" Jordan asked.
"Sure."

Trish said. "Today won't work for me, the Westminster Library Committee is meeting at my house at

4 o'clock. I'll contribute by renting you a car so you won't have to drive one of yours in case you're seen."

"Good enough," Cay nodded. "Does anyone want that last bagel?"

Chapter 18

"Jordan, what is this?" Cay pointed at the hood of a very small bright blue car.

"It's a subcompact. It's all the rental company had left, except for some big boats. It's maneuverable, and easy to park. What more do you want?"

"For starters, I want something that doesn't scream, 'Look at me! I'm a cute tiny car!' We agreed to sleuth, Jordan, not audition for the clown car act at the circus. How am I going to get into that thing?"

"I think it's a pretty good fit. For once I can see over the dash without my pillow," said Jordan. "Usually when I sit down in a car, I disappear. My legs are long and my body is short. Besides, the rental car was Trish's idea, just in case the cops were tailing us or Mary Alma spotted us, so you can blame her when you see her."

"You sound like a cheap novel, Jordan."

"Thank you. It's a gift."

"I'm supposed to get into that seat? My rear end is wider than that, you know."

"Stop complaining. Squeeze in and let's go, we're wasting time. Did you bring a disguise? I doubt Mary Alma would recognize us from the party, but you never know."

"This is all I could find," Cay said, removing a curly blond wig from her purse. "My niece left it in her old dress-up box in my attic." Cay pulled the wig on over her short brown hair.

"For God's sake, take it off! You look like Harpo Marx! Maybe we don't need disguises." Jordan put on her huge Chanel sunglasses, wedged herself behind the wheel, and started the engine.

They had agreed to rendezvous at the Publix closest to Mary Alma's condo. Cay left her Volvo in the lot, went in the front door of Publix, pushed a shopping cart around some, then ducked out the rear loading door, clearly marked "store employees only."

Jordan had positioned the rental car near the Dumpster. As Cay pushed herself into the car Jordan said, "Take the rotten lettuce off your shoe before you get in. And tell me you didn't put on those damned socks with Sherlock Holmes' spyglass on them on purpose!"

"Dress for the occasion I always say. Help, I'm sitting on the seatbelt fastener, and I can't move. Not to worry if there's an accident. I couldn't possibly go even one inch. They'd have to bury me in this thing. How did you find Mary Alma's address, anyway?" Cay asked as she struggled with the seatbelt.

"Well, as we suspected, Mary Alma's name isn't in the phone book, so I thought, 'What would be regularly delivered to her apartment?' I struck gold with the newspaper. I put a vacation hold on the paper, and I gave them a false address. When they said they didn't have a subscription at that address, I asked them what address they did have for Ms. M. A. Harwick, and voilá, easy as pie."

"Jordan, that doesn't make sense. If they'd been delivering the paper to a different address than the one she gave, she wouldn't have been receiving her paper, and . . . oh, never mind."

"It was good enough for the guy on the phone, and it's good enough for me," Jordan said. "Her condo's right up here on the left."

"Now, what?"

"We should wait awhile, I guess. I'll park so we can see the entrances to the building and the parking garage. If she doesn't show up, we go inside and see if we can find her condo." Jordan rolled down the windows and turned off the car engine.

Cay looked around. "I'm sure there's someone at the desk guarding the elevators. They'd never let us in, anyway. And if by some miracle we got up to her condo, what then?"

"I haven't gotten that far. Do you want me to do everything? I found her address, we're here. You think of something." Jordan stretched and repositioned herself on the car seat. "We have to help Andrea, and Mary Alma surely looks like the logical murderer to me. Unless we want to see Andrea in the pen or worse, we're going to have to do some serious detective work."

Cay said, "Jordan, turn the AC back on. It may be October, but with the sun out, the weather's turned hot.

"You know, I was thinking, if Broadway made a musical and called it "*Atlanta*," they would make Andrea a 'Roxy Heart' type. Let's see, who would play her? I know, Jerry Hall! It could revive her career. Maybe they could get Mick to play the lawyer. They're too old, of course, but it would have kind of a crypt-keeper edge to it."

"That isn't funny, Cay. This is a life-and-death matter."

"I know. I just can't resist casting real life, can you? You say to yourself, 'Oh, he would be played by Brad Pitt, and she'd be Susan Sarandon - that sort of thing."

"There are very few people in my life who would be played by Brad Pitt, I assure you. Walter Matthau maybe," said Jordan.

"I think he's dead."

"Exactly. In the story of my life, I want to be played by Goldie Hawn," said Jordan.

Cay looked at Mary Alma's condo building, "Kathy Bates would play my role. She can look great when dressed up and frumpy at other times. We should have brought coffee."

"Where would we put it?"

"Good point. Look! Isn't that Mary Alma's car? The little silver one at the light. She must've come out of the garage."

Replacing her sunglasses with a pair of high-powered Janssen binoculars, Jordan said, "It's her all right, let's go!" She threw the binoculars between the seats.

Mary Alma set a brisk pace down Peachtree, weaving in and out of traffic and turning onto Tenth Street toward Georgia Tech. It was all Jordan could do to keep her in sight. Once they entered the Tech campus, Jordan had no idea where the silver Porsche had gone.

"Damn! Every street on this campus ends in a parking lot," Jordan said. "Cay, keep looking for her. We didn't go to all this trouble to lose her." They were backing out of a dorm lot when Cay spotted Mary Alma's silver porche, driving toward the pool on the far side of the campus.

"How do I get over there?" Jordan was nearly shouting. "Oh, hell, who cares," and she jumped the car forward over the curb, headed between the dorms, over a grassy patch of lawn, skirted a couple of oak trees, and bounced back onto the road. "Drastic times require drastic measures or something like that," she said under her breath.

"Where did you learn to drive, Jordan? If I had false teeth I would've lost them! Stay on the roads, please." Cay had a death grip on the dash.

Mary Alma was about to turn right onto Marietta Street and head back north. "What is she doing?" Cay asked. "What's over there?"

"Maybe she's getting some furniture reupholstered. Lots of fabric wholesalers are around here." The silver Porsche ducked down a road on the left without signaling and Jordan almost missed it.

"Slow down, Jordan. Maybe she's spotted us, although I can't imagine why."

Jordan pulled into the lot of an auto glass company about thirty feet from Mary Alma's car and parked behind a truck. She grabbed the binoculars, got out of the subcompact, and peered toward the driveway where Mary

Alma stopped. A man in work overalls headed toward their bright blue car and Cay got out to intercept him.

"Good afternoon," she said.

"Can I help you? Hey, what's she doing?" he asked pointing a fat cigar in Jordan's direction.

Jordan had taken up a position by lying across the truck hood to steady her binoculars.

"Birds!" Cay said. "We work for the Audubon Society and we had a report that a very rare bird was in this area. We're checking it out. Find anything yet, Lulu?"

"Oh yeah?" he said. "Birds? Well, this lot is for our business, so as soon as you've seen your 'bird,' we'd like it if you'd move your car."

"Lulu, time to go, dear," Cay called. With no response from Jordan, Cay hissed, "Get in here right now."

"Huh? Me?"

"What a spy you make," Cay whispered, squeezing into her seat. "We should offer you to whoever the bad guys are. You'd shut 'em down in a day. What did you see?"

"Mary Alma went in that tan building over there. I'm going to drive by and see what kind of business it is."

Cay squinted. "They are all tan buildings, Jordan. Okay, keep moving, but don't drive past. Park across the street. There!" Cay pointed to a building with the driveway running along the side. "Park up close to the building. Maybe we won't be so easy for Mary Alma to spot when she comes out. The parking lot she's in is empty. Since it's Sunday it's pretty dead around here. Pardon the expression."

"So what is Global Tool and Die, do you think?" Jordan stared at the sign on the front window of the building Mary Alma entered. "Blinds are closed. I don't see anyone else in there."

"We can Google it," Cay said. "That might tell us something."

"Say Google Global three times in a row. I dare you." Jordan grinned. "Any way if we Google it, that means we have to wait until we get home. If Mary Alma leaves soon, I think one of us should go inside. Pretend we're lost or something. Just look around. See if anything stands out."

"What would we be looking for?" Cay asked.

"I don't know. You have a creative mind. You'll think of something."

"Me? I'm supposed to go in?"

"We have to share the work here, Cay. You can't just ride shotgun. You have to do some of this sleuthing, too."

"I diverted the guy at the glass place, didn't I? And pretty cleverly too, if I do say so myself. Maybe we should call Trish while we're waiting."

"Good idea," Jordan said, pulling out her cell phone.

"Hey, Trish, we hit pay dirt, I think. We followed Mary Alma to a building off Marietta Street. I don't know . . . . I don't know . . . . Cay's going to go inside and check it out when Mary Alma leaves. Uh-huh . . . . Maybe. Call you later."

Cay grabbed Jordan's arm. "Okay, here she comes."

Mary Alma opened the door of Global's office and stepped out. She went back inside for a moment and let the door close. Reopened it, got in her car, checked her make-up, put on lipstick, then roared into reverse and headed back toward Marietta Street.

"What do we do now? Wait?" Cay asked.

"Just a few minutes. We don't want the scene to get cold."

"Jordan, you watch too many detective shows. Cold? How would we know whether it's cold or not?"

"What are you going to say when you go in?" Jordan asked, ignoring Cay's question. "You should practice, so you can look around at the same time and not worry about what's coming out of your mouth."

"Well, I could say that I was looking for Ajax Maintenance Service, and say I thought this was their address and do they know where Ajax is located. And I could ask to use the phone book. If I had to call somebody, I could call you. And then I could ask to use the bathroom."

"Not bad, Cay. Very good, in fact. Are you ready?"

"As ready as I'll get," Cay said. Jordan pulled across the street into Global's parking lot. Cay got out of the car, smoothed her jacket and slacks, and entered the building. Jordan turned on the radio. To pass the time she sang along with the music. She drummed her fingers nervously on the wheel, looked for gum in her handbag, changed the radio station, found a nail file, fixed the nail that had been driving her crazy, and practiced deep breathing exercises.

"C'mon, Cay," she implored under her breath. "Please come out. Oh, God, I hope there's nothing bad going on in there. Maybe we did the wrong thing. C'mon, c'mon c'mon."

Eventually Cay came through the door, giving a cheery wave to someone inside. She resettled herself in the car and Jordan pulled out of Global's lot.

"Well? Are you going to tell me what happened?"

"Not much, actually. Jackie works behind the desk and has been there six years. Her son is really cute - she has a framed school photo of him. Global makes little metal parts for various kinds of drills - big drills, not your home handyman kind of thing. And oh, yes, there's a framed photo on the wall with a bunch of guys standing by a big dead fish, and the same dead fish, presumably, is mounted on the wall. Not much of interest there, except one of the guys in the picture is Sonny Simmons and another is Mag Cramer."

"So what else is new? All these rich guys play together. Who do you think owns Global?"

"My guess is that it belongs to Mag," Cay said. "There were some trade magazines in the bathroom, and the subscription labels all said 'Global Tool and Die,' except one, and that one said 'Cramer Industries.' Oh, there was another interesting magazine, *Horse Breeder*. The label was torn, but I'd swear it said 'Simmons', and the address was Global."

"Now that *is* interesting," Jordan said. "Sounds as if they not only played together, Sonny and Mag worked together, too."

Chapter 19

Andrea took her attorney Lanier Poole's fashion advice, and showed up at Ogden's law office in a charcoal pin-striped Karen Millan suit. She colored her hair a darker blond with discreet highlights and styled it in a French twist. Andrea assumed, as did Lanier, that people would be watching her, especially after that horrid article in the newspaper, and she didn't want to provide any more fodder for the gossip mongers.

Ogden's office looked like a successful lawyer's office should, to Andrea's way of thinking: Oriental rugs, glorious Chinese porcelains, and deep pile comfort wherever you turned. She was served coffee in a paper thin porcelain cup bearing the name of the firm artfully scripted into the green and gold border. The air held a faint fragrance of potpourri, which would not be the smell one associated with Lanier Poole's office, but Ogden Williams served a different clientele.

Andrea was uncharacteristically on time, and after a short wait, was escorted into Ogden's suite by a young woman wearing Ann Taylor and pearls. Paneled in carved cherry and lined with law books, it inspired confidence. The smell of the pine logs blazing in the fireplace would comfort any client. Ogden greeted Andrea warmly, taking her hand in both of his. Pleasantries were exchanged, and Andrea took a seat in a leather wing chair pulled up near Ogden's desk.

"Have you seen Lanier Poole yet?" Ogden asked.

"Yes, I have, and I think we'll work well together. His office certainly doesn't have this atmosphere, I must say." Andrea glanced around the luxurious office meaningfully.

"No doubt," Ogden chuckled, "but you aren't a typical client, although he has had certainly his share of high-profile clients, and has done well by them. Very well, indeed."

"That's reassuring to hear," Andrea said smiling at the same young lady placing her coffee cup on a side table.

Ogden adjusted his glasses. "Perhaps we should get right to Mr. Simmons' - Sonny's - will."

"I remember it was a pretty simple affair, much like mine."

"That's true."

Andrea noticed little beads of sweat forming on Ogden's forehead, although the room was not excessively warm. "Ogden, what's going on here?" Andrea asked. "Is there some kind of problem you haven't told me about?" She was getting nervous. "For heaven's sake, tell me what's up."

"Perhaps I should just tell you what the will says. As you know, it provides for some small bequests and the rest to you and your children. Really just to you, because two of the children are minors, and you will understand Missy's position more fully after I read the will to you."

Ogden cleared his throat. "Unfortunately . . . ," and Andrea felt as if she were strapped into a luxury leather-padded thrill ride, plummeting down a vertical slope. Through the wind rushing around her ears she heard, ". . . there are no assets to speak of. Maybe a thousand or two, but everything is mortgaged and leveraged up to the . . ." and Andrea stopped hearing anything. The room was spinning. In a moment it went black. She came to with a cold towel on her forehead and the young woman's pearls dangling in her face. She was patting her hand and saying "Mrs. Simmons" over and over.

Embarrassed that she had fainted, Andrea waved the young lady away. "I'm fine, really. I didn't eat breakfast. I was in such a rush."

"Should I call a doctor? Or someone else?" Ogden asked, his forehead densely furrowed. "I'm so terribly sorry, dear. I should have cushioned the shock. This was all my fault."

"Nonsense. Let's just forget about it, please." Andrea's voice shook.

"I'll find you some crackers, and some water," Ogden's assistant offered.

"If you could bring me a Co' Cola, that would help a lot," Andrea whispered. "The jolt of sugar and caffeine, you know." The assistant hurried off. Turning to Ogden, Andrea said, "Does this mean I'm broke? What in the world happened to all of Sonny's assets? His real estate investments? What about the house?"

"I'm afraid the bank owns the house. Sonny had a second mortgage on it. The monthly interest alone is over twenty thousand dollars. Oh, money will come in from some of Sonny's projects for a while, but it all has to service the debt. At least it is supposed to, but we can probably juggle a few things for a couple of months, and then..."

"And then the shit hits the fan. Am I right?" Andrea asked.

"Pretty much. That would be a fair characterization."

"Wait a minute. Sonny told me more than once I would be better off financially if he were dead. What about his life insurance? Surely that will make a difference, won't it? What about the casino in Biloxi he gave me?"

"Andrea, Sonny was in such bad shape financially he had to default on his insurance premiums several months back. After the hurricane struck the Gulf Coast, the casino was destroyed. He had no insurance on it, either. I'm so sorry. You know, if he had lived, he would have done one of his famous magic tricks and everything would have continued as usual, but, well, I know this is a shock. I'm so very sorry."

Andrea took a deep breath and reached for the Coke.

Chapter 20

"Bless you for coming over and holding my hand, Trish." Andrea hugged her cousin.

"My pleasure, Darlin'. I'm going to start a fresh pot of coffee." Trish filled the grind and brew with water and beans.

"Oh, Trish, I feel so bad dragging you into this mess, but I don't know who I can trust or where else to turn." By now, Andrea's voice was going up the scale to a full-blown wail.

"Andrea, Andrea, calm down. It's all right. Tell me what's goin' on."

"I'm broke. There's no money."

"Didn't you just come from Ogden's? Did Sonny cut you and the children out of his will?"

"No, nothing like that. I mean he was very generous in the will. He didn't cut me out. Sonny left a little money to his secretary Isabelle, which was only right after what he put that poor woman through for all of these years, but there's almost nothing left. I mean nothing, zero! Ogden says, I'm going to lose the house and all of our properties and assets. I won't even be able to pay the children's tuition," Andrea sobbed.

"Andrea, I can hardly believe it." Trish poured two cups of coffee and joined Andrea at the kitchen table. "We need to think this through. There's got to be an answer. Did Sonny stash money anywhere? You know, in the bookcase, the sock drawer? I always hide my chocolate fix all over my house, in my car, at Art and Soul."

"I don't think Sonny hid anything in the house. He wouldn't have told me, anyway." Andrea blew her nose. "Wait! Sonny has a safe! He had a safe put in the library behind that big ol' painting of him with his race horse. Maybe there's some money in there!"

"You have to get it open right away. Do you have the combination?"

"No. I don't remember him ever talking about it. I could look in his desk."

"Yes, and if it isn't there, you should call Isabelle. Just tell her there are some family papers you need to look at, and you've misplaced the combination. Ask her to search the office if she doesn't know where the combination is. Did Sonny have a safe deposit box?"

"Just the one we had together, at least as far as I know, and there is nothing important in it. Just our passports and birth certificates. Sonny didn't trust banks, or me." Andrea's smile was sad.

Trish finished her coffee and put it down on the granite counter. "All the more reason to check the safe. Tell you what. I'll come back tonight and bring some food. You have to eat and you can't be in the mood to cook. We can take the painting off the wall and at least take a look at the safe. Is it okay if I bring Jordan and Cay? It may take the four of us just to lift that huge painting."

"Sure, why not. The more the merrier, and I trust them not to talk. Besides, one of them might know something we don't about opening safes, especially Jordan. Jersey girls seem to have all sorts of out of the ordinary, useful information. Especially of the criminal sort." Andrea's smile was much more hopeful, and she felt better. At least she had a plan, even if she had almost no hope of finding anything of value in the home safe. A couple of hours later, her feelings were less upbeat. Nothing in Sonny's home office indicated the existence of a combination to the safe. Her call to Sonny's secretary, Isabelle, was equally fruitless, sending the poor woman off on a search that yielded nothing.

While Isabelle was still on the phone, she asked Andrea, "Did you know the police were here, at the office, looking through Mr. Simmons' things? They had a search warrant, so I didn't have any right to keep them out. I waited, though, while the officers were here, and they didn't seem to be interested in anything in particular."

Had the police known, they might have been interested in some of Sonny's files and his date book, and maybe his Rolodex. Isabelle felt the office would be much tidier without them, so she took them home with her as soon as she heard of his murder. *You simply never know,* she thought, *when these things might be useful.* She was grateful there was no computer in his office, since that would have been the devil himself to move.

"Gosh, Isabelle, I never even thought of the office. Did the police take anything?"

"No, there was nothing for them to take."

"My goodness, I'm so glad you were there with them. Thank you so much, Isabelle."

"Glad to help, Andrea."

Andrea knew Sonny had an incredible memory. Maybe he took the combination to the grave with him and didn't actually write it down where it could be found.

Andrea didn't know what else to do before the LitChix arrived, so she took a long, scented bubble bath. Her mind wouldn't stop whirling with questions. As she relaxed in the warm water, it came to her how she might get the safe open. *What I need is a safecracker. But how do I get the contact information for such a person? I Who would even have the phone number of a safecracker?*

* * *

Trish arrived promptly at six. Cay and Jordan pulled up about half an hour later. Trish spent the first half hour feeding Andrea's children. They were old enough to be embarrassed by all the talk about their parents, and were grieving their father's death. There wasn't much Trish could say to comfort them, but her fried chicken and sweet potato biscuits went a long way toward making life more normal.

Mary Marshall was plugged into her iPod, but tears were slowly streaking her make-up. As Trish passed her some fried chicken, she gave Mary Marshall an affectionate hug.

"Oh, Aunt Trish, I hate this. Daddy's dead and Mama's in trouble. When are things gonna be normal again?"

Trish sat down beside Mary Marshall and wiped her tears with a Kleenex. "Oh, baby, I don't know. I am sure everything will work out somehow."

EJ looked up from his plate and said, "You both are nuts if you think life will ever be normal again. That's impossible."

"EJ, we're family," Trish said putting her hand over his, "we've got each other and together we'll get through this horrible ordeal. Life may not be the same, but that doesn't mean it won't be good again."

Mary Marshall and EJ finished their dinners and retreated to their rooms and computers, where they silenced the outside world by text messaging and web surfing well into the night.

Trish put out the grown-ups' dinner of Florida Pompano baked with green beans, ginger flavored carrots, and garlic new potatoes still warm from the oven.

"Trish, this smells wonderful. I do not know how you do it," Cay said. "Everything you cook is delicious. You could be a caterer or at least write a cookbook."

"Cay, if you think my cooking is good, one of these days I am going to take you and Jordan to a Townsend family reunion in Florida and give you a southern food baptism. You won't be able to eat again for a week. Andrea knows exactly what I mean. We eat in a pavilion by Hart Springs and there are at least ten tables filled with every country dish you can imagine."

Jordan asked, "By the way, where is Claudia tonight? I was afraid she would join us for dinner, and I don't think we wanted to talk about these things in front of anyone else."

Andrea answered. "As luck would have it, she asked for the night off and I told her that would be fine."

Trish served her Aunt Ethel's chocolate cake with coffee. Jordan finished first. "Okay, I'm done. Now, what's the deal?"

Andrea cleared her throat. "I suppose Trish has told y'all I don't have any money. I'm broke. That wasn't Sonny's intention, but he borrowed a lot and some deals went bad, and he was just plain out of money. If he hadn't been murdered, we probably would have kept going. Sonny could pull more rabbits out of a hat than a magician, but with his death, all his debts will come due, and there is no money to pay them.

"The most pressing problem I have right now is cash. I need to find out what's in Sonny's safe in the study, and I want to do it quietly. I definitely don't need any more publicity. With my luck, I'd have Geraldo on my doorstep with a film crew ready to do a TV special from my den. No, I want this to stay among us, but I do need help opening it."

"Do you know how to crack a safe?" Jordan asked. "If you don't, that could be a problem."

"I've thought about that," Andrea said, "and I have a plan, but let's take a look at the safe first. Who knows, Sonny might not have even locked it or maybe with four of us, we can figure it out together."

As they finished dessert, their discussion turned to Andrea's living arrangements. The LitChix decided Andrea and the children should not stay in Chateau Soleil. Claudia would be there to check on the house daily and see that everything was in order. If the bank foreclosed or people continued to ride by and gawk at the house, it would be better if Andrea and her family were comfortably living elsewhere.

"There's no question," Trish said. "Y'all will move in with Trey and me. My son and I are alone in that big house since John's death. There's an apartment over the garage that's going begging, so you and your family can be with us and still have your privacy. I won't even consider anything else."

Andrea didn't protest. "What in the world would I do without you," she said. "I don't know if I'll ever be able to make it up to you, Trish."

"There's no 'making up' among family," Trish said. "Just tell the kids to pack some clothes, get their computers and electronics together, and we'll move Friday afternoon, before the football game. I can take some small things in the meantime. If we move things over the course of several days maybe the neighbors and the police won't notice."

Jordan started to clear away the empty plates.

"Thanks, Jordan. I'll do the dishes later," Andrea said. "Leave everything where it is for now. We should probably get that horse painting off the wall and see the safe behind it. That way I'll know what we are dealing with."

The LitChix and Andrea walked into the den and stood before the enormous painting of Sonny and one of his winning Thoroughbreds.

"That's one big mother," Jordan said.

"Jordan!" Trish said.

"What's the matter? I didn't say anything bad. You know, the mother of all paintings."

Cay frowned. "Do you actually kiss Jim with that potty mouth, Jordan?"

"Very well, according to him." Jordan grinned wickedly.

Andrea spoke in a take charge voice, "As they say in Lake City, 'times a'wastin'. Let's get started. Cay, you and Trish take that end. Jordan and I will take this one."

"Wait a minute," Cay said. "When we get it off the wall, where are we going to put it?"

"Good point," Trish said. "Let's move some furniture so we can lean it up against the sofa."

It took the four women considerable scooting and tugging to clear a path to the sofa, and much more to move the painting away from the wall without leaving marks. Finally it was free; they lowered it slowly to the floor and slid it into place.

"That wasn't as heavy as I thought it would be." Cay said. "Just awkward."

Jordan collapsed in a nearby chair. "God, Cay, there were four of us but my side of the painting was plenty heavy."

"Well, let's take a look." Andrea moved in close to the brushed gray metal front of the safe. It was about two feet square, flush with the wall. There was no dial or handle visible.

"I've never seen anything like this," Trish said. "Of course I haven't seen many safes, but I don't know what to make of this one." They stared at the piece of inscrutable metal as if it were the monolith from *2001*. They tapped it and pressed it, but nothing would make it release its secrets. A narrow metal band at the top identified the safe manufacturer. A long number was inscribed on it, presumably some sort of identification.

"You may be stuck." Cay said, peering at the mysterious safe. "You have to contact the manufacturer. There isn't even a place for a key."

Andrea looked intense. "It may come to that. Hmm, I have another possibility. Trish, I'll call you tomorrow. If I say 'Let's make dinner plans,' that means you call Jordan and Cay and y'all be here at six. Park in the garage. I'll be watching and let you in. If you can carpool, that would be good, but if not, well, it's four stalls, and I'll be sure there's room."

Cay asked, "I know we want to keep this private, but why so secretive?"

"For one thing, I wouldn't put it past the police to tap my phone. I don't even use my cell phone because I heard anyone can pick up those conversations. If everything works the way I hope it will, I'll have another person here and, that person will no doubt prefer anonymity."

"I think you are beginning to enjoy this just a little," Trish said, not without some alarm.

"I wouldn't say I enjoy it, but I'm discovering some survival skills and starting to take charge, and it is making me feel better. We'll see how I feel after tomorrow night. Trish, I need to conduct a little private business with you. Could you come out to the kitchen with me? We won't be a minute," she said to Jordan and Cay. The two cousins left the room.

Cay muttered, "This is getting to be pretty heavy. I don't know if I'm ready for all of this mysterious stuff. It's fine in books, but in real life, well, I don't know."

"I think it's exciting," Jordan said. "Who can't use a little excitement in their lives?"

"Me, for one," Cay said. "I like the quiet life. That's why I work with books. My life isn't boring to me. It's so peaceful."

"Maybe Andrea will get this thing open tomorrow," Jordan said, gesturing toward the safe, "and you can go back to the simple life."

"Fine with me," Cay replied.

Chapter 21

"Lanier, I have the silliest question to ask you." Andrea was using her most seductive telephone voice. She had called Lanier Poole very early, afraid he would leave for court and wouldn't be able to talk with her until late in the day. She was calling from Starbucks with a pre-paid go phone. She would not put it past the police to tap her house phones.

"I have some family papers I'd like to get to that are in our safe at home. In all the confusion, I've forgotten how to open it. It's very state of the art. I want to be discreet because of the ridiculous press coverage and police snooping, so I haven't called a locksmith or the manufacturer. Do you know of anyone I could employ who might have some expertise in opening safes? Strictly on the up and up, of course. Just a simple job, a contractual arrangement." She didn't want to say too much, just enough for Lanier to get the picture.

After a moment Lanier came up with the name John and a telephone number. "John has cleaned up and gone straight, so you aren't going to get him in any trouble, are you?" Lanier asked.

Flustered, Andrea replied, "Why of course not, Lanier. It is my safe." When she realized he was joking with her, she said, "You are a devil. My sense of humor is at a very low ebb, as I am sure you can understand. I do thank you. It should make things easier."

The minute she got off the phone she dialed the number Lanier gave her. When she got an answering machine she tried to speak in a businesslike manner, but was beginning to feel shaky from nerves and coffee. After she hung up she thought, *did I sound crazy? I emphasized I needed a call-back soon. He probably thinks I'm a nut job. He's never going to call me.* She opened her purse to put away the note with John's phone number. When the cell rang a moment later she jumped and answered immediately. "Yes?"

"Is this the lady who called about a safe?"

"Yes. Yes. Lanier Poole told me you might be able to help me. This is totally an honest job. I need to open my safe in my home. It's just that it's . . ." Andrea realized she was babbling.

"You don't need to explain, lady. Where is this safe located? I'll need the address." Andrea told him. "And when do you want it opened?" Andrea answered she would really like it soon, like maybe sevenish tonight. John didn't question the urgency or the evening hour. Matter of factly, he stated his price. Cash. Andrea sucked in her breath and agreed. *Trish better be able to come up with the money.* This was more costly than Andrea expected when she asked her cousin for a loan the previous evening. With the amount in her own account plus Trish's money she would just barely have enough, but it would leave her no cushion.

"This is a very high tech safe," Andrea said. "No dial, no key, just a flat surface."

At the other end of the line, John smiled. He liked to stay current. That was why he was considered the best. He visualized packing his bag for his evening's work. A tuning fork might be all he would need, but if that was not enough, he had back-up methods. He was looking forward to getting back in the game.

* * *

Andrea called Trish. "I'm at Starbucks."

Trish said, "I almost didn't answer your call because my cell read "private number." What's that all about?"

"I got a pay-as-you-go phone. There's no record of the calls that way. It sounds as if you are eating something."

"Just some M&Ms. Omigosh, Andrea, you continue to surprise me. How did you know about that kind of phone?"

"Oh, Buck and I use them all the time so no one would ever see a record of how many times we talked." Andrea flipped her hair out of her eyes. "Dinner tonight is a go. And the other thing we discussed, can you do that by tonight, too? Trish, you're literally saving my life, I cannot believe how wonderful you've been."

For the rest of the day Andrea was so nervous she barely accomplished anything. She put some of her clothes along with Mary Marshall and EJ's into shopping bags, so she could send the bags home with Trish. Shopping bags seemed much less conspicuous than suitcases. Andrea carefully wrapped her best jewelry and tucked it into a couple of designer purses. She put these at the bottom of a Saks Fifth Avenue canvas tote and topped it off with her favorite black suit. She didn't want to speculate what might actually be in the safe, if indeed this John person could get it open. Just thinking about it was more stress than she could bear.

The Chix were prompt and arrived in two cars. Cay drove alone because the library project she was working on was too far away for her to carpool with Trish and Jordan and still get to Andrea's by six. Andrea was on the lookout for the Chix and opened two of the four garage doors as each car pulled up so all vehicles remained securely out of view. She nervously hugged each one of them as they came into the house. She urged them to sit down in the kitchen to hear her plans.

"Ladies, I've hired a safecracker!" she began.

"Andrea, you haven't!" exclaimed Trish.

"It's not what you think. Give me a chance to explain." Andrea told them about her phone call to Lanier, and her conversation with John. "This is my home and my safe, after all, and I'm entitled to at least know what is inside it, right? I could never look inside by myself, I'd be way too nervous. That's why I wanted my friends here with me. Who knows what I will find in there? There is probably nothing important or helpful, but I have to try." Taking a tray of little sandwiches out of the fridge Andrea said, "Here, have some hors d'oeuvres. Hope you don't mind party leftovers. They've been frozen for a while, but they're still perfectly good. By the way, I think it would be better if you stayed out of sight while John is here. I don't want him to get edgy."

"*Him* get edgy?" Cay asked. "This guy is a criminal, Andrea."

"Well, not anymore. He's an honest citizen now, just making a buck like everyone else. Lanier wouldn't have given me his name if he thought he was dangerous."

"I guess you'll be wanting this," Trish said, taking a thick envelope from her purse with an empty York peppermint wrapper stuck to it.

"Oh my, thanks Darlin'." Andrea put the envelope into a kitchen drawer and the candy wrapper into the trash. She patted Trish's shoulder. "He should be arriving pretty soon now. I told him to drive to the back and come in the kitchen door so he wouldn't be seen. Where should you girls hide?"

"Well, I want to hear what's going on," Jordan said. "I want to know how he plans to open that thing."

"I agree. Besides, we need to be close in case he decides to rob you," said Cay. "Good grief, Andrea, he could kill you and steal goodness knows what. And where are the children? Are they going to walk in on this?"

"Really, I've thought this through. Mary Marshall and EJ are staying overnight with friends, and I don't think John's going to rob me if Lanier knows he's here."

The LitChix decided to stay in Andrea's sitting room with the intercom on. If they heard anything scary, they would race down the stairs with EJ's baseball bat. As they entered Andrea's room, Andrea spotted John's headlights in the driveway and dashed downstairs.

When she opened the back door, he said, "Mrs. Simmons? I am John Cho."

Andrea had not expected him to be Asian, so she was momentarily taken aback, but she recognized his voice from the phone. John was well dressed in a dark sport coat and gray slacks and carried a legal-type briefcase with him. He asked to see the safe.

Andrea expected some reaction when he saw it, but John said nothing.

"You may stay in the room," he said, "but you must be absolutely quiet. When the safe is opened, you can pay me the agreed amount and I'll leave. Is that suitable?"

Andrea nodded.

"I never look at the contents of a safe, for my own security," he added and gave a little smile. "With this type of safe, it will never be permanently unlocked. Close it and it will automatically lock again."

"So you know about this type of safe," Andrea said, feeling elated.

"Of course." John turned toward the wall and looked at the safe again for what seemed to Andrea a very long time but was perhaps only two or three minutes. Then he took a small metal bar and a rod from his briefcase. Carefully, he held the bar in his left hand and struck it with the rod. A faint lingering tone was heard, but nothing happened. He reached back into his briefcase and took out another bar, struck it once, twice, and waited. This time a low hum was heard and the safe door popped open an inch.

John stepped back, and returned his instruments to his briefcase. He said, "And now it is yours."

"May I ask what you did? That was just amazing." Andrea couldn't take her eyes off the door, slightly ajar.

"Trade secrets," he said pleasantly. "Works on tone."

"I can see that, but you were so fast. It looked so simple."

"Fast, yes. Simple, no," he said. "And now my payment."

"Of course. Just a second, please. Wait right here, I'll be right back."

Andrea dashed to the kitchen for the envelope, then returned to the study and counted out the money. She figured he made about a thousand dollars a minute, and fervently hoped something inside the safe justified such an expense. Andrea walked Mr. Cho to the back door, thanked him profusely, and let him out, locking the door behind him.

Andrea yelled into the intercom, "He's gone. The safe's open. Let's look right now."

The LitChix nearly tripped over each other coming down the stairs.

"Don't get too excited," Trish said. "I don't want you to have a big disappointment."

"That was so fast and quiet too." Jordan said. "I couldn't hear a thing."

Andrea warned, "Just don't touch the safe. The door is only slightly open and it will lock again if it closes. We have to be careful."

"Then don't let me anywhere near it," Cay said. "If anyone accidentally closes it, it would be me."

They tiptoed into the den and lined up reverently in front of the metal square on the wall. "Well, should I?" Andrea asked. She stepped forward and carefully put her fingers between the door and its frame so it could not accidentally shut. "Gather round, ladies. Here goes."

Cay said, "I have the crawly feeling in my spine that I get at horror movies. I hate this kind of suspense."

"You want me to get the popcorn?" Jordan asked.

Cay glared at her.

Andrea opened the safe door and everyone stood there in silence. Then Andrea handed out a package to Trish. Her voice muffled by continuing to face the safe, Andrea said, "Is that what I think it is?"

"If you think it is money, you're right." Trish's voice was hushed. "How many of these packages are there?"

"Lots and lots. Give me something to put in the opening so we can prop the door."

Jordan found a ruler in the desk drawer and some tape. "Maybe you can tape this in place so it won't fall out."

"I can't," Andrea replied. "My hands are shaking too much." Jordan gave the tape and ruler to Trish. "Here. You're the grown-up. You do it." So far no one said anything about the bundles.

Trish carefully taped the ruler in place while Andrea held the safe door open. Then Andrea said, "I have to sit down. I'm serious. I'm getting light-headed." She sat in an armchair and started to cry. "Do you know what this means?" she asked, pointing at the package that Trish had put on an end table.

"You have money," Cay said.

Andrea nodded. "Lots of money! I'm not broke after all. We can't let news of this get out. Sonny's creditors would take it all." All of her emotions of the day, and the previous week came flooding out, and Andrea sat in the chair and sobbed.

"Oh, Andrea, I can only imagine how relieved you must feel," said Cay. She helped Trish and Jordan carefully remove bundle after bundle.

"We have to count the money and hide it somewhere. Andrea, you should get it out of the house tonight. You can't put it back in the safe, and you don't want it anywhere around here."

"How much do you think there is?" Andrea asked, having just about cried herself out.

Trish turned to Andrea. "I've looked at only a few bundles, but most seem to have fifty thousand dollars in them. One had at least a hundred thousand. I don't know. There could be several millions here." Everyone stopped what they were doing.

"Are you shitting me?" Jordan asked. "Several millions? Andrea, that's wonderful. You'll be okay. More than okay. But Trish is right. You can't let the money stay here. I say we clean out the safe, put these bundles in garbage bags, and tape them up so they are as compact as possible. Then we'll put the painting back on the wall, eat something, and decide where in the hell we are going to hide several million bucks. It should be a snap."

For the first time since discovering the money, they actually laughed.

Chapter 22

"Sonny sure liked to buy in bulk, didn't he?" Trish said as she and Andrea entered the storage room. They looked for garbage bags to hold the cash from the safe.

"I always thought he bought so much of everything because he grew up poor back home in West Virginia. Kinda like he was always afraid of running out of something." Andrea gestured to the long shelves of juice, beans, soup, and . . . garbage bags!

"These are perfect," Trish said and reached for the bags. "We can fill them up so they're not too heavy for us to carry. We'll tape them and label them."

Andrea raised an eyebrow. Trish added, "Not with anything obvious, like 'Cash' or 'Hidden Dough.' More like 'Love Letters' or..."

"That's a heck of a lot of love letters," Andrea said. "We can decide that part later. Meanwhile, where can we put them? I can't leave them here, and you can't take them because I'll be living with you. Do you think Jordan or Cay would hide them?"

"All we can do is ask." Trish took an extra large box of industrial strength bags off the shelf. They headed back to the den. All four sat on the floor to figure out how they could package the money manageably.

"Wait a minute," Andrea said. "Before we start taping these up, I want to take some out. Enough to pay you back, Trish, and enough for me and the children, for emergencies..."

"And for manicures," Jordan said. "Don't forget manicures."

"For all of us," Andrea said, smiling, "A girl's day at the spa, on me. We deserve it."

"Where, exactly, are we going to hide the money?" Cay asked.

"That's a good point," Andrea said. "Trish can't keep it, because I'll be at her house."

"And I can't keep it," Jordan said, "because I don't have any place to hide it. When Jim's home, which, granted is not very often, the man roams everywhere. He has business records in the attic and who knows what in the basement. I'd be a nervous wreck. That leaves you, Cay. You live alone."

"But I don't want it," Cay said quickly.

"Nobody wants it, Cay, but somebody has to hide it," Trish said. "Be a good sport."

Jordan said, "Besides, you must have good places to hide stuff in your house. It's full of interesting nooks and crannies. You win the prize, Cay. When we pack this up, we'll put it in your car and then we'll all go to your house and look for a place to hide it. It'll be fun. Like a treasure hunt in reverse."

"Lucky me," said Cay. "Okay, but if I start to take a lot of expensive vacations, oh well."

They spent nearly an hour sitting on the floor, laughing, strategizing, and stuffing bundles of bills into garbage bags. When they were finished they folded the bags neatly and wound duct tape tightly around each. The bags were heavy but it was possible to move them to the garage without much difficulty.

Cay reluctantly opened the back of her Volvo station wagon. "This old car has carried some mighty odd things," she said, "but this takes the cake." One by one, they heaved the bags into the back of the Volvo, spreading them into a more or less even layer a couple of feet high.

"We should cover this with something," Cay said. "For once, my car is relatively clean. Andrea, you must have an old blanket we could use."

"We have a couple of old bedspreads, I think. I'll get them."

Trish went with Andrea and they came back lugging two king sized bedspreads, one from a zebra print phase and something dark plaid. They spread them across the black garbage bags and Andrea ran back to the storage room and produced a cooler, which she tossed on top. "It looks more casual this way, very picnicky."

Jordan glanced in the back of the Volvo, saw the zebra print bedspread and asked, "What is it with you, Andrea, and all this zebra shit?"

Andrea sighed. "It's just one of my phases. Be glad that you weren't around when I went through the patriotic phase and everything was red, white, and blue. It made you want to stand up and salute."

When they were finished loading the car, Jordan climbed in next to Cay. Trish and Andrea got into Trish's Land Rover for the caravan across town to Cay's little house near Lullwater. Andrea was careful to leave a number of lights on when she left the house and to put her hair up under a knit hat. She sunk down below the car window in case the police were watching and taking note of how many people arrived and left.

All went smoothly until they passed Dusty's Barbecue at Briarcliff and Clifton Road. Trish was in the lead, and she noticed a police car sitting in Dusty's parking lot. At that moment, the blue lights came to life and the cruiser pulled out right behind Cay and Jordan.

"Oh, my word," Trish said under her breath. "It's a policeman. I think I'm going to be sick."

"Trish, don't you fall apart now." Andrea said. "It's my money. I haven't done anything wrong."

"What do we tell them if they find it? That we are just taking it out for a little ride?" Trish's voice began to tremble.

In Cay's car, there was dead silence. Finally Cay said, "We have to pull over. Just act nonchalant. Two girls out for the evening. He may not even be stopping us."

"Oh, that sounds great," Jordan said. "For once I don't plan to say a thing."

Cay pulled into the shopping center parking lot on her left. The police car did not follow. But when Trish turned in at the next entrance, the policeman pulled alongside, got out, and stepped up to her window. Cay and Jordan strained to hear, but the traffic noise made it impossible. It was evident the cop was looking at Trish's license. He walked around the car, shining his flashlight at about bumper height as he went.

"What do you think he wants?" Jordan whispered. "Do you think Andrea looks suspicious in that hat?"

"Probably not. The police see people in the most bizarre clothing. A knit hat isn't odd. It's cold enough."

Jordan noticed Andrea seemed to sink down in her seat until only the top of her head showed. "Now she looks suspicious," Jordan said.

The policeman returned to the driver's window, had a brief conversation with Trish, got into his black and white, and headed back toward Dusty's parking lot. No one in either car moved. They had entered another dimension and all four women remained frozen. The world seemed to move around them. Eventually Cay drove her car alongside of Trish's Land Rover. Trish was sitting with her hands on the wheel staring straight ahead, and Andrea was still burrowed into her seat.

Cay put her window down, "What did the cop want?"

"He said my right front headlight was weak. Dim. He said I should get a new one soon."

"That's all?" Jordan asked. "He stopped you for that?"

"Slow night, I guess." As soon as Trish said that, Andrea started to laugh. She laughed so hard tears ran down her cheeks. She rocked back and forth in her seat, nose running, hiccupping, completely given over to the release from the stomach-churning panic of the past few minutes. Trish tore open a Kit Kat.

"I'd say let's stop for a drink and get settled down," Jordan said, "but if we push our luck, somebody will steal Cay's car while we were in the bar."

"Let's just go," Cay said. "I want to get home."

Cautiously they pulled out of the parking lot and drove under the speed limit and arrived at Cay's house without further excitement. Lacking a garage, Cay pulled as far as she could up her driveway and hoped the tall shrubbery around the side of the house shielded the Volvo. Trish parked her car as close as she could to Cay's. They walked the few steps to the only entrance that was ever used, the back door. The warm homey kitchen and the joyful greeting from Cay's sweet-tempered shaggy mutt made everything seem almost normal.

"We have to get going," Cay said. "We need to find a place to hide the you-know-what and then *put* it there. It's going to take a while and it's already way past my bedtime."

Jordan nudged Cay. "Cut the code-speak. Your house isn't bugged, so you don't have to watch what you say, Cay."

Trish said, "Well, let's look around. I don't see any place in this room that's big enough, do y'all?"

They went upstairs to the small bedrooms, which contained armoires instead of closets. They dismissed the idea of trying to haul the heavy bags up the ladder to the unfinished attic, then rejected the basement for the same reason.

"Okay, think," Trish said. "We didn't parade all the way over here for nothing. There has to be a place to hide this, this stuff."

"You're all talking like we're bugged, or something," Jordan said. "It's making me nervous."

Cay looked around. "The only other place I can think of is the summer kitchen." She walked out the back door through another door on the right and flicked on a bare bulb. "I never use this little area. It would make a good mud room if I gardened more. It used to be open for summer cooking, and at some point it was closed in, but nothing was done to it to make it really useful."

"What's that?" asked Trish, pointing at an old white chest marked Amana.

"A freezer," Cay said. "I think it still works, too, although it's as old as dirt."

All four gazed at the horizontal white box with the rusted silver latch and the distinctive Amana script.

"My grandmother's first TV was an Amana," Jordan reminisced.

"It's your freezer. You open it," Andrea said to Cay.

"Why do I feel like I'm in the road company of *Arsenic and Old Lace*?" Cay asked. The handle was stiff, but eventually yielded. Cay opened it, shutting her eyes and averting her head.

"What do you expect to find?" Trish asked.

"I don't know. I just can't imagine there would be anything in there I would want to find. Somebody else look. Please."

"Okay," Jordan said. Trish, Jordan, and Andrea all peered inside. Jordan gasped and muttered "Oh no, for the love of God! The humanity!"

"What? What is it?" Cay screamed and jumped back letting go of the freezer top. It slammed shut with a thud.

"It's nothing, you baby. I was kidding," Jordan laughed. "Actually, it looks pretty clean, and it doesn't even smell bad. I'd say we've got a hiding place."

For the second time that night, they hauled bundles. They arranged them neatly in the freezer, coming within a few inches of the top.

"We have to put something on top of all this," Cay said. "Something that looks like food."

"Then let's get some frozen dinners," Andrea said. "Is there an all-night grocery around here?"

"There's a Kroger down Ponce de Leon," Cay said.

"First we better see if the freezer gets cold. It would be horrible to put food in it and have it rot," Trish said. She took the heavy cord and plugged it in, wincing in fear that she would blow a fuse and plunge them all into darkness. Instead the lights dimmed briefly and the freezer began to hum. No particularly alarming sounds were heard.

After ten minutes, Cay stuck her hand inside. "Yup, it's getting cold, all right. That's a real trooper." She gave the Amana a little pat. "So who here is going grocery shopping?"

"I say we all go," Andrea said. "After all, you're going to have to leave sometime. Although maybe you should put a padlock on the door tomorrow, just in case."

The four piled into Trish's car and headed to the twenty-four hour Kroger, where they bought all the Weight Watchers and Lean Cuisine meals in stock. Cay was warned she couldn't eat any unless they were promptly replaced, to keep the nice even layer on top of the very cold cash beneath.

Chapter 23

"I haven't heard anything new, have you?" Mary Alma poured hot tea for Claudia and coffee for Lenora. "Either the police are mighty slow or they don't know anything about us."

"Something is definitely up with Andrea," Claudia frowned. "She said she was taking the children and moving in with her cousin, Trish Townsend. She did tell me she was very concerned about me and where I would live. I told her I would stay in the house as long as it is possible. Also told her she needed not worry, because I already had a place I could move to. That seemed to reassure her." Claudia took a sip of tea. "Andrea has always been so sweet to me. But it's strange she would leave Chateau Soleil to move into a garage apartment. Even if it is only temporary."

Lenora said, "Maybe she's lonely. That house is huge."

"I don't know." Mary Alma said. "Andrea never seemed like someone who would give up a fancy house. But no one has been arrested, and you don't read anything new about Sonny's murder in the paper, not after that big Sunday spread. Do you think Andrea shot him? We know *we* didn't have a gun, so who did?"

Mary Alma had to admit she was edgy. They thought Sonny was alive when they left him in the pool the night of the party. There were too many loose ends. She had invited Claudia and Lenora to her condo to discuss the situation and to talk about what, if anything, they ought to do.

"That line in the last Sunday's paper about how he was shot through the throat was a complete shock," Claudia said. "I don't know what to think about that. Was he shot before or after he fell into the pool? I didn't hear a gun shot."

"Neither did I," said Lenora. "Who could have shot him? I can't believe that Andrea would be that calculating."

Mary Alma added, "Or that she had such good aim. Who knows? Maybe she was a crack shot down there in Hicksville or wherever she came from. Country people are always good shooters."

"Excuse me," Lenora said. "I'm from the country and I don't know one end of a gun from the other. You shouldn't generalize about people, Mary Alma."

"Oh, chill, Lenora. I just meant Andrea certainly had a motive, she had the opportunity, and maybe she had the method. Those are the three things the police always look for in mystery novels."

"Then why haven't the cops told the press anything more?" Claudia asked. "Maybe they know something they aren't telling. That's another thing they always do in mystery novels and on TV."

"Maybe Andrea hired a hit man," Mary Alma said.

"I know her better than the two of you," Claudia said, "and I can't believe she would have Sonny killed. She had plenty of reasons to be mad at Sonny, but I think she truly loved him."

"You sound like a romance novel." Mary Alma didn't like the idea of Claudia or Lenora going soft. "It's amazing what lengths people will go to when pushed far enough. Witness the population of this room."

"Well, I for one want to get out of town until this whole thing dies down," Lenora said. "Besides, I didn't give him enough poison to kill him. Just enough to make him disoriented and unbalanced. It was the two of you who choked him and smacked him over the head before he fell into the pool."

"Let's stop arguing," Claudia said. "The fact remains that none of those things killed him. The bullet right in the Adam's apple did it, that and the broken neck when he fell, which we could also attribute to the shot."

"That's true," Mary Alma said. "The police are probably not even interested in all the things we did. Curious, maybe, but not looking for us. All we did was muddy the waters. They want the shooter. I think Lenora is right. It's a good time to take a little vacation to someplace with no extradition treaties."

"Amen," said Lenora.

"What am I expected to do?" Claudia asked. "Do you expect us all to take a little vacation?"

"To some place with beautiful beaches?" asked Lenora.

"And palm trees?" added Mary Alma. "I don't see why not. No one specifically told us to stay here, and we aren't subpoenaed to testify about anything."

"Not yet, at least," Lenora said.

"Good point. I guess things could pick up at any time. If we are not here, we can't be subpoenaed."

* * *

A few blocks northwest of Mary Alma's condo, Andrea, Trish, Cay, and Jordan were similarly deep in conversation. Each was wearing a blue velvet robe with Spa a Trois embroidered in gold on the breast pocket.

"You should try the Plum Pink," Andrea said to Cay. "It would flatter your skin tones." The manicurist reached for the bottle of Plum Pink polish.

"Not so fast," Cay said. "I don't have skin tones." To the manicurist she said, "Just a natural color, please."

"In other words, something that makes it look like you haven't had a manicure," Jordan said.

"Exactly, so when it peels off, as it will by the time I go to bed tonight, it won't be so obvious."

"Well, I think this was a wonderful idea," Trish said. "Thank you, Andrea. This is just the kind of break we need. Kind of a mini-vacation."

"I do feel a little more relaxed. By tomorrow night the children and I should be completely moved into that darling apartment you have, and so far no new catastrophes have surfaced. I want to stay as far away from the police as possible, but I'm dying to know if they have any new information. Maybe I should call them. I don't want them to think I'm uncaring, or worse yet, guilty, only because I'm not pushing them to find Sonny's killer."

"That is a problem," Jordan said. "Maybe you should call tomorrow and say something about being concerned about the progress on the case and how frightened you are that the killer is still at large."

"I think you ought to ask Lanier Poole first." Cay cautioned. "He might not want you talking to the police about anything."

"You're right. People are always getting themselves in trouble on TV for blabbing to the police when they shouldn't. I'll see what he says. It really isn't fair for them to keep me in the dark. For all I know, some gunman could have his sights trained on me this very minute, and I would never know."

"There's a comforting thought," Jordan said. "Just a minute." She turned and addressed the manicurist working on Cay's nails and read the name plate on her dark blue uniform. "Mimi, before we get any further along here, do you think we could break for lunch? We'll do the rest of the manicures after we've eaten. I think we ordered the chicken salad plates with white wine."

Mimi nodded, but thought that these women should decide what they were doing and not inconvenience everyone else with their whims. However she smilingly left the room to request their lunch trays be delivered.

"Sudden hunger pangs? That certainly came on fast," Cay said. "How am I going to eat with wet nails?"

"Blow on them. I sent her off for the lunch order because I realized our conversation was solid-gold gossip, and since Andrea has been so careful to keep a low profile, we don't want to ruin it with one manicure. Now we will be able to talk in peace. Andrea, when I so rudely interrupted, were you referring to the hit man theory?"

"Who else could have shot Sonny? It was silenced, right on target from a pretty good distance, and with apparently split-second timing. It sure wasn't some local out shooting at squirrels."

"Squirrels don't come out at night. It would have had to be a 'possum," Cay said.

"Well, if you aren't Little Miss Rodent," Jordan said.

" 'Possums aren't rodents. They are marsupials. Nocturnal marsupials."

"It doesn't matter what they are, Ms. Animal Planet. No one is going to pick them off with a rifle, especially not in Buckhead," insisted Jordan.

"A silenced Norwegian military rifle," said Andrea.

"How do you know that was a Norwegian military rifle?" asked Trish.

"It was in the coroner's report. Didn't I tell you? Lanier got it, and that is what it said. Sonny was struck by a single shot from a rifle used at one time by the Norwegian army. The police know because they have the bullet and it's very distinctive. That sure sounds like a hit man to me."

"A Norwegian hit man," Cay said.

The trays arrived, beautifully set with china, sterling silver, and crystal, placed on delicate wooden tables with a single red rose in a bud vase on each.

"Thank you. This looks lovely," Trish said to Mimi. "I'm hungry, even though it's early. That was good timing, Jordan."

As soon as she was sure Mimi was out of hearing range, Cay said, "I've lost my appetite. To think that someone was out there while we were at the party is just so weird. Wouldn't anyone standing down at the opposite end of the pool from Sonny be seen by everyone?"

"Remember, there were no lights back there," Andrea replied. "For heaven's sake I was back there with Buck and I didn't see a thing."

"As I see it, there are two places he or she could hide. Either in the pool at the deep end, maybe crouched down, or up in a tree."

"That's good thinking, Trish," Andrea said. "If he were in the pool, he would have had to shoot upward. Up in the tree, he might have been just a few feet off the ground. He would have had to be above Buck and me. There is a big branch that heads right straight out toward the pool. Maybe he could have stretched out along it."

"Now there are two more questions," Cay said, between forkfuls of chicken salad. She had forgotten all about her fresh nail polish. "Why did the hit man - hit *person* - think Sonny would appear behind the house, and who hired him?"

"Somebody would have had to lure Sonny back there," Jordan said. "Who would that be?"

"Well, Sonny only moved for two things," Andrea said. "Sex and money. So it could have been either, or both. Maybe that person wrote the third note on the pink scented paper. That sounds more planned than writing on a cocktail napkin."

They ate silently for a while. Sonny's stars must have been in very bad alignment that night, because it was undeniable that a whole lot of people wanted him dead, and accidentally or not, they picked the same time and place to carry out their plans. Only the hit man really mattered, though, and perhaps whoever got Sonny in position for him. That person could lead the police to the real killer - the person who hired the hit man.

"I just had an awful thought," Cay said. "What if the people who strangled him, and did all those other things to him also hired the hit man? Maybe for insurance. The newspaper said there were apparently several people back there with Sonny before Sonny was killed. Maybe they pooled their finances and bought themselves a hit man. I hear they are expensive, and a really good one probably costs, what? A hundred thousand? More? Maybe it was a group effort."

"Why all the dramatics?" Trish asked. "The Hermes scarf, the panther statue and so forth?"

"Maybe they each had an axe to grind, so to speak." Cay said. "That would also account for the barbecue sauce. It wouldn't kill him, but it would make a statement."

"What would it say?" Jordan asked Cay.

"Maybe something like, 'Keep your gol'durn redneck paws off me.'" Cay exaggerated the southern accent. "Or maybe 'I'm sick of you thinkin' barbecue sauce on filet mignon is gore-*met* food.'"

"Cay, you put it so poignantly," Trish said. "If we hadn't been together the whole night I would have thought you did it. However the barbecue sauce could also indicate the murderers thought Sonny was a pig. Or it could have symbolized that all men are pigs, if we want to take it to the next level."

"Speaking of taking things to the next level, I think we need to get a ladder, climb up to that tree branch and see if anything's there," Jordan said. "Maybe some fabric, or hair - anything that could show that someone was up there and it wasn't Andrea."

"Not a bad idea," Cay said. "I'll hold the ladder."

After lunch the LitChix and Andrea continued with their manicures and pedicures. Having a plan in mind gave them little need to continue the conversation in areas that would tempt any gossips listening for news.

"There are two things I really don't like," Cay grumbled.

"Only two?" Trish asked.

"Okay, we all know I am a bit set in my ways, but the first thing I don't like is anyone putting makeup on me. They always make me look like an extra in *Night of the Living Dead*, And I don't like anyone approaching my feet with sharp objects." This was said as a muscular blonde named Ingeborg started paring the calluses from Cay's feet, using an instrument that looked like it could open clams.

"Cay, you love it." Trish laughed. "I can tell."

Chapter 24

"That was such fun," Trish said. "Thanks again, Andrea." They were pulling into Andrea's driveway in Trish's Land Rover to pick up a few last minute things for Andrea and her children. Trish stopped her car. "What's going on? What are the police doing here?"

Two police cars were parked in the driveway, one blocking the front door and the other preventing access to the garage.

"This doesn't look good," Cay said, burrowing into her seat.

"Should one of us call Lanier?" Jordan asked. "It's 4:00 and his office doesn't close until 5:00."

"Not yet," Andrea said. "Let's see what the police want. It might be nothing."

Bongiovanni had been slouched down in his seat, his hat tilted over his eyes. Presumably he had been there for some time and decided to nap. He got out of his white Ford Crown Victoria as Trish turned off the ignition. Andrea heaved a sigh and got out of the passenger side of the car. Before she could say anything, Bongiovanni said, "Andrea Simmons, you are under arrest for the murder of Elliot Earl Simmons, Jr. You have the right to remain silent..."

"I am *what*?" Andrea said in disbelief. "You can't be serious!"

Bongiovanni continued his litany. "...the right to have an attorney appointed for you. If you cannot afford . .."

"*Now* we call Lanier," Jordan said. "Who has his number?"

"It has to be on Andrea's speed dial," Cay said. "Trish, get her phone out of her purse and call him."

Trish fumbled around in Andrea's Louis Vuitton hobo bag for a moment before coming up with the skinny little Razr phone. "Drat, I've never used one of these. How does it work?" Her fingers felt cold and clumsy. She could hardly work the tiny buttons. "Here it is, I think. Oh, dear Lord, I hope so."

Trish's attempt to call Lanier was greeted with a secretary's voice.

"It's an emergency. I have to speak to Mr. Poole immediately," she said. "Andrea, his client, Mrs. Simmons, is being arrested right this minute."

"I'm sorry ma'am. He is in court and his cell won't ring. He checks his messages all the time. I'll text him and he should call you in a few minutes."

"A few *minutes*?" screamed Trish. She was beginning to cry. "The police are here in her driveway *right now*! I don't even know where they are taking her."

"Don't worry. Mr. Poole will know all of that. Just calm down and trust him to do the right thing. Mrs. Simmons is in capable, experienced hands."

"Be that as it may, right now she is in the hands of the police! Ask him to please call me back as soon as he can. I'm her cousin, Trish Townsend." She recited her cell and home numbers.

By this time, Cay and Jordan were standing next to Trish's car, feeling utterly helpless. Two uniformed police officers stood by, as if Andrea would make a break for it.

"I can't believe you people came here as if she were a common criminal," Cay said indignantly. "It smells like somebody wants publicity."

"Hush, Cay," Jordan admonished. "It won't help us if you get arrested, too."

A police officer handcuffed Andrea, who was trying to remain calm. "Trish," she said over her shoulder, "look after the children. And don't forget Mr. Chanel."

"You have nothing to worry about, dear," Trish said. "I called Lanier. He'll take care of this situation soon."

"It reminds me of the French Revolution," Cay whispered loudly. "Poor innocent Marie Antoinette taking the rap because she was a high-profile woman."

Jordan squeezed Cay's arm. "Shush, Cay. These guys have no sense of humor."

"I wasn't trying to be funny."

Bongiovanni put his hand on the top of Andrea's head as she got into the back of the police cruiser.

"Why do they do that?" Cay asked.

Jordan answered her. "Some 'perp' must have cracked his head on the door and charged the cops with roughing him up, so they made it a rule. That's all I can figure."

"Andrea, don't you worry." Trish called out waving frantically to her cousin. "We're here for you!"

The cruiser headed down the driveway, Andrea gazing back through the rear window.

"This is so sad I could cry or spit or both," Trish lamented.

"Andrea's beautiful manicure gone to waste."

"Jordan, that is so insensitive," Cay said.

"No it's not. It's just I know the value of a buck. Those are ten expensive fingers, and for what? To impress the felon in the next cell? Wonder if her color will clash with that tacky orange jumpsuit? That's enough reason for us to spring her right there. Orange never was her color."

"What do we do now?" Cay asked, intentionally changing the subject.

"Well, I know what I have to do," said Trish. "I have to be sure the children don't hear about this before I can tell them. Sonny's death, combined with all the publicity, has been a lot for them to bear. Teenagers don't like to show that they are affected by anything, but they are, and I hurt for them."

"But if they find out by accident, it will be worse," Jordan said.

"You're right," Trish said.

"Are we alone here at the house?" Jordan asked, looking around and reapplying her lip gloss.

"Is Claudia's car here?" Cay asked.

Jordan walked back to the garage and peered in the windows. "Nope, she's gone. C'mon," she called to Cay and Trish. "This is our chance."

"Our chance for what?" Trish asked, hurrying to keep up with Jordan as she disappeared around the back of the house. "What do you have in mind, Jordan?"

"Who knows how many chances we'll have to be here alone? We want to look around the crime scene, remember? We want to see if there was a hit man or woman who could have been up in the magnolia tree. Now is the time, ladies."

"You're right," Cay said. "What do we do first?"

"I suggest we start with our theory and work backward. If someone comes…"

Trish interrupted, "Remind me again of our theory."

"Our hit man or woman idea," Cay said. "If there were a hit person, he or she would have had to be on a low tree branch, aiming toward Sonny. Anywhere else and he would have been seen by Andrea and Buck or by the culprits who were pouring barbecue sauce on Sonny."

"So, how are we going to investigate that theory?" Trish asked.

"Easy," Jordan replied. "We're going to get up in that tree and see what we find."

"Once again, 'we' doesn't exactly cover it," Cay said. "You can get up in the tree, Jordan. Or you, Trish. I will steady a ladder, take notes, sing a song, whatever you need, but my feet aren't leaving the ground."

"Fine," Jordan said. "I'll climb the tree. It isn't far up, after all. I just need something to stand on to get up there."

As they talked, they walked toward the big magnolia that provided the trysting place for Andrea and Buck, and perhaps also shielded Sonny's killer.

Trish looked over the pile of construction supplies in the area of the pool house. Now, with all construction stopped, the workmen had cleared out their tools and equipment, and that included ladders.

"We should have checked the garage before we came down here," Trish said. "I'll bet there are ladders in there. And I have Andrea's keys because she left her purse in my car, so we can get in."

"I think I can get up there without a ladder," Jordan said. "Back home in Jersey, I used to ride horses, some pretty big ones. If one of you can give me a boost up, I think I can get right up on the most likely limb."

"Okay, show me what you want me to do," Cay said with a sigh. Jordan showed her how to bend her knees and then weave her fingers together, and make a sort of a cup for Jordan to step in. Then, with a well-coordinated push upward, Cay would boost Jordan toward the limb. Jordan would grab the branches just as she would a horse's mane, and sling her leg over the main branch, arriving astride in one swift movement.

"You must be kidding," Cay said. "We are here to find evidence, not leave it. How long since you've performed this maneuver and were you wearing skin-tight jeans at the time?"

"It has been a few years. Besides the laundry shrunk these pants."

Cay snorted. "Bet it's been twenty years since you rode a horse. I don't think this is a good idea. I'll volunteer to go find a ladder."

"One try, Cay. I know it will work, and we don't know how much time we have. I don't think we want to have Claudia see us crawling around down here, or, God forbid, a policeman sent to watch the place."

"I'll do it," Trish said, taking off her Calvin Klein jacket and handing it to Cay. "I know a thing or two about climbing trees. We climbed plenty of big ol' live oaks and magnolias in the summer when I was a girl, and this one is easy." She went to the trunk of the tree and looked up into the branches. Trish grasped a smallish branch above her head and pulled herself up into a split in the trunk about four feet above the ground. Then she found the limb that extended toward the pool. It had some small sucker branches at its base, which she used to steady herself as she carefully slid her right leg over so that she was straddling the limb. As her foot scraped along the tree she thought, bye, bye Ferragamos, you have been good and faithful friends.

At the same moment, Jordan was thinking, *we'll have to get that burgundy shoe leather off the tree or it could be bye, bye Trish!*

"One of you stand on either side of me so if I start to tip you can push me up." Very slowly Trish inched forward. "It's pretty dark up here. I wish I had more light."

"Can you see anything at all?" Jordan asked.

"Maybe, I don't know."

"I'll toss you my penlight," said Cay. "Good catch, Trish!"

It was apparent the hit man would have needed to crouch forward to get a clear view, but this was undoubtedly the place the shot had come from. Trish's eyes were getting more acclimated to the dim light and Cay's penlight helped. While she wouldn't admit that she was nervous about her perch, she felt a bit insecure and whole lot less flexible than she had been as a child in rural north Florida.

Looking carefully up and down the branch, trying to focus inch by inch, she noticed a broken twig that looked unnaturally dark. "I'm going to move forward about a foot," she said to Cay and Jordan. "I see something that calls for a closer look."

Trying to lift herself up as she moved along the limb so that she wouldn't leave any fibers from her own slacks, Trish took her time inching toward the discolored spot. Once she was close, she wasn't sure what she was looking at.

"What is it? You've been up there long enough to see if anything is there."

"Pardon me, Cay. It's not like I'm Gil Grissom."

"Do you like him too?" Jordan asked. "I just love his little chipmunk cheeks and the way he peers over the top of his glasses."

"Who in the world are you talking about?" Cay asked.

"You know, CSI," Jordan huffed. "That's what we're doing here, a crime scene investigation, except we don't have any of their cool equipment."

"I could use some cool equipment right now," Trish said. "This sure looks like blood to me, and a couple of threads are stuck to this twig."

"Blood? You found blood?" Cay asked excitedly.

"I don't know for sure. It's dark, sort of reddish brown."

"Can you stick your finger in it?" Jordan asked.

"Why would she want to do that?"

"Because if we could get a little off on something, maybe we could find out if it is blood, maybe even whose blood it is. I know about DNA."

"That's not a bad idea," Trish said. "I have a card from the spa in my pocket. Maybe I can get it out and then . . ." She was quiet while she wriggled a little to reach the card. She pulled it free. "Here goes nothing," she said, carefully pressing the plain back of the card against the dark spot. "A good idea, but I don't think the blood is wet enough to show up. What we need is a real CSI person to come out and look at this. For all we know, the police already looked at it and dismissed it. It could have been from a raccoon or something."

"A raccoon in a sweater or shirt? You said there were threads," Cay reminded her.

"I think I'll come down. Let's ask Lanier what to do. This is beginning to hurt in ways I can't possibly describe." Trish worked her way backward on the limb and carefully let herself down.

"I'm impressed," Jordan said. "I thought you were too ladylike to climb up there."

"A southern lady does what she has to," Trish said. "Even ruin a perfectly good manicure."

Chapter 25

At five p.m., Mary Alma tuned into the local TV news. At five after five she put in a conference call to Lenora and Claudia.

"Pack your bags. We are leaving tonight."

"Why now? What happened?"

"Andrea Simmons has been arrested for Sonny's murder, and we don't know what else the cops might have up their sleeves. We can't risk staying in town. Be at Peachtree DeKalb Airport at eight tonight. Go to the Epps' hangar and they'll direct you to the plane.

"A passport is good but probably not necessary. Warm weather clothes, as many as you can get in your suitcase. Take as much cash out of your ATM as you can. Figure the rest out for yourselves. See you at eight."

"But where are we going?" Claudia asked. "I can't just leave town and desert Andrea in a crisis like this."

"If you aren't there, we leave without you." Claudia and Lenora were cut off as Mary Alma quickly hung up and started another call.

Lenora raced around her apartment to pack. She didn't have a lot, so packing didn't take long. A private airport, she thought. I wonder what that is all about.

Claudia was terribly upset by news of Andrea's arrest. *This is awful*, she thought. *We all know she didn't do it, at least we are pretty sure, and we're running off to safety while she's in jail. Surely the police won't keep her. How can they? Oh, dear I was supposed to stay and watch the house.*

Claudia's concern for Andrea was eclipsed by her fear for herself, and she began to pack a bag. It was fully dark by the time Claudia arrived at the Peachtree DeKalb Airport. She left her car in the Lindberg MARTA lot on

Piedmont Road and took a cab to the airport. She doubted that the transit police checked the lot very often for cars left an unusually long time. She didn't want to take a cab from Andrea's and alert the police if they were watching the house.

Lenora watched the cab pull in and Claudia get out before she got out of her own car. "I don't know what to do with my car," she said to Claudia as soon as she saw her.

"Lenora, I have an idea for your car. I'm sure we can find someone around here willing to put it somewhere, for a fee of course. We will work that out inside."

Lenora felt great relief. Claudia seemed very calm and organized, the very characteristics that made her so valuable to Andrea. She might be quaking inside, but outside Claudia was smooth as silk.

Last to pull up was Mary Alma. The car was unfamiliar to Claudia and Lenora, a dark blue Rolls Royce that slid in parallel to the front office of Epps charter service. The driver got out, an older man in a navy blue jacket and pants, and held the door for Mary Alma, who exited the car all smiles and charm.

"Wow, is all I have to say," Lenora said. "Is that yours?"

"This? This car? No, afraid not. This is Mag's little baby. Isn't it darlin?"

They were astounded when Mag Cramer pushed himself out of the other rear passenger door, nodded at everyone without introducing himself, and marched inside the hangar.

When Claudia recovered her voice she said to Mary Alma, "Lenora needs help with her car and I think you are the woman who can provide it." She explained the problem.

Mary Alma made a note of Lenora's address, gave it to the chauffeur together with Lenora's keys, and said,

"Don't worry. Your car will be put somewhere inconspicuous but safe, your keys mailed to you. I will let you know how to find out the car's location from Mag's chauffeur when you return." Mary Alma gestured toward the driver.

"Let's go, ladies." It was Mag, in high spirits ushering them in the door and through the small building, and out the other side to the tarmac. A gleaming white plane awaited them, its steps beckoning.

"Are we getting on this?" Lenora asked Claudia.

"I guess so. You know as much as I do. I'm mystified."

A pretty young woman in a camel colored suit appeared at the top of the stairs. "Welcome aboard," she said. "Take your seats and dinner will be served as soon as we reach cruising altitude."

"Cruising to where, I'd like to know. When do we find out what is going on, Mary Alma?" Claudia asked.

"I'm sure y'all are puzzled, but I will be happy to bring you up to date once we're in the air. Let's get going." Mag was usually a man of few words, but he looked and acted as if he were going to a party instead of transporting potential fugitives, to who knows where.

When everyone, including Mag, was settled into luxuriously deep leather loungers, Claudia swiveled around to admire the cream colored rice paper edged in thin strips of brass covering the walls and the tables and doors of dark swirling walnut, polished to a mirror gleam. The overall effect was reassuring, relaxing, and, most of all, rich. There was an attendant for each guest, and they handled every job, from stowing the luggage to seeing that seats and belts were adjusted correctly, with pleasant expressions and silence. A Chopin piano concerto played almost inaudibly in the background. The plane taxied into position on the runway, and before they knew it, they were hurtling into the sky, destination still unknown.

"Now really, Mr. Cramer," Lenora began.

"Mag, dear, please. But go on."

"Well then, Mag, please tell us what's happening. We were just talking to Mary Alma earlier about flying off to some sunny place to avoid, er uh, certain problems . . . ."

"Don't be flustered, dear. I know all about your 'certain problems.' "

"You do? Mary Alma, I thought this was all hush-hush. You never told us anyone else knew." Lenora was feeling a little betrayed.

"Before you go blaming Mary Alma," Mag said, taking a glass of champagne from the waiter and handing it to Mary Alma, "let me tell you what happened."

"Let me tell, Mag," Mary Alma said. "I do owe everyone an explanation.

"Earlier this fall, right after we first met at the salon, I ran into Mag at a charity event. It was over at the Renaissance or the Radisson or some such place."

"The Ravinia," Mag interjected. "Go on."

"The Ravinia, that's right. Well the party was boring as hell so I headed to the bar and who should I find there but Mag, who was doing the same thing I was doing - escaping a lot of drivel about sailboat racing and salmon fishing in Scotland. Of course we already knew each other, and he said I looked sad. I said I wasn't sad, just bored, but then after a couple of vodka tonics, I confessed that I was a little upset, and I told him a few things Sonny had done to really break my heart. Of course I didn't tell him it was *Sonny*, but Mag knew, because Sonny's reputation had gotten around."

"A little something before dinner?" a steward asked, placing a silver tray of canapés on the table in the circle of chairs. Accustomed to being the one passing the trays, Lenora appreciated the service. Now it was her turn to choose from little quiches, shrimp on circles of toast, and an icy bowl of caviar with shaved hard-boiled egg and onion, along with a basket of crackers. She realized she was hungry and it was now well after dinner time.

"If I can interrupt just once more to take your dinner order," the steward said, offering choices of Kobe beef, lobster Newburg, and a vegetarian platter. The women who seldom ate a meal of red meat suddenly found their inner carnivore and all ordered the beef.

"Excellent choice," Mag said. "Go on, Mary Alma." He said this in a tender, paternal way, as if he were proud of her narrative to the group.

"As I was saying," Mary Alma continued, putting down a toast-point piled with caviar, "I was pissed, and I said, 'That is a man who just needs killin'. A woman betrayed should take revenge.' Well, you can imagine my surprise when Mag said, 'I couldn't agree with you more.' I thought he'd assume I was joking, but he took me seriously, so we started to talk about it, in a kind of abstract way. Mag said that Sonny, by then we were calling him by name, was like a rogue elephant, wild and out of control, no longer useful to the herd. Nobody trusted him. He was making dishonest deals and causing the whole development picture in downtown Atlanta to be questioned, which hurt Mag and other major developers. In addition, Sonny was bragging and swaggering around and maybe even had the mob involved in that oil rig debacle. Then Mag said, and I remember his words exactly, he said, 'You know what they do with rogue elephants, don't you? They shoot 'em!'"

Mary Alma giggled and grinned at Mag. "Well, one thing led to another. We talked about it for a while but the next day I thought it was just bar talk and nothing more would come of it, with Mag, that is. We were still going ahead with *our* plans," Mary Alma said, and gestured to include Claudia and Lenora.

"Anyway," she continued, "one day out of the blue, before the Panther party, Mag called me and said he thought he'd arrived at a permanent solution for 'our problem,' as we called Sonny. He suggested I ask some attractive young friend of mine to slip Sonny a note with 'meet me by the pool' and a time on it, to get Sonny alone. Well, I told him that great minds think alike because Lenora was already going to get him back there so we could teach him a lesson. Lenora spiked his bourbon and Coke just enough to disorient him. It was easy for Claudia to whack him on the head with the panther statue, and I choked him with Andrea's scarf. I also executed the *coupe de grace* by pouring barbecue sauce on him."

Lenora interrupted Mary Alma. "We each had our reasons to get even with Sonny. He raped my mother when she was just a teen-ager helping Aunt Berry cater a party in Buckhead. He never even cared he fathered a child. I was furious when he complimented my blue eyes, since I got them from him!"

Mag stared at Lenora. "No wonder you hated Sonny." He shook his head. "Claudia, what's your story?"

"My story is remarkably similar to Lenora's. The difference is I fell for another man's line and when I told him I was pregnant, he left me. Being a good Catholic girl, I quit college, give birth in secret, and place the baby up for adoption. Sonny's unfeeling behavior toward Andrea and all the women in his life was too much like my own awful experience. I saw the opportunity to do something about a no-good, wicked, cheating man. I agree with Mary Alma. A woman betrayed should take revenge."

Mary Alma cleared her throat. "Well, to get back to that night. Mag was just mostly concerned about the time, and pretty soon I said, 'Okay, Mag. I've got it. Eleven-thirty.' I thought that was that. Well, come to find out that there was a hit man back there, which was pretty scary. Claudia and I were right smack in the middle of everything when Sonny was shot. It's sure lucky that guy was good, because if he had been a few inches either way...."

"Just points up the need for really good communication," Mag said, "but all's well that ends well." And he lifted his glass in a little toast.

Chapter 26

"I guess that explains some things," Claudia said, "but I still want to know where we're going."

Lenora said, "I have to admit it, Mary Alma, I thought we were all in this equally, and now it seems you were just using Claudia and me the night of the party." Lenora cast a glance at Mag. "What's really going on here? I don't get it."

"You're right Lenora. I was getting worried we weren't going to find Shangri-la, where we would be safe from the law, if, God forbid, it should come to that."

Mag interrupted, "Mary Alma was fumin' and fussin' and goin' nowhere, and I knew the perfect spot. Hell, I own the perfect spot."

Claudia stared at Mag. "Okay, so where is this perfect spot?"

"Have you heard of the island of Santa Zipporah?" Mag asked. Claudia and Lenora shook their heads 'no.' "I thought not. It's not hidden, not even a secret, but not many people know about it. It's a few square miles of sand and palm trees near the Dutch Antilles. For a long time, the closest airport was on Bonaire, if that's any help. The Dutch and the Spanish traded the island back and forth for centuries. Both of them settled on Santa Zipporah, and about twenty years ago I bought it and built a resort, Hacienda Zipporah." Mag shifted in his seat.

"My resort is quiet and private and first class. There's no television, and we try to avoid phones. Of course the reception for cell phones is nonexistent, which helps." He snapped his fingers and asked the steward to give everyone champagne. "We hope our guests become so satisfied and relaxed by their surroundings that they forget all about the outside world. My staff does maintain short-wave in case someone is ill or injured and the local clinic can't handle it. Only private planes are allowed into the airport, and the mail plane stops at the southern tip of the island a couple of times a week."

"Are we staying at your resort?" Lenora asked.

"For the time being, yes," Mag answered. "I imagine y'all will want to see how things play out back home. There're some attractive cottages around the island if it turns into a long-term stay. Let's just wait and see."

"Isn't it a little hard to wait and see without communications?" Lenora asked. "How do we keep up with the Atlanta papers from there? You just said there's a need for really good communication."

"You've been listening." Mag smiled patronizingly. "Sharp girl. I have my own little communication system, not available to anyone else on the island, so you can stay fully informed."

"Mag owns a satellite," Mary Alma said. "It's spinning around up there somewhere," she pointed up at the ceiling of the plane.

"How did you work that?" Claudia asked. "I didn't know private citizens owned them."

Mary Alma tucked her legs up onto the seat cushion. "It's Russian, and all it took was cash."

"Mary Alma," Mag said in mock dismay, "you can't give away all of my secrets. Anyway, it's time for me to get to work, so I'll retire to my office for a while and ya'll enjoy yourselves."

With that, Mag went toward the back of the cabin. His office was luxurious in every sense, but what couldn't be seen was even more important: a titanium mesh shell beneath the wood and wallpaper trimmings to assure that Mag would be safe in case of any unfortunate security breaches. An impenetrable safe room with full satellite communications made him at least as protected as the President, perhaps more so. He enjoyed the comparison.

"Mary Alma, have you been to Hacienda Whatever?" Claudia asked.

"No, I haven't. I'm as eager to see it as you are," she said. Cutting her steak with a fork and savoring the incomparable smoky sweet flavor, she said, "Oh, this is good! This is really good."

"Dessert?" The steward wheeled in a cart loaded with fruit, cheese and a spectacular Black Forest torte. Mary Alma had some of each.

* * *

If Claudia, Mary Alma, and Lenora were in a state of nervous anticipation as they flew into the late evening sky, Trish Townsend in Atlanta began her evening in a state of nervous dread. She had to tell Andrea's children, EJ and Mary Marshall, their mother had been arrested for their father's murder. She called and told them they needed to be home for dinner and was amazed they complained very little. Every minute would bring them closer to a news program or a mouthy parent secretly happy that someone else was having misfortune.

When the back door slammed. Mary Marshall, EJ, and Trey tossed their book bags onto Trish's kitchen counter, they seemed relatively normal. A bit sullen, a little sarcastic, and therefore normal for teenagers. The early evening news had that bad photo of Andrea splashed everywhere, and drooling accounts of the crime and the alleged murderess.

How lucky, Trish thought, *teenagers have little interest in news other than who 'hooked up' with whom, as they so charmingly put it.* If, after her news, EJ felt he couldn't face his teammates, Trish had decided he could stay home and not play Westminster's football game against Banneker scheduled for later that night.

Trish put dinner on the table in the kitchen. Her family always liked the comfort foods of meatloaf and applesauce. That, along with lima beans, twice-baked potatoes, and caramel apple pie should put them in a good mood.

Mary Marshall came to the table first, announcing she would have to eat fast because her friend Kelly was picking her up in *like* forty-five minutes and she still had to *like* pick out an outfit and *like* put on her makeup. She continued a list of her obligations to beauty and style. Trish tuned her out, grateful nevertheless that the fourteen-year-old was talking up a storm. As soon as EJ and Trey appeared, Trish sucked in her breath and began.

"EJ, Mary Marshall, Trey, I have some news, and it will not be easy for y'all. EJ, please take those things out of your ear and listen to me. As I was saying, what I have to tell you is not pleasant news."

"Eeeuuuw!" Mary Marshall let out a sound of disgust as she poked her fork at the slice of meatloaf on her plate. "What is this? I don't eat brown food."

"It's meatloaf and it's good," Trish said, growing impatient. "Please don't interrupt. This isn't easy for me, children." At the word 'children' Mary Marshall rolled her eyes, "Your mother has been arrested for the . . ." and here Trish could not say murder, "for the death of your father. Of course we all know she didn't do it and the truth will be out soon, but meanwhile that's what happened today."

"Mom's in jail?" Mary Marshall asked in a high voice.

"Way to go, Momster," EJ exclaimed, pumping his fist in the air.

"EJ!" Trish shouted. "You apologize, right now! Your mother is not a monster." Trish felt tears well up behind her eyes.

"Not 'monster', Aunt Trish, *Momster*. Oh, never mind. I think Mom is cool. So is that what you wanted us all together for?" Trish heard the preposition at the end of the sentence and it bothered her. But considering the circumstances she kept it to herself.

"Yes, it is," she said. "This is serious, EJ. This isn't a TV program, it's real life. Your mother is in trouble for something she didn't do, and we all have to help her."

"How long will she be there, Mom?" asked Trey. "Can't she be released on bail like they do on TV?"

EJ responded quickly, "I don't see what I can do. It's not like I can break her out of jail."

"EJ, I'm amazed at you! I wanted you to know if you feel like you need to skip the game tonight, it's all right. If you are too upset…"

"Mom, EJ is the *starting* quarterback," Trey cried out. "There's no way he can skip the game."

"Upset? Hell no, Aunt Trish. I mean heck no. I mean I'm sorry Mom has to spend the night on one of those stinky jail beds, and I wish she could be at the game, but that doesn't stop me from playing football. We went to the game after Dad's funeral, remember? If we did that, why would a little arrest stop everything? I'll eat after the game," EJ said and pushed away from the table, plugging the tiny speaker back into his ear.

Trey got up from the table and followed EJ out the door; shaking his head at the very idea of EJ missing tonight's game for any reason.

Trish was speechless, wondering where reality was for these children. Certainly not in actual life-and-death struggles. Maybe it existed in the contests on perfect grass under the lights, or perhaps not even there.

Mary Marshall had said nothing. As soon as her brother left the table, she asked, "May I go now, too? I have to get ready."

"Yes, of course. Go ahead." Trish was gratified only by Mary Marshall's use of "may" instead of "can", but that was very little comfort. With a feeling of grief washing over her, she scraped the plates into the disposal and gave a bite of the meatloaf to Mr. Chanel, who was scurrying around at her feet. Even he seemed disinterested in Trish's meatloaf, picking up and dropping bits a few times, then leaving them behind, slightly chewed and rejected. Trish sighed and grabbed a couple of chocolate kisses from the back of her silverware drawer.

I wish I could fly off to some tropical island, Trish thought, *and pretend that this whole mess never happened.*

* * *

I wish this whole mess had never happened, Lenora thought, looking out the porthole at the moonlight on some wispy clouds below the plane. *I'd like to be home in my robe and slippers eating carryout. Well, I've made my bed, I guess.* Lenora began drifting off to sleep, cradled in the soft reclining seat. She awoke, to find a cream colored cashmere blanket lightly covering her, and to hear the gentle, almost crooning voice of one of the attendants announcing they would land in five minutes.

When the door to the plane popped open, the warm damp air was a shock. It had been a chilly mid-October night when they left Atlanta. Now she heard the sound of the sea, saw millions of stars, and felt embraced by warmth unlike anything she had ever known. There were hands all around, taking their luggage, guiding each of them down the steps and into open cars. Were they in some kind of Jeep? Mary Alma, Lenora, and Claudia got into one car and heard Mag say, "I'll see you ladies at the Hacienda. I'll be right along."

"That's all there is to it?" Claudia asked Mary Alma. "No customs? I didn't even see the airport."

"Oh, the airport is down there," the driver said, pointing to a darkened runway. "Closed for the night."

The little caravan pulled away from the plane, with Mag and the luggage in the lead Jeep. The warm air brushed their faces. The only light came from the moon reflecting on the water and from three sets of headlights. Scents both sweet and spicy were everywhere, mixing on the air, drifting from the foliage that lined the road on the side opposite the beach. And the beach: it appeared shimmering white in the moonlight, a perfect ribbon, extending as far as the eye could see.

They didn't realize they had reached the Hacienda until the Jeeps stopped and men took their bags and helped them step down into soft grass. A few lanterns lit the way, but Lenora saw no grand gates, no tiki torches, no huge lobby like most tropical resorts.

Mag said, "I arranged for each of you to have a cottage. Follow me." He picked up a lantern and walked a few yards before he hung the lantern on a hook and opened a door. "Lenora, this one is yours. Claudia and Mary Alma, you're right down the walkway." He spotted a momentary reaction of surprise from Claudia.

"Did you expect Mary Alma and me to share a cottage? She's a lovely woman, but I am a thoroughly married man, and I plan to stay that way. Why, if Melanie so much as suspected I was unfaithful to her, she'd hunt me down and kill me with her bare hands. You gotta love that in a woman." Mag chucked. "No, Mary Alma is a kindred spirit who has a lot of potential, but our relationship is strictly platonic."

"'Course I flirt with him a little bit, anyway," Mary Alma said, gently nudging Mag in the ribs. "That's what makes the world go 'round. Come on Claudia, let's get see what your cottage looks like. Good night, Lenora," and she headed down the seashell path, lined with bushes and vines with fragrant flowers.

Lenora stood in her cottage's entrance and looked around. Most of the teak furniture was simple, covered with deep soft cushions. The walls were covered in grass cloth printed with subtle palm fronds. On the floor jute accent rugs completed the tropical look.

Lenora explored the bedroom. The four poster bed was swathed in sheer white mosquito netting, although there were no mosquitoes. The room was painted a soft pearl color. The soothing sounds of the ocean could be heard through the sliding glass doors. The bed was piled high with pearl colored pillows.

This is the finest place I've ever been, Lenora thought. *I could easily have gone my whole life and never experienced this elegance.* She went into the bathroom, ran a warm bath and poured in some of the gardenia scented bath crystals contained in shell shaped urns. Some of her earlier doubts began to fade. *I wonder how long it will take for all of this to seem right,* she wondered.

Meanwhile, Claudia's thoughts were not as peaceful. She and Lenora now knew way too much about Mag's role in Sonny's death. *Why would he trust us with so much damning information unless he had a plan for our silence? What is he up to?* Although Claudia didn't anticipate a restful night, she was asleep minutes after her head touched the cradling down of her pillow.

Chapter 27

"Oh, Trish, thank heavens I got you." Andrea's voice sounded far away.

"This is a bad connection. I can hardly hear you. Andrea, are you all right?" Trish flipped on the phone's speaker function to improve the sound.

"I'm fine, or as fine as I can be, under the circumstances. How are EJ and Mary Marshall? Did you tell them?"

"I had to," Trish replied. "If they found out from someone else, it would have been awful."

"You did the right thing. How did they take it?"

"I think they took it very well," Trish said, remembering EJ's cavalier attitude and Mary Marshall's open lack of interest. "Teenagers are pretty resilient."

"I talked to Lanier. Thank you for calling him. He was very comforting."

Not hard to be comforting when you are not the one in jail, Trish thought.

"He sort of laid out the plan for the next few days, but I was so rattled by everything that happened I can hardly remember it. I do know he's going to get me in front of a judge first thing Monday for a bail hearing. He'll call you, because I told him one of my friends would put up the money for bail."

Trish understood Andrea was alluding to the cash in Cay's freezer.

"Did you say Monday? What happens between now and then?" Trish asked.

"Not much, I guess. I'm stuck. Lanier will get the prosecutor on the phone and push this thing ahead, but no judge will hear it before Monday, so here I sit."

"Andrea, that's terrible. Do you need anything? Do you want me to come see you? Are you in any danger?"

Andrea laughed. "From what I can tell, it's more dangerous out where you are. Oddly enough, I've met some really nice women. In fact I am beginning to see our justice system is totally unfair to women. Some of them made just one mistake."

Trish wouldn't characterize murder as a mistake, but she let it go.

"The most ridiculous things are the felonies. One woman here wrote a rent check because her husband swore up and down he'd deposited the money, but the check bounced, so they arrested her and charged *her* with a felony. Where's the justice in that, I ask you?"

Trish was pleased and surprised Andrea's social conscience was kicking into gear, but that did not allay her concern about her cousin being in jail over the week-end. The next couple of days would not be easy.

"The LitChix will be there Monday, Andrea. Right in the front row."

Andrea brushed back her hair and shifted the phone to her other ear. "That reminds me. Lanier said he will ask you to bring some suitable court clothes for me. Pack a little bag with my black suit, the one I wore to Sonny's funeral, the low-heeled black pumps, clean undies and so forth. Forget the jewelry. They made me take it all off and locked it up when I got here. I'm not letting that happen again. Oh, don't forget makeup and my Shalimar. And a hand mirror."

"I'll take care of everything, Andrea. Please don't worry. I love you. You're like a sister to me, and I won't let you down."

"Thanks, Trish. I've to go now. Women are lined up to use the phone. Give EJ and Mary Marshall a kiss from me. Tell the other Chix how much I appreciate everything they are doing for me. See you all Monday in court.'Bye."

Trish didn't mention to Andrea that she, Cay, and Jordan had done a little snooping and found a possible clue to the shooter. When she told Lanier about the possibility of blood on the tree limb, she couldn't tell how interested he was from his response, only told her he would pursue it. She realized she had to be satisfied with that for now.

Trish finished dressing for the Westminster football game, not looking forward to an evening of smiling and pretending all was well. She knew her mind wouldn't be on the game, but she had to be there for the children. The thought of Andrea spending a long week-end sleeping in a hard narrow bed on rough sheets, hearing the sounds of prisoners' shouts reverberating throughout the cells, was disturbing and very sad.

Andrea, on the other hand, saw the evening ahead of her from a different perspective. While those who had been in the system before tended to be closed and wary, all was new to Andrea. She found her surroundings enormously interesting. Nothing could be further from her Buckhead life than these women wronged by men they had foolishly loved, women cheated out of their money and lives by drugs, alcohol, and men. Despite the difference in circumstances, the relationships and behavior were nothing new to her. Prison was a dressed-down version of what she saw in Buckhead. She was a good listener and truly concerned. Some of the things women told her made her cry.

This is terrible, she thought. *This injustice has got to stop. Someone needs to speak up for these women.* Sitting on a metal folding chair in a common room, wearing an orange jump suit that did nothing for her looks, Andrea experienced the kind of conversion that some find in church.

When I get out of here, she vowed, *I am going to do something so these women don't get here in the first place.*

Thinking about the future took her mind off the fact that in a few hours she would stand before a judge and plead not guilty to the murder of her husband.

* * *

When Lanier Poole returned Trish's phone call Friday evening, shortly after his return from court, he was incensed to learn Andrea had been arrested. He thought his understanding with the prosecutor allowed Andrea to turn herself in at a mutually agreed-upon time. This was blatant showmanship, maybe even a little class resentment, and definitely the kind of hubris Lanier wouldn't let pass.

Lanier immediately called Detective Bongiovanni. "Jerry. I hear you arrested a dangerous criminal today. A beautiful woman, a mother, no less, grieving for her husband. You must have been quaking in your Florsheim's."

"Lanier. I thought I would hear from you. What can I do for you?" Bongiovanni's reply sounded a little smug.

"Well, you could have honored our agreement to let the lady turn herself in. Funny, we never even got a request. Out of the blue, there you and a small army are sitting outside Mrs. Simmons' door."

"I don't know who you had that agreement with, but it wasn't me," Bongiovanni replied gruffly.

"That's right. It was with your boss, ol' 'Straight-shootin' Miller Cantrell. Isn't that what he calls himself? 'Miller,who-has-never-so-much-as-looked-down-the-barrel-of-a-gun Cantrell' would be more like it. Miller owes me one!

"On a different note, I suspect your crime scene investigators may have been a little perfunctory, shall we say, when they investigated the Simmons' property. It has come to my attention that some evidence might have been overlooked. I am taking my independent lab boys to

Chateau Soleil as soon as it's light, and they are going to get to work."

"You can't do that," Bongiovanni protested.

"The Simmons home is no longer an active crime scene," Lanier replied. "It has been tramped over by your men. Nevertheless, I might have some new evidence to look at that your people haven't destroyed yet. You're welcome to be there if you want. Just remember, you have to share like a good boy, and if there are any samples, we divide them. In fact, it's better that way. Rather than one report absolving Mrs. Simmons, we'll have two." And he hung up.

Lanier knew that nothing he would find, with the exception of the signed confession of the killer, would absolve Andrea, but it could cast doubt, and just a sliver of doubt was all Lanier Poole needed. When he was through with cross-examination in trial, that sliver would be wide enough to drive a Mack truck through, with a little extra room on either side.

Now to call his lab people and get things lined up.

Chapter 28

Trish felt she had fallen down the proverbial rabbit hole. Jails, bond hearings, murder trials - all unthinkable only a few short weeks before were now the stuff of daily thought and conversation. Planning for Andrea's first appearance before the court on Monday had taken on the characteristics of a mad hatter's tea party.

After six rings, the number she speed-dialed was picked up. "Jordan, I've talked to Lanier, and he says we should be outside the courtroom no later than eight. That's AM. Do you know what that means?"

"We get our coffee to go?" Jordan spoke sleepily, having been awakened from a satisfying late Saturday afternoon nap.

"No, it means Monday morning gridlock downtown, that's what it means. I won't risk being late by having to find parking and walking over to the courthouse. Jordan, I want you to drive and drop Cay and me off. Then you can park . . ."

"And hoof it over by myself, right?"

"Yes, more or less. But Jordan, we really need you. Not just anybody can negotiate that kind of traffic. Some people would just lose it."

"So, my time spent on the Jersey Turnpike finally pays off," Jordan said, still yawning.

"Well, you are the most . . . aggressive driver I know," Trish said.

"Moxie," Jordan said. "You gotta have moxie. Most of these Atlanta drivers don't know how to play the game. They bolt and dart every which way. You have to focus and plow straight ahead."

Once Jordan was lined up, Trish called Cay.

"Lanier is going to ask for bail, of course," Trish said. "He thinks he has an agreement with the prosecutor, but he thought he had that before about the arrest and it didn't work. Anyway, it will be up to you to put up the money."

"I'm assuming we're talking about the *special fund,* am I right?"

"Yes. If the judge sets a million dollar bond, and Lanier thinks that is what the prosecutor will ask for, you'll have to put up one hundred thousand. Ten percent. That's the way it works."

"So I stuff a hundred thousand in my purse, go into the courthouse where they make you open your purse in front of everybody and check for anything strange, and then march up to the courtroom."

"That's about it," Trish said.

"I was being sarcastic, Trish. Do you think they're going to let me in with that wad of cash?"

"I don't know why not. It's not a weapon or illegal, is it?

"Why can't we give it to Lanier and let him take it in? Attorneys don't have to open their briefcases."

"I'm not so sure of that, nowadays. But anyway, he can't appear to be paying his client's bail."

"It wouldn't look like that," Cay replied. "I'm sure lawyers have deeds and mortgages and cash and stock and all sorts of things that their clients use for bond in their briefcases."

"Cay, just do this, will you? Lanier said *we* need to bring the money, and you have the money. We may not even need it if, God forbid, the judge denies her bail and makes her stay in jail. I don't even want to think about that."

"All right, I'll be a sport, but if anyone asks what all that money is doing in my purse, I'm going to point to you and say 'She'll tell you.' "

"Fine. I'll think of something." *Please just let us get through Monday and have it all over with. I feel like I'm a hundred and ten years old.*

* * *

If there was anything Lanier hated, it was getting up early, especially on a Saturday. He got up early on Saturdays all the time, but repetition had not made him hate it any less. He made himself a pot of coffee, grabbed some of last night's leftovers, and was out the door to meet Bongiovanni at the Simmons' place. He didn't want the cops to get there first. No telling what they might do.

"Officer. Good to see you on the job. Lanier Poole." he said, handing the policeman his card. "I am here to meet Detective Bongiovanni, as it happens, to discuss some of the finer points of discovery in the case involving this very property." He could see the young man struggling to keep up.

"I don't think anyone…"

"Of course not. Not just anyone. You are one hundred percent on the money about that. Good job. As I was saying, we are meeting here about some issues of concern to us both, and I am going to want you to send the detective right down in back to meet me the instant he arrives. Got that? The instant! This can't wait, son. Matter of life and death! Fine man, your detective. I have my investigative team right behind me," Lanier gestured to the black van pulling in. "And they are going to go back there and set up and wait for the main man to arrive."

The officer looked confused enough to make Lanier feel that he'd bought at least a few minutes, so he strode purposefully to the rear of the house. His investigators moved even more quickly and were already setting up their equipment under the magnolia. Trish had been very specific when she described to Lanier the location of the possible blood on the magnolia branch. Already the small collapsible ladder was up and an investigator was standing on it, leaning over the branch but not touching it, scanning back and forth with a special light that made blood glow blue.

"We have something here," she said. "Definitely blood. I don't think it has been disturbed, so their guys probably didn't find it."

"Good enough," Lanier said. "Now let's wait for the detective and his GBI team to get here."

Of course, nothing said that the blood was left the night Sonny Simmons was murdered, or that it could be matched to anyone who might throw some doubt on Andrea's guilt, but it was worth a try.

Lanier was standing in the driveway, sipping his coffee from a thermos and stamping his feet in the damp morning cold when the detectives pulled up, accompanied by a crime scene investigating unit. Helen Morrow got out and introduced herself to Lanier.

"I don't think I've had the pleasure," he said. "I have some extra cups in the car. Would you like some coffee?" Lanier didn't offer any to Bongiovanni.

"No thank you," Helen replied. "Let's get on with this."

"Well, I'm sure your sharp techs over there can tell us the answer to that, Detective. Of course they missed it the first two or three times they investigated, but no problem."

"Did you ever think it wasn't there the first two or three times?" Bongiovanni asked.

Lanier just shrugged, sipping his coffee and walking toward the magnolia. "Your investigators' notes should tell whether they climbed up in this big ol' tree, and, if so, whether they found blood. Have you checked their notes yet?"

It was Bongiovanni's turn to parry with another question. "And how exactly did you find out about this blood, or alleged blood?"

"A tip. As I told you, a tip. From a reliable source."

Bongiovanni sneered, "Yeah, right.

"Why, detective, I thought you used tips all the time. A 'Huggy Bear' kind of thing."

Bongiovanni shrugged, but a few moments later Lanier heard Detective Morrow explaining to him, under her breath, who Huggy Bear was in the *Starsky and Hutch* lexicon.

"As if I had time for dumb old TV cop shows," Bongiovanni mumbled.

There ensued a discussion of which team would look first, who would take the first sample, and who would disclose what to whom. It was agreed that each party would notify the other of the results of their separate lab findings, because, as Lanier put it, "This is in the interest of justice, right Detective? It's not a game with winners and losers." Of course Lanier knew that justice belonged to the party with a royal flush plus an extra ace up his sleeve, for insurance.

Chapter 30

"Trish, you know you really are the meaning of the word *genteel*," Cay observed. "This room, the food, everything you do is so, so classy."

"Why, thank you, Cay," Trish said with a laugh. "Since this house belonged to two generations of Townsends, I'm blessed John's family had such exquisite taste." The den was Trish's favorite room, with its blue toile club chairs and aged mahogany bookshelves and paneling. Her collection of blue and white export China porcelain completed the look of traditional elegance. With a fire blazing in the fireplace the den felt safe and snug - the perfect place to meet and talk over a very stressful subject.

"It helps to marry well, doesn't it," Jordan said, reaching for the brie and crackers. "Where is Andrea?"

"She was supposed to be here by now. She has only to come over from the apartment over the garage. I'll call her on the intercom. I can't wait to get started thinking of ways to help exonerate Andrea. Just because she got out of jail on bond does not mean her troubles are over. We haven't seen anyone official working hard to prove her innocence. They aren't even trying to find another suspect. It's up to the LitChix to solve Sonny's murder. Amateurs do it in the mystery books we read all the time. We can't let Andrea down."

"Who's letting anybody down?" Andrea spoke from the doorway. "I'm so sorry to be late. I was on the phone with Miss Adeline, and, well, you know how she can carry on. I know I've really neglected her - all of Sonny's family, in fact- and I'm trying to make up for it. I haven't been thinking of anyone but myself and my children. Poor old Miss Adeline and Vergy are sitting up there in Possum

Pocket, wondering what is goin' on. I wanted to bring them up to date and comfort them as best I could. It's amazing with all the publicity and accusations against me not one of Sonny's family thinks I killed him. They have been so supportive."

Andrea was uncharacteristically low key, wearing very little makeup, her hair in a pony tail. She wore a pale blue warm-up suit no designer logo or label in sight.

"Shouldn't Claudia be here, too?" Jordan asked. "I'm not her biggest fan, but she might have some helpful observations."

"That's the oddest thing. I can't get in touch with her. I'm worried. She has been so devoted all these years I cannot believe she would simply disappear and leave me and the children right now."

"That's strange all right," Trish said. "I drove in yesterday and rang the bell, but the only person around was a security guard. I think the police put him there. Anyway, I peeked in the garage, and her car was gone. I asked the guard if he had seen anyone with her description and he said he hadn't, but of course that doesn't mean anything. It's very disturbing."

Trish walked to a closet and pulled out a dry erase board on an easel and some markers.

"Cool," Cay exclaimed. "Just like *House* on TV."

"I thought we could make a diagram of all the people we think could have anything to do with Sonny's murder, and figure out where they were at the time he was killed. Then at least we would have a beginning number of possible suspects besides Andrea." She stared at the blank board. "We have to consider the methods, the opportunity, and the motive. Killing someone takes a lot of hatred."

"Or fear," Jordan interjected.

"That's a good point. Lots of people had a reason to hate Sonny, and some had a reason to fear him, I suspect. Sorry, Andrea. I know this has to sound awful to you, but we have to face the facts. Clearing you of murder is our first priority now."

"I know, Trish, and you're right. Who knows how many people Sonny destroyed."

"Let's make a chart," Trish said. "Does anyone have a suggestion of how to start?"

"Oh, goody," said Jordan. "I loved making web diagrams in school. Why don't you let me organize the crime?"

"Be my guest." Trish handed Jordan a marker. "Come right on up here and lead the way."

"I'm not sure if this will help, but what if we put Sonny's name in the center and put the names of everyone we can think of who might want him dead all around him, like this, and then figure out which of those people were there, who hated him enough to kill him. We can color code those. The first person has to be Mary Alma Harwick. She was obviously furious at the Panther party. Her name should be in red."

Jordan turned to Cay. "Cay, you overheard Mag Cramer after the funeral saying some questionable things to another man. And those magazines you found in Global Imports indicate that Sonny and Mag were pretty close if Sonny was getting mail there. Sonny could have been a threat to Mag, so I'll add his name in green."

"Don't forget," Cay said, "Sonny was shot by some-one who was apparently an expert marksman. Probably a professional hit man."

"Or hit woman," Jordan interjected. "Let's keep it fair."

Cay frowned. "Or hit woman, then the person who hired him or her didn't even have to be at the party."

"That's true," Trish said, "and that's the one person who really counts. How can we figure out who hired the hit person if it could be everyone who was there or someone who wasn't?"

"Wait!" Jordan said. "You know who should be helping us and isn't? That mousy secretary of Sonny's. What's-her-name. I'll bet she knows a thing or two. I don't believe Sonny was murdered in some passionate outburst, in spite of all those hokey things like the barbecue sauce and the scarf. Somebody hired a hit person because he or she had a whole lot to lose and the crime was planned way in advance of the party. That probably means the murder had to do with business, and who would know about that better than what's-her-name?"

"Isabelle. Isabelle O'Brien," Trish said looking to Andrea for affirmation. "I think you're on to something, Jordan. Maybe you should call Isabelle, Andrea."

"What should I say? Do we want her to come over here? Should we offer to go to her house?"

"Let's think that over while we start on supper," Trish said. "I've made an antipasto and some bruschetta. We can go to the kitchen and serve ourselves. I'll put up TV trays in here."

"You have TV trays?" Cay asked. "What a relief. I'd been thinking you were too perfect. But I bet they are really, really nice TV trays."

"That's funny. They were on sale at Wal-Mart. Wine anyone?" Trish asked. "Or, if you prefer, I have San Pellegrino, with lemon."

"Oh, this is too good," Cay said. "What's for dessert?"

"Cay, how can you even think about dessert?" said Jordan laughing."

"I always save room, and Trish always makes dessert," Cay said. "So, what is it?"

"If you must know, it's a pound cake with pear confit."

"Pear confit!" exclaimed Cay. "I don't even know what that is and I love it."

"Okay, ladies, let's put our heads together while we eat." The Chix and Andrea returned to the den with food piled on their plate. "How should Andrea approach Isabelle? We don't want to scare her off," Trish said.

"Isabelle has always been so protective of Sonny," Andrea added. "I can't say anything that would make her think we are trying to make him look bad. Nothing about dirty deals or enemies. Don't you think?"

"How about starting off by asking about Isabelle's health, how she's holding up, that sort of thing," Cay suggested.

"That's good. And I could ask about her mother. She's a huge part of Isabelle's life - probably her whole life now that Sonny's gone. Then maybe I could say the police are focusing on me and only me for Sonny's murder and that would have upset Sonny very much. He would have wanted me to have every tiny piece of evidence, no, wait, tiny piece of information that would help catch the real killer."

"And," Jordan added, "you could tell her there might be clues that you would recognize, and could you please go through Sonny's papers with her."

Andrea put down her soup spoon. "Are we going to ask her to come here? Could she even bring everything she has? It could be boxes of stuff, for all I know. I doubt she would leave her mother home alone, and Trish's house would probably intimidate her."

"You'll have to play that one by ear, I think," Trish said. "See how she sounds and go from there. You're blessed with great people skills, Andrea, and the right words will come to you as you talk to Isabelle."

"Oh, I don't know," Andrea said. "How will I know if she sounds like 'I'll be there with bells on and Mother be damned,' or 'I don't plan to leave the house or Mother alone now or ever.' "

"Have faith in yourself," Jordan said. "After all, you are the girl who charmed Lanier Poole into giving you a safecracker, and look how well that turned out. I'd be very confident, if I were you."

"Ready to make that phone call, Andrea? You don't want to wait until it's too late," said Trish. "I doubt Isabelle stays up for the 11 o'clock News."

Andrea took her cell phone from her pocket. "I have Isabelle's home number in my directory."

"Hello? Isabelle? This is Andrea . . . . I can hardly hear you. Could you speak up a little, please? . . . . Slow down, Isabelle. Tell me what has happened . . . . I'll help you, but I have to be able to understand you first. Take a deep breath. Now calm down. It'll be all right. Speak slowly and tell me why you're so upset . . . .

"Wait a minute. Isabelle, slow down, dear. I don't understand what you are trying to say . . . . You found what in Sonny's office?

"Keys to a safe deposit box? I already looked in our box. Sonny didn't have - oh, a key to *another* box. In your name. Oh, I see. Isabelle, should I come over and take a look at this?" A long pause while Andrea listened and glanced at the Chix. Then she repeated, "Isabelle, should I come over?" Another pause.

"May I bring some friends with me? They are helping me sort out Sonny's affairs." She looked at the ladies and smiled. "All right. We'll be right there . . . . No, of course not. I should have called *you* sooner. Now don't be so upset. I'll see you in a few minutes, Isabelle." Andrea hung up. "That woman needs a valium."

"Who doesn't?" said Jordan.

Cay sat on the edge of the chair. "Well? What was that all about? For heaven's sake, we are practically drooling in anticipation."

"Apparently, Sonny kept a safe deposit box in Isabelle's name. She said she discovered the key in an envelope in one of the files she took from the office. She went to the bank and emptied the contents. There were some important papers inside and a cassette tape. Then she started crying and said the information they contained was so awful and she doesn't know what to make of it. She would have gone on and on, so I think it's best we go see what she's got for ourselves. Right now."

"No dessert? No pear confit?" Cay asked.

"Really, Cay. I think this is a little more important." Jordan said. "We'll have desert when we get back. Whose car should we take?"

"I hate to suggest it, but we should probably take mine," Cay said. "She lives on Deering or someplace over that way, doesn't she? There's a lot of gentrification around there, but a lot of the little older places, too. My wagon probably wouldn't be as conspicuous as your snazzy cars."

"Okay. The Volvo it is," Trish said as Jordan cleared the trays. "Let's freshen up and move out. Leave the dishes Jordan, I'll straighten up later. Grab your coats Ladies, and let's head out."

Cay turned on the radio to NPR to drown out the rattle in the engine, "Don't worry. The car's fine. Ignore the noise. Just showing her age a little, that's all."

"You should also have someone look at the shocks," Jordan said.

"Hey, after half a million miles, your shocks wouldn't be so good either," Cay replied. "Besides, I like to feel the road."

"Feeling the road is one thing. Having it jolt your fillings out is another," Jordan said, bouncing forcefully off the seat as Cay's car hit a pothole.

"Don't knock the car. This old Volvo has been good to us more than once. Now, just settle down. We'll be there in no time." Traffic was lighter than usual, so they arrived at Isabelle's well before nine.

Andrea said, "This gives us plenty of time to look at what Isabelle has without delaying her bedtime too much, I hope. She sounded like she could use a good night's sleep."

"From what you said, I think a shot of vodka and a shiatsu massage at Spa a Trois would be good medicine," Jordan said, "but that's just me."

Cay found a place to park on the street near Isabelle's driveway, and they walked up the uneven concrete steps to the front door. The woman must have been waiting, because as soon as Andrea knocked, Isabelle flung open the door and pulled her inside, the entourage following closely behind. Although the tiny living room possessed too few seats to accommodate them all, it quickly became obvious the action was in the dining room anyway. They gathered around a small stack of envelopes on the table and Isabelle tried to explain why she was so distraught.

"Andrea, as you know, I always held Sonny in high esteem. The very highest. I felt so protective of him. I know that sounds foolish, but it's the truth. But what I found out is so awful. It must be true, but I still can't believe it."

Andrea put her arms around Isabelle's shoulder. "There, there. Let's have a look at what you found." Andrea could hardly wait to put her hands on the items on the table, but she didn't want to dismiss poor Isabelle's grief.

Isabelle wiped her eyes, blew her nose, and said, "Here, let me show you. I have them in order, I think."

The first envelope held three letters. The first was from Sonny to the head of the construction company building a Gulf Coast petroleum rig. It specified the materials for him to use in the massive off shore rig. The second letter was from the construction company foreman telling Sonny that the specs he had given them were inadequate and would never withstand a major storm. The third letter was Sonny's reply, threatening consequences not only from him but from Cramer Industries as well unless construction proceeded exactly as he was told.

"Mag was in on this?" Andrea said amazed.

Isabelle, her voice quivering said, "Do you remember what happened to the Gulf Coast rig? It went down in a hurricane. One hundred fifty men lost their lives. And the China Gate tunnel? It collapsed on the workers while still under construction. Not all of Sonny and Mag's projects failed, at least not yet," Isabelle continued, "but all were put together with inferior materials. The construction companies objected, but Sonny said Mag would ruin them if they complained. Some did, plenty of lawsuits against Sonny were pending when he was killed. But some contractors complied, and several disasters were directly related to Sonny's demand that they use cheap goods, according to the letters in these envelopes."

Andrea said, "This explains why Sonny was broke when he died, but I don't see how this information can clear me of his murder, even though Sonny destroyed enough lives to make at least one person want to kill him."

"And then there is this," Isabelle said, opening another manila envelope. Out dropped a cassette tape and an envelope addressed "To Whom it May Concern" in Sonny's handwriting. In a strong voice Isabelle began reading:

"I, Elliot Earle Simmons, Senior, want it known that if I die under suspicious circumstances, Magnusson Cramer has threatened my life on numerous occasions, one of which is documented on the tape accompanying this letter. Mag and I had a disagreement over several investments (documents in envelope). When I reminded him that I had evidence of his involvement in projects built to substandard specs in order to increase his profits, he stated that he would have me killed if I tried to use that evidence against him. As it is now structured, no one would ever know he was involved."

"Here is the tape," Isabelle said, "but I don't have a tape player. Maybe one of you has one." The old-fashioned cassette lay in her hand.

Andrea asked, "Does anyone have an old tape player this would fit? We have to hear it. I don't know if they even make those players any more."

"I know where one is," Cay said. "I have an old tape player in my Volvo."

Everyone grabbed a coat and headed back to the car, including Isabelle.

"Will your mother be all right?" Trish asked. "Should she be left alone?"

"She's as tough as nails," Isabelle said hurriedly, "and I wouldn't miss this for anything."

A stringy polyester spider web and a lopsided cardboard skeleton decorated the front door of the bungalow next to Isabelle's.

"I forgot! It's almost Halloween," said Trish. "I always decorate for Halloween, but this year, I completely forgot."

"Don't worry, dear. Life's scary enough." Isabelle gave Trish a little pat on her shoulder.

Cay pulled up her trouser leg. "I've got on black sox with orange pumpkins on them to celebrate the season. See?" Jordan groaned.

The five women piled into the Volvo. Cay turned on the engine and the heater to alleviate the late October chill. She put the tape in the player. The first voice was Sonny's, giving the date and time and saying that he had taped a telephone conversation with Mag. He said that in the event anything happened to him, everything should be given to the police.

"Wow," Cay said under her breath.

Andrea was shivering, in spite of the warmth in the car from the heater and from so many heavy-breathing occupants.

The static and other sounds on the tape made it evident that Sonny was on the phone and Mag was speaking.

"If you think I'll let you bring down Cramer Industries you're crazy. You're right. You have enough information to finish me off. No more government contracts, no more wife, and no more society pages, as you put it. And you think I'd let that happen?"

Then some remark came from Sonny that sounded like an expletive, but he was too close to the microphone to be intelligible.

Mag was speaking again. "You poor bastard. I can have you taken out so fast you'd never see it coming. You think I don't know people who kill for a living? You think it would be the first time? Remember Richards? Do you really think he had a fishing boat accident? You better look over your shoulder, Sonny. If you even hint that you intend to point a finger at me, you're a dead man."

There was more on the tape, but it was essentially blustering by Sonny. When it was over, Cay pressed "rewind," and carefully took it out of the dashboard player. "Once again, the Volvo comes to the rescue," she said.

The rest of the group sat transfixed as they contemplated this latest bombshell.

"Isabelle, do you have any brandy?" Jordan said breaking the heavy silence. "Because if you don't, I saw a package store just down the street and I'm going to buy some. We need some help in trying to absorb this."

"Brandy? My dear, how do you think I've endured Mother all these years? Come inside and let's see what we can find."

Chapter 31

"So what do I make of that?" Bongiovanni asked, hanging up the phone.

"Make of what?" Morrow replied, sounding distracted. She was filling out police reports, a seemingly endless job, and wasn't much interested in conversation.

"That Trish Townsend woman invited me to dinner. She was cryptic. She said she had come across some information the police should have."

"Isn't she the tall blond one? I think she's a rich, pushy woman with too much time on her hands."

"She said she was inviting you to dinner too, Morrow."

"In that case, isn't she that striking, clever woman who is Andrea Simmons' first cousin?"

"The very same. I don't think it would violate ethics or anything else if we went, do you? As long as Andrea Simmons isn't there. Townsend isn't a suspect."

"Not my problem. I don't go out in the evening unless it's with my kids. I have little enough time with them as it is. So you'll have to go all by your lonesome, I guess." Morrow knew Bongiovanni wanted to go. She could see the loneliness all over him sometimes. His children were grown and needed him less all the time, and his longing for his late wife was almost palpable. "Go ahead. I won't tell. You deserve a night out."

"This wouldn't be a night out," Bongiovanni said, sounding slightly defensive. "She said she has something for me - something the police should have."

"She couldn't bring it here?"

"I don't know. I didn't ask."

"Whatta cop. You're all over it, Jerry. Atlanta is safe."

Trish called Morrow extending the dinner invitation to her.

The LitChix heard her say, "I do understand, I'm a widow and a single mom myself. Maybe another time."

Trish hung up the phone. "Helen can't make it, but Jerry can."

"Helen and Jerry, is it? Oh, my," said Andrea, lying on the couch, "you've gotten chummy all of a sudden. Ooh, I shouldn't have talked. My head . . . ." Andrea repositioned the cold towel on her forehead.

"Serves you right for drinking all of that brandy," Trish said. "I thought you and Isabelle were trying out for *Girls Gone Wild.*"

"Who would think something that tasted so good could pack such a punch," Andrea moaned. "Never again. You don't look worse for the wear, Jordan. By the way, did you or Trish notice all the romance paperbacks in Isabelle's bedroom? When I went to the bathroom I had to walk through her bedroom and I've never seen so many bosoms and pecs in one place in my whole life. Floor to ceiling bookcases, filled."

"All very interesting, but Cuz, you have to get yourself in gear, headache or not. You have to take those papers to Lanier's office and get a copy, hold on, make that two copies, of the tape."

"Why two copies?"

"The original for Lanier, a copy for the police, and a copy for safekeeping. For now, why don't you find a safe place to tuck away a set of the papers with the tape?"

"I want to bring the main course for dinner," Jordan said unexpectedly. "Eggplant parmesan. I have a wonderful recipe, from a dear old friend. It would give a good Italian boy a taste of home."

"If you really want to, you certainly are welcome," Trish said smiling. "Goodness, I won't know what to do with myself with nothing to cook."

"You can make a fabulous desert," Jordan said, "and tell Cay to bring the garlic bread and salad. We ought to do some of the work, you know."

Trish had one more call to make. "Isabelle? Detective Bongiovanni agreed to be here Thursday night at seven sharp. Can you make it? Andrea says she can be at your house by six so she can meet your mother before you leave. That way your mother will get to know her a little before they settle in for the evening. Andrea also said she'd bring dinner for the two of them." Trish tucked the phone under her chin and started pulling out her good China.

"Mother eats like a bird," said Isabelle. "She probably won't even notice the food, but that's very sweet of Andrea. I'm so excited. I get out so seldom, and you girls are just such fun. I hope the detective won't be mad that I didn't find the tape right away and then waited to do something about it."

"I'm sure he won't be mad, Isabelle. We're all very happy to have it. This evidence should clear Andrea of Sonny's murder."

Isabelle paused. "I hope Andrea's feeling well today. She put away quite a lot of brandy last night. It can really sneak up and bite you, if you know what I mean."

* * *

Activities certainly expand to fill the time, Trish thought. It was almost five. What had she done with the hours, besides make dessert, set her table, and go out to buy Chianti and fresh flowers? Trish was looking forward to having a man in the house again, even a man in whom she had no romantic interest. A man coming to dinner, even Detective Bongiovanni, made it feel special somehow. She missed doing the little things she used to do for her husband.

Andrea pulled in a little after five and came through the back door, complaining about the horrendous traffic. "But," she said, "mission accomplished. Here are two copies of the original tape. Lanier's secretary was very helpful, making one for your 'Jerry' and one for safekeeping. Lanier kept the originals. I feel so relieved. Of course there was no time to go over all of this with Lanier because he got back from court late and had a client, but I'm sure these things will make a huge difference in the case. Now I have to run and get ready to go to Isabelle's. I'm looking forward to spending an evening with her Mother. It will be relaxing for me."

"He isn't 'my Jerry,' " Trish called after Andrea, as she headed outside to the apartment stairs.

"He isn't?" asked Jordan, coming in the back door with a huge pan of eggplant parmesan. "Then do we all get dibs on him? I like him. He seems like a good cop with the right accent," She put the pan on the kitchen counter. "Do you think this enough?" she asked.

"Enough for twenty at least."

"You haven't eaten *this* eggplant parm. There may be some left over, but not much. Keep the leftovers for the kids. Just don't tell them it's a vegetable."

Andrea had barely gone up the stairs when she came back down, wearing jeans and a sweater and carrying a down coat over her arm.

"How cold is it supposed to be?" Trish asked. "You look like you're headed to the Arctic."

"It's supposed to get down to forty tonight, and in my book, that's the Arctic."

"Poor baby," said Jordan. "You should experience a Jersey winter. I used to walk through snow up to my elbows. Oh wait, that was *Fargo.*"

"No, thanks. I'm a southern girl through and

through. I could never live anywhere magnolias don't bloom. See y'all later," and she was out the door.

"Wait. I thought she was taking dinner with her to Isabelle's mother," Trish said.

"That means she's getting take out. What else?"

Cay was the last to arrive, carrying a big bowl of salad and a long loaf of French bread tucked under her arm. "I feel uncomfortable about this. Don't you? Bongiovanni is a cop; he isn't Andrea's friend. In fact, it's his job to try to put her away, and we are feeding him dinner? Should we even be talking to him?"

"Listen, Cay," said Jordan, "if you want to go home now, it's okay. Bongiovanni isn't stupid, and he wouldn't be coming over here if it weren't kosher. Now's your chance. Go if you want to, but leave the garlic bread."

"Are you kidding?" Cay said. "And miss your eggplant parmesan? You couldn't get me out of here with dynamite. Besides I wanted to see how low cut your neckline would be. That's how I judge your interest in a man.

"Do you all think I should have offered to pick up Isabelle and given her a ride? If she isn't accustomed to rush-hour traffic, it may be a shock to her."

"Isabelle insisted on driving," Trish said. "I tried, but she wanted to drive, and that was that."

"We have time before Isabelle and Bongiovanni get here," Jordan said. "Let's sit down and go over what we know."

"Just as important, what we want to know," Trish said. "We can't be too pushy, but if we're going to continue to help Andrea, we have to learn as much information as possible from Jerry."

"Are we planning on playing the tape for Bongiovanni?" Cay asked.

"Not unless we all want to pile into your Volvo again," Trish said. "No, I think we should let him listen to it on his own, at police headquarters hopefully. And of course we'll tell him Andrea gave the original papers and tape to her lawyer. He'd expect that anyway."

"Let's see. We know that Sonny and Andrea had a fight upstairs during the Panther party," Cay said. "Thanks to Jordan, we overheard them and heard a slap."

"And we know Andrea lost one of her artificial nails during the fight and the nail was found in Sonny's shirt fringe," Trish continued.

"There's also the whole thing about Buck. He and Andrea were doing the nasty under the magnolia tree at the far end of the pool at about the same time Sonny was killed. Andrea's shoe prints were all over the place." Jordan was ticking off the evidence against Andrea on her fingers.

"We can't forget the blood Trish found on the tree limb. That's my favorite, because Trish climbed that tree with such dignity," Cay said. "I'm not sure it exonerates Andrea, but it certainly was exciting."

Jordan continued. "And the notes. There was a note that was found on the ground, written on Andrea's stationary, about meeting her at the pool house. We know she wrote it to Buck and he must have dropped it. The question is, do the police believe her story. Another note was found in Sonny's pocket. It was written on a cocktail napkin about meeting someone at the pool, but we don't know who wrote that one. When the police questioned Andrea about the notes, she explained the first one to Buck, but didn't know anything about the one on the cocktail napkin or the third one on pink perfumed stationery."

"Wow, Jordan," Trish said. "You have really been thinking about this in a lot of detail. What do you think the story is with the scarf and the barbecue sauce?"

"Those things continue to puzzle me. Sonny was also hit on the head with a heavy panther statue, and the autopsy said he had some drugs in his system, a kind of a poison, that might have disoriented him. I don't know what to think about the barbecue sauce . . . ."

Cay said, "I stick by my opinion that the barbecue sauce was just plain anger. Someone saying he was a pig. Plenty of people would have held that opinion. Especially women."

"But when it came down to killing him," said Trish, "it was the bullet that got him in the throat, and the fall that broke his neck. He couldn't have been shot by the same person who poured the sauce on him and all the other stuff."

"Happy accident?" Jordan asked. "Several assassins or would-be assassins at the same time? I can't help but remember when Vergy freaked us all out at the cemetery by having that vision, or whatever it was. Didn't he say something like, there will be one accused but many will be involved? Maybe the old codger does have 'the sight' after all."

"Wouldn't that be amazing? But I don't know," Trish said. "It's the hit man or the person who hired him who are the real killers, and the material Isabelle gave us seems to say Mag Cramer was the one who hired the hit man - okay, or woman. We have Mag's motive, in his own words, no less. We know the hit person had the opportunity, and we know his method. That seems pretty clear to me, but we have to be sure it is equally clear to Jerry."

Jordan said with an exaggerated sexy voice, "I'll hop up on his lap and explain it *all* to him!" Then she grinned.

Chapter 32

Discussion was interrupted by a knock at the back door. Trish hardly recognized the woman standing there with a pleasant look of expectation on her face.

"Isabelle? Is that you? My goodness! You look so different," she said, taken aback by the younger-looking, more chic secretary. "Is that your car?" Trish didn't mean to sound amazed, but the burgundy Cadillac seemed a bit luxurious for Isabelle.

"I don't have anything else to spend my money on, and Mother likes to be comfortable when I take her riding. If she's not, she complains something fierce." Isabelle glanced into the hall mirror, flipping her new hairdo. "Do you like my haircut? After you girls left last night, I saw myself in the mirror, and I looked so old and drab I thought 'Why don't I perk myself up a little? A change would be good for me.' So this morning I took Mother and we went to one of those quickie cut places at Peachtree Battle. I told them to cut off the whole thing. I've had that bun for more years than I'd like to say, I just wanted a new look. It feels so light and free. I should have done this years ago. The stylist suggested some color, but I'm not ready for that, yet. Maybe next time," she said with a giggle.

"Guess what else we did?" Isabelle didn't wait for a reply. "When we were going into the grocery store, I saw a nail salon right there, so Mother and I both had manicures! Can you believe it? Everyone there was speaking in Vietnamese, I think, and I didn't understand one word. I've never done such a frivolous thing in my whole life, but oh my, it was fun!"

Trish led the way into the den. "Well, come on in and show everyone the new you. We're still waiting for Detective Bongiovanni."

Isabelle's appearance was greeted with great enthusiasm. "Whoa! You look amazing," Jordan exclaimed.

"It's a good cut for you," Cay said with approval. "It takes ten years off you, at least. You'll love the freedom of short hair."

Changing the subject, Trish said, "Isabelle, we don't want you to be intimidated by the fact that Detective Bongiovanni is a policeman. Just tell him what you told us. Sonny left you a letter to be opened in the event of his untimely death. When you read it, you discovered the safe deposit box. When you opened the box, you were confused and upset. Andrea called you to find out how you were doing, you were relieved because you planned to call her. You told her what you knew and gave her all the papers and the tape."

"Yes, that's just the way it was," Isabelle said. "You don't happen to have anything to drink, do you? Maybe a little wine? I feel all out of breath after that drive. The traffic was just as bad as you said it would be, maybe worse, so I'm glad I left when I did." She took the glass of white wine Trish handed her and downed it in a couple of gulps. Trish didn't offer a refill. She didn't want Isabelle tipsy when it came time to recount her story.

A few minutes after seven, Detective Bongiovanni pulled into the driveway. Trish hurried to open the front door.

"Hi, Jerry, please come on in," she said, smiling. "I'm so glad you're here. Let me hang up your coat." Before he removed his coat, he handed her a bottle of wine.

"Here," he said. "I don't know if you are a wine drinker, but . . . "

"Indeed I am. We'll have this with dinner. Thank you for being so thoughtful." Trish took his heavy topcoat and hung it in the coat closet, but not before she caught the odor of cigarette smoke on it.

"Every one is in the den. Right this way." Trish could sense Bongiovanni was looking around as he walked a step behind her. *I forget this house is impressive*, she thought, glancing at the Gracie hand-painted wallpaper, partly covered by ancestral oil portraits. The antique Chippendale chest with Louis XIV upholstered chairs on either side contributed to the old money look of the entry.

Jerry was greeted warmly as he walked into the den, and Trish made the necessary introductions. "I guess you have met all of us before," she said, "but under unpleasant circumstances. I thought you might have forgotten who was who."

"Remembering who is who is my business," Bongiovanni said with a twinkle in his eye, "but you ladies would be unforgettable in any circumstances."

Fortunately, he didn't see Cay roll her eyes.

"It's nice to hear someone who can tawk right," Jordan said, smiling broadly. "It's been a while."

"It's been a while here, too," said Bongiovanni. "So where you from?" A conversation about familiar locales in New Jersey ensued, which seemed to satisfy them both enormously.

"Wait until you taste the eggplant parm tonight. I made it from a recipe of an old friend. The tomato gravy would have been better with Jersey tomatoes, but what can you do?"

"Maybe we ought to explain what it is we want to give you," Trish said, "or rather Isabelle wants to explain what she has, before we start dinner. Then we can have wine and not worry we'll forget something important."

Isabelle stood right on cue. She picked up the papers and the tape from the end table and told the detective exactly what Trish had said earlier, almost word for word. She finished with a particularly soulful look and said, "I won't get in trouble, will I? There was just so much going on and I was so upset I wasn't sure what to do exactly. I'm so sorry I didn't have this information for you sooner."

"No," Bongiovanni said. "I don't think you could get in any trouble, Isabelle. Let me have a look at these papers. May I?"

Isabelle handed him the papers in the order she had shown them the previous evening. Bongiovanni gave them a cursory look, then his eyes tracked back while he gave them much more careful scrutiny.

Isabelle explained, "The letter that says 'To whom it may concern' applies to the tape recording. I guess you'll have to play the tape at your office, but it records Mag Cramer on the phone with Sonny, and he talks about knowing a hit man and having Sonny killed." Isabelle's eyes started to water and her voice got higher pitched. Trish handed her some tissues. "I'm sorry. This is still so upsetting to me. I worked for Sonny for years and years and never dreamed he was asking me to keep records that were lies, and all these tragic things were happening." With this, Isabelle began to cry, and Trish got her a glass of water.

"You've done the right thing, Isabelle," Bongiovanni said.

"You should know that these are copies," Trish added, gesturing to the materials on the table. "First thing this morning, Andrea took the originals to her lawyer, Lanier Poole, who kept them and made copies. But Isabelle wanted to do what Sonny asked, which was to give the tape to the cops as he put it."

"I always prided myself on being a good secretary," Isabelle said with a snuffle, "and that is what he wrote for me to do."

If the tape and the documents are real, this is quite a bombshell, Bongiovanni thought. There was probably no way they could continue to charge Andrea with Sonny's murder if all of this new information proved to be true.

"I tried to visit Mag Cramer at his office yesterday with a few follow-up questions, but his secretary said he was out of the country. Anyone have any ideas about that?"

Trish said, "Claudia, Andrea's assistant is gone too. Claudia was supposed to stay in Chateau Soleil and keep an eye on things, but she isn't there. Her car isn't in the garage. Claudia has always been so faithful and so very fond of Andrea and the children. It's downright peculiar she wouldn't have notified Andrea if she were going somewhere."

Jerry took out his notebook. "It does seem odd, and quite a coincidence. Perhaps I should look up some of the others I interviewed and see if they have disappeared as well."

"Now I'm really worried," said Trish. "If Claudia's absence has anything to do with Mag, and if Mag is as bad as this tape suggests, maybe she's in some kind of danger. Though I can't imagine those two have any connection with each other."

"It's definitely something to pursue," Bongiovanni said. "For the police to pursue, that is. Not to put down the enormous help you ladies have given us, but leave the investigation to us, okay? Police work can be risky. And I think I am getting dangerously close to discussing an ongoing investigation with you, which I cannot do."

Duh, Cay thought. *He all but patted us on our little female heads. Would they have the blood sample from the tree limb without us? Not even these tapes and papers. We've done at least as much as the cops.* Aloud, Cay said nothing.

Jordan, on the other hand, did not feel patronized. She was enjoying the cadence of a voice from home. How she longed to get him alone, to ask where he went down the shore for the summers, if he remembered . . . She was brought out of her reverie by Trish's suggesting they go in to the dining room for dinner.

If Trish had been concerned about Isabelle's drinking a bit too much and becoming a loose cannon, she needn't have worried. Isabelle drank only two sips of the Chianti that accompanied dinner and was the quiet and somewhat shy woman she was known to be. Jordan and Jerry, they all called him 'Jerry' now, dominated the conversation with recollections, primarily of their teenage years, a shared love of do-wop music, and the Feast of San Genero in little Italy; the sausages, peppers, and onions; the cannoli, the Virgin carried through the streets with dollar bills stuck on her.

Jordan glanced at his wedding ring and asked, "How has your wife adjusted to living in the South?"

"My wife . . . my wife is deceased. She was a caterer. A wonderful cook." The tone of his voice changed.

"Jeeze, I'm so sorry," Jordan said. Everyone was making murmurs of sorrow.

"She was killed in one of the twin towers on 9/11. The one day in her whole life she went into the World Trade Center to meet with a client. She was going over the details of the party she was to cater for his company. She was so excited. This was going to be the first big deal event for her business. Eighty-first floor, she never had a chance."

Jordan's eyes started to tear. This was too close to home. No one from the tri-state area lacked some personal connection to that tragic day. So many people bore a sadness that never really healed. "I am so sorry, Jerry." She reached her hand out to touch his arm. "I lost a close friend in the second tower, and she wasn't supposed to be there that day either. I can't get over how many people were not there who were supposed to be, and how many were there who weren't supposed to be. This eggplant parm is my friend Susan's recipe. We taught together in East Orange. She was Susan Didimenico Murphy. When I moved to Atlanta, we talked to each other on the phone for over fifteen years."

Jordan shook her head, as if to clear away the memories and said, "Okay, stop. We're all going to be OK. Jerry, your loss was so much worse than mine. Your wife! Omigod."

The tone of the dinner became more somber. Talk was mostly about Atlanta, and what it meant to be a transplant. The topic of colder winters in Jersey was pounced on with enthusiasm, and the weather from past years was avidly recounted.

Thank God for the weather, Cay thought, *the one topic that can take us through any awkward situation.*

Jordan's remarkable eggplant parmesan was devoured, as she predicted, leaving no leftovers for the kids.

"My contribution to this meal is dessert," Trish said. "Why don't I make coffee, and we can go back to the den and eat in there." They all stood when Bongiovanni said, "I feel embarrassed about asking this, but would you mind if I stepped outside for a smoke? I gave it up years ago, and had been real good about it, but I picked one up that morning and now I can't stop. Don't even want to."

"I won't make you stand outside in the cold, Jerry," Trish said, as much as she loathed the smell of smoke in the house.

"That's all right. I'd like to. I like the cold air. I miss the Jersey winters."

"I'll go with you," Jordan volunteered. "Fresh air feels good after dinner. Trish, don't clean up or even think about it. I'll do that later." She went to the closet in the foyer to retrieve their coats. "We'll be right back," she said over her shoulder.

Outside, Bongiovanni offered her a cigarette. "No thanks. I gave it a fling when I was a teenager, but never liked it."

"So, are you married?"

"Yes. I married my college sweetheart. He's away on business right now, just as he always seems to be."

"Jeannie and I were childhood sweethearts. When we in the fourth or fifth grade, we told everyone we were going to get married." Jerry took a long drag of his cigarette. "Everyone thought it was very cute, and ten years later, we tied the knot. There was never anyone else for either one of us. Never will be.

"After she died, I decided I couldn't take the pain. I was a cop; I had a gun; I could just end it. But of course, I had our kids, and I couldn't do that to them, so I decided that I'd wait. I wouldn't give up the idea; I'd just wait until they got through college. Then I thought even that was too soon for them. I'd wait until they were married, had their own families. Then I thought I'd hate not to see Jeannie's grandkids. And so it goes." He flicked cigarette ashes onto the grass.

"Did moving here help any?" Jordan asked.

"Maybe. Sometimes. Sometimes I wish I could go to the old places, just for a little while."

"I've been here a long time, but I will always miss Jersey. I go back pretty often to get my 'fix'. I love the way it smells down the shore, the kids I hung out with at the Dairy Queen, in fact, I miss the whole Jersey scene. Oy, if we don't cut this out we're going to go back in Trish's sobbing. You about finished smoking?"

"Yeah. Yeah, let's go back in." Bongiovanni looked around for a place to put the cigarette butt. He stuck it in a tall iron pot holding a neatly trimmed evergreen near the French doors into the den.

As they came in Jordan called, "Cawfee ready yet?" Her Jersey accent had become more prominent since sharing fond memories with Jerry.

"Perfect timing. Sit down and I'll bring in the dessert." When everyone was seated, Trish carried in a silver tray with a chafing dish over a little sterno heater. The scent of oranges filled the air. Next, she returned from the kitchen carrying another antique tray with five frosty silver bowls, each filled with a tall mound of French vanilla ice cream.

When Trish placed a cup in front of each guest, they noticed a depression in each rounded scoop. Finely grated nuts and pieces of chopped, brandied fruit were scattered on the sides. "Don't taste yet," Trish said. She poured a stream of the hot orange-scented liquid into one depression at a time and quickly lit each with a little Bic. It flamed up and spilled down the sides of the ice cream. "My tribute to Italy on this night of Italian food: Ice Cream Mount Vesuvius."

"Ladies, we really should write a cookbook," Jordan said.

"If I wrote down the names of all the good food delivery places in Atlanta, would that count as my contribution?" asked Cay.

"Stop it, Cay," said Jordan. "You are an *interesting* cook! Just because you don't like to cook, doesn't mean you can't when the mood hits. I bet you have a lot of delicious recipes."

The ice cream and coffee disappeared quickly. "More coffee?" Trish asked.

"None for me, thank you. I hate to be the first to leave," Isabelle said. "I've had a wonderful time, but I don't often drive after dark, and Mother will be expecting me."

"Why don't you let me drive you home?" Cay offered. "I need to be going, too. It would be much safer, and we can get the cars straightened out tomorrow."

"Oh, dear, I don't know."

"Of course I could always give you a lift in *my* car," Bongiovanni said. "I even have a blue light I could put on the roof."

"That would probably give Mother a heart attack," Isabelle said, only half joking. "Well, Cay, if it isn't too much out of your way, maybe it would be best if you drove."

With Cay and Isabelle gone, the gathering broke up quickly. Bongiovanni expressed his genuine gratitude for the dinner and hospitality. He said he was surprised by how much he had enjoyed the evening and each of the women. He patted the manila envelope, saying anything that helped bring out the truth was of critical importance, and he would begin to examine all the evidence with his partner and the chief first thing in the morning.

"And if you can," Trish said, "maybe you can find out where Claudia is. The longer she's gone, the more worried we are."

Bongiovanni nodded and got into his car.

Turning to Jordan, Trish said, "I think it went pretty well, don't you? We didn't really learn anything new, but that was to be expected, I guess. He can't talk to us about the case. It wouldn't be ethical."

"We did learn one thing," Jordan said. "Mag is gone too, and I think that is really odd."

"Do you think Claudia is in cahoots with Mag somehow? Oh, I'd never believe that."

"Stranger things have happened, Trish. Maybe she's not in cahoots. Maybe she found out something Mag didn't want her to know, along the lines of what's on that tape."

"That's even worse. Mag is unscrupulous. You don't think he'd have her killed too, do you?"

Jordan shrugged. "I don't know. I hope not. I hope she has the presence of mind to watch herself, wherever she is. Mag is no one to be toyed with, that's for sure."

Chapter 33

The tapping on her door seemed to get louder, and Claudia could hear Andrea saying, "Claudia, I need you. Where are you? Please help me." She struggled to get up, pushing the comforter aside, looking for her clock to see what time it was. She must have overslept. The light was so bright. Slowly her eyes focused on the carved detail on the four poster she had fallen asleep in the night before. "Miss, Miss, do you want breakfast?" the voice outside the door was saying.

"Just a minute, please," Claudia called, her voice sounding thick. Her memory of the incredible previous day and night began to come back: her flight with Lenora and Mary Alma on Mag's jet to this tiny, exclusive island and her introduction to the luxurious Hacienda Zipporah. Her night had been filled with troubled dreams of being chased by a panther, Sonny swimming in his pool with black and white scarves trailing behind him, and someone telling her she had beautifully manicured hands, except for the blood on them.

Claudia sat up in bed and looked at her hands. The dreams were so real, but her hands were clean and unstained. Again, a knock and a sweet feminine voice calling, "Miss . . . ."

Claudia hurried to the door and opened it. A young woman stood outside, really only a girl, holding a tray with a teapot, cup and saucer, and a bowl of fruit that must have been selected for its beauty. A small basket held little muffins, whose warmth exuded a perfume of guava or mango. "The main breakfast is served in the dining room," the girl said, "but you might want something to start the morning." She put the tray down on the glass topped table, bobbed her head, and quickly left the room, closing the door quietly.

Claudia had to sit for a moment and think. *Why was she here? Everything happened so fast. First, Andrea was arrested, then someone panicked. Who? Was it Mary Alma who was so anxious to get away and insisted Claudia and Lenora go with her? Then there was Mag. She suspected Mary Alma was having an affair with Mag Cramer. How could she? Hadn't that woman learned anything about married men from Sonny Simmons? Mag wasn't any different, and Mary Alma should be able to see that.*

And this place. It was the sort you read about in magazines but never saw in person. Everything was of the finest quality. Claudia was sure the sheets were Pratesi. A well-made bed in this place no doubt cost the equivalent of a small car. Andrea used Pratesi sheets too, and on all the beds at Chateau Soleil, not just her own. That was one of the many things which endeared her to Claudia. Andrea wasn't selfish in the least, and if she enjoyed something, she wanted everyone else to enjoy it, too. Of course, it wasn't as if Claudia were hired help, she told herself. She was much more like family, at least family on Andrea's side.

Claudia felt an actual ache when she thought of Andrea. She missed her and felt painfully guilty for having left in her time of need. *Family wouldn't do that,* she thought. *How could I? She must be frantic, wondering where I went, what happened to me. Mary Alma was so convincing, but I should have stayed home and looked after Andrea.*

Claudia was deciding what to do next when she heard another knock at her door. Lenora called, "May I come in? Claudia? Are you awake?"

"I'm awake. I'm just trying to get my bearings," she said, opening the door.

"You haven't touched your breakfast," Lenora exclaimed. "It's wonderful. Do you mind?" she asked, picking up a tiny muffin and popping it in her mouth.

"These are straight from heaven. I'll have to get the recipe for Mrs. Berry."

"About that," Claudia said. "How long are we supposed to stay here? What if they pin Sonny's murder on Andrea? What do we do? We can't let her be convicted. We should have planned this a little better."

"Well, the fact is that we are here, there is no extradition, and it is a lovely place to be, as far as I can tell. Oh, you know they won't convict Andrea. She'll be okay."

"How do you know that? I need to find out what is going on and tell her I'm safe. I need to apologize for running off like this."

"You must be crazy. Of course you can't contact Andrea. You can't contact anyone. We covered that on the way here. We are only really safe as long as no one knows where we are. No extradition treaty is one thing, but do you want to wear a big sign around your neck saying 'Look at me! I'm guilty?' "

Claudia started pacing. "I think we overreacted, thanks to Mary Alma. You know the newspaper said Sonny was shot, and he broke his neck when he fell. That pretty much exonerates us, I'd say. We could claim we were pulling a prank."

"Do you really think anyone would believe that the whole thing was a prank? Claudia, you have been watching too much television, too many of those dumb reality shows. Mary Alma was right, and she was kind enough to persuade Mag to bring all of us here."

Claudia sat down. "Was she being kind or was she just protecting herself? Maybe she didn't want to leave anyone in Atlanta who could implicate her. Furthermore, I cannot believe that someone of Mag's stature would tell you and me of his involvement in Sonny's death. There's something wrong about that. How can he trust us to not implicate him in this crime?"

"I don't think you give Mary Alma and Mag enough credit. Let's get off this grim topic and enjoy the day. I'll see you in the main dining room. Hurry up. I want to explore the island."

Lenora seemed carefree as she twirled out the door. *She could at least say she missed her mother*, Claudia thought.

Mag and Mary Alma were leaving the dining room as Claudia entered. Now when Claudia looked at Mary Alma, she wasn't sure if she was seeing a friend or an opportunist who had used her. She felt confused and hurt, and she didn't know what to do about any of it.

"Wasn't that the most wonderful sleep of your entire life?" Mary Alma asked as they passed. "This place is pure magic," she said, giving Mag a little tickle.

Disgusted, Claudia looked around for Lenora, spotted her sitting at the table Mag and Mary Alma had just vacated. She decided she wouldn't alarm Lenora by repeating her wish to go home or her opinion that hiding out on the island was wrong. She wanted to keep an ally. Instead, she said, "Lenora, you're right. After breakfast, let's take a walk and see some of the island."

"I have a better idea," Lenora said. "Let's take bicycles. We can see a lot more that way. There's a little sign outside saying bikes are available in a hut near the path. It'll be fun."

Claudia could not remember the last time she rode a bicycle, but if that would make Lenora happy, that's what she would do. "I'd like to write a card," she said. "I wonder where they have them."

"You mean like a post card? With a picture on it? You're not in the Bahamas, honey. They want this place to stay secret. For heaven's sake, Claudia, why did you come with us if you didn't want to disappear, at least for a while?"

Claudia was wondering the same thing, but she shrugged and changed the subject. "I'll need sun block if we are going to ride bikes. I'm going back to my room and put some on. I'll meet you at the wooden bench on the path to the dining room. Fifteen minutes?"

"Give me a little longer. There's no schedule, Claudia. Can you believe it? Doesn't it feel wonderful? I am going to look at the buffet again, and then I'll meet you, but if the food looks good. I'll be here more than fifteen minutes."

For her part, Claudia didn't like to be without a schedule. She liked to know how things were going to proceed and to feel in control, not just floating around at loose ends as Lenora apparently preferred.

As Claudia left the dining room, she decided to turn to her left, away from her cottage, and walk down to the beach. She could follow the beach and turn back up toward the cottages, approaching them from the rear. The air was so soft and sweet, and the water made the gentlest sounds as it lapped the sand. *This really is a paradise,* she thought, and under different circumstances, she could feel relaxed and happy here, but all she felt now was anxiety and tension. She constantly worried over what Andrea must think, what she must be doing, what awful things could be happening. Mainly she worried about her own future - if she had one.

Claudia was so absorbed with her mental images she walked farther down the beach than she intended and lost track of which cottage was hers. They all looked the same from the back, and were set at angles that confused her. She chose a pathway between the third and fourth cottages. *At least it will take me around to the front,* she thought, *and I can get my bearings from there.*

Claudia walked between flowering hedges alongside one of the cottages. She didn't think it was hers because the shutters were propped open from the bottom, in the Bermuda style, and she was sure her shutters had been closed when she left her room. Then she heard Mary Alma's voice coming from the window.

"You're really disappointin' me, Mag darlin'. You said nothin' at all about gettin' rid of anybody. I'd never have insisted you bring Claudia and Lenora if I thought you were going to kill them."

Claudia stopped in her tracks. Slowly, she looked around to see if anyone was nearby. She took a couple of steps so she couldn't be seen from the window, and pressed closer to the hedge, which turned out to be prickly in spite of its fragile-looking blossoms. The sun was getting hot, but Claudia felt freezing cold. Mag was apparently on the far side of the room or in the bathroom, because Claudia could barely hear him and could barely make out his words.

Mary Alma's words, however, were crystal clear.

"Well of course you did, Sweetie, and I never once objected to that, did I? After all, Sonny could have brought you down with a word. Why, if the details of that deal in the Gulf ever got out, your whole empire would be toast, and we both know it. That guy you paid to do the job was well worth the money. And let's not forget Sonny treated me like you-know-what. He was a man who dearly needed killin'. Let's be honest, you did the world a favor. But these two are nuthin' to you, Mag. They don't even know the whole story.

Mag's voice interrupted. He sounded louder for a moment and then a door shut. Maybe they were leaving the cottage. Claudia took a deep breath. She made her feet and legs propel her away from the cottage. She turned back toward the ocean, trying to see through the tears that were blinding her. She had to act calm, and she needed to tell Lenora. Their lives were in danger, and she had to convince Lenora she wasn't making up a wild tale because she was homesick or having second thoughts. She concentrated on walking toward the beach and back to the dining room.

Claudia had no idea how long it had been since she left Lenora at the table. As she entered the room, she saw Lenora was still there. A considerable amount of food was set in front of her, so she wasn't going anywhere anytime soon.

Chapter 34

The sun was almost overhead when Lenora joined Claudia on the wooden bench near the path to the beach.

"Sit down, Lenora, I have to tell you something."

"Have you been crying?" Lenora asked. "You dashed out of the dining room so fast, I was a little worried, although not worried enough to leave breakfast. It was fabulous. You should have stayed."

"Lenora, hush! I'm sorry, but I have to talk to you. Just listen for a minute. There's something between Mag and Mary Alma. I walked by her cottage on the way back here earlier, and I heard them together."

"Well, you shouldn't be so upset about it, Claudia. Things like that happen."

"No! Things like what I heard do not just happen." Claudia lowered her voice. "I heard Mary Alma talking about how Mag had Sonny killed and she was arguing with him not to kill us. But she wasn't arguing very hard, I can tell you that."

"Kill us! Why in the world would he want to do that? You must have gotten it confused."

"I didn't get anything confused. We are a liability. Mag's safe here indefinitely, if necessary. No extradition, remember? If he and Mary Alma are lovers, she's going to keep his secret. But do you think he plans to let us die of old age, having lived a life of luxury and never setting foot off these few acres in the ocean?"

"Why can't he just take us home?" Lenora asked.

"Because Mary Alma doesn't want to go home and face an investigation. What we know could send Mag to prison. Sooner or later someone would talk. Mag told us way too much and he has to be afraid of us. We are so naïve. He can't keep us alive, Lenora, and he was talking about it to Mary Alma."

"I'm not ready to agree this is true, not just yet, but if it is, what are we going to do about it?" Lenora's voice was taking on an edge of anger.

"I don't know." Claudia started to cry again. "If Mag's going to kill us, there would be no point in waiting. I thought maybe I should talk to Mary Alma."

"No! That's the last thing you should do. If she has taken up with Mag, she is not our friend. Let's think."

"Do you believe me then? I was right under Mary Alma's window, and I could hear her plain as anything. I'll show you. There's no rule about where we can walk. Come with me." Claudia felt a lot better.

They walked back past the dining room, toward the beach and then back toward the cottages, passing their own and turning at the hedge alongside Mary Alma's. Claudia put her finger to her lips and moved in close to the hedge. Lenora followed.

The shutters were open as before, but no sound came from the room. They were about to turn back toward the beach when they distinctly heard Mag say, "My God, you're a feisty little thing." He gave a little yip, presumably as Mary Alma demonstrated her feistiness.

"I'll bet you were the one who thought up that crazy plot to scare the hell outta Sonny. C'mon, you were, weren't you? You said it was Lenora, but Lenora's too dumb and Claudia is too timid. It'd take a fiery little bitch like you…" He was interrupted by some muffled giggles followed by sounds of thrashing about.

"The minute you told me what you wanted to pull off, I knew you were the woman for me. I like a gal with spunk. Sorry I took such a risk to execute the kill, sweet thing, but I hired the best, and I knew you would be all right. You got him out by the pool, right on cue. You are something else, girl, I'll give you that." There was more rustling of sheets, then silence.

"Mag, do you hear something? Outside the window. I swear I hear a noise. Go look."

Claudia thought her feet would never start to move. Lenora had already taken off toward the beach, and Claudia wanted to follow but felt rooted to the spot. After a moment, she walked a few steps, then ran to where Lenora had plopped on the sand and was furiously starting a sand castle.

"Get over here!" she hissed at Claudia. "Start digging. Now!" Claudia made some half-hearted attempts to scoop sand in a heap, and Lenora said loudly, "This is so much fun. I haven't done this since I was a little girl." She looked over Claudia's shoulder and waved. "Mag! Mag! Come build a sand castle with us. We need a bucket for water."

"What are you doing?" Claudia whispered. "We don't want him with us."

"Remember what they say about secrets," Lenora said. "If you can't hide, make a spectacle of yourself."

Mag gave a brief wave, looked around, and headed back toward the front of the cottage.

"Do you think he knows it was us?"

"He probably suspects," Claudia said. "Okay. Do you believe me now? Thank you Mag, for proving my point. Is that all those two talk about?"

"It may be all they have in common," Lenora said. "And yes, I believe you now. We need to get the hell off of this island."

"How? Sprout wings?" Claudia asked.

"Let's do what we'd planned. Get bikes and ride around. Maybe we'll get an idea."

The bikes were old and single speed but adequate for the sandy paths. Getting their bearings, they figured they were more or less at the northern end of the island.

Riding south, villas gave way to small houses and a few little shops. A couple of them looked as if they might cater to well-heeled visitors, but others evidently served those who staffed the Hacienda.

"Didn't Mag say something when we first got here about a mail plane? I know he did," Claudia said. "It was something about a pontoon plane, landing at the south end of the island."

"Yes, I remember that now. I was so tired, it seems as if I dreamed it."

"Let's see if we can find out when it comes in. Maybe we can ask in this shop. Custom Bikinis. Just what we need. Let's hope someone in there speaks English." They parked their bikes in front of the bikini shop. "Look rich," she said to Lenora. "And don't use our names."

They walked into the shop, casting a cursory glance at a display of fabrics and sample swim suits. A young woman behind the counter gave them a broad, perfect smile. "How may I help you ladies today?" Her words revealed a slight British accent.

Claudia said, "Oh, just browsing, I think. Perhaps we need more suits. What do you think?" she asked Lenora.

"I know I do," Lenora said.

"Would anyplace around here have magazines or newspapers?" Claudia asked, all the while examining a tropical print bolt of cotton. "I'm bored with what I have."

"If they don't have any at the general store, then I'm afraid you're out of luck. No one else carries reading material," the saleswoman said.

"Oh, I've read everything I brought," Claudia moaned. "When do new ones come in?"

"The mail plane will come on Friday. The pilot brings everything the guests need. Usually the magazines are *People* and *Time* and *Paris Match*, and *The Guardian*, plus a few other papers. Sometimes special papers come in if Mr. Cramer requests them. You can make a special request, if you like."

"Those choices are just fine," Claudia said. "What time does the mail delivery arrive?"

"Hard to say. A lot depends on weather, or if he has to ferry someone to a hospital or whatever. Around ten, usually."

"Oh, is it one of those pontoon planes? I love those. I want to see it land. Where does it land?" Lenora was trying to be casual.

"Over near the beach," she said, gesturing loosely behind the general store.

Claudia said, "Well, it's almost time for lunch, so we need to get back. We'll come back soon with an order," and giving her warmest smile, Claudia hustled Lenora out of the shop.

"What? What's wrong?" Lenora asked.

"I was afraid you seemed too interested in the plane. We can't arouse suspicion."

"I don't know about you, but I'm going to make myself a new best friend on Friday, and he is going to fly us right off this island. Dumb, indeed. You'll see, Mag Cramer."

Chapter 35

"Andrea, turn on the TV right now. FOX News."
Trish was speaking into the phone so fast Andrea could
barely understand her.

"Good heavens, Trish. What's wrong? Slow down."
Andrea picked up the remote and clicked. "What channel?"
she asked.

"Thirty-seven. Quick."

Reporters could be seen jostling with each other for
the best positions. The background on the screen was dim,
but one woman's face could clearly be seen. It was
Claudia!

"Dear God in heaven," Andrea said, sinking into a
chair.

A female reporter was sticking a mike in Claudia's
face. "Do you suspect a slave ring?"

"No. Mr. Cramer has a lot to answer for, however.
He told us he arranged the murder of an Atlanta
millionaire, Sonny Simmons, and he threatened our lives.
We will swear to that. If we hadn't persuaded that brave
pilot to take us off of Zipporah, well, I don't think we'd
have been around much longer." The reporter turned
toward the camera.

"There you have it, ladies and gentlemen. Here in
Miami, these two courageous American women have
barely escaped the clutches of billionaire Mag Cramer, and
a possible slave ring. This is breaking news, and we'll stay
with it. For Fox News . . . ."

Andrea returned to the phone. "Slave ring? Wasn't
that Lenora next to Claudia? What in the world is going
on?"

"You know as much as I do. At least we know where Claudia is, and that she's okay. I've got to call Jordan and Cay," and Trish hung up.

Big and Bobby Lee, Andrea thought. She immediately dialed Big and got his wife. "Merla, darlin' how have you been? I was just thinkin' about you and Big and how I needed to get you on the phone, and now, today there is this shocking news on TV . . . . No, not on the *Today Show*, On Fox News . . . . Have you seen it? Two women accused Mag Cramer of plotting Sonny's death . . . Mag Cramer. He's a very powerful Atlanta businessman. One of the women was Claudia Bannon. You know her. She's my personal assistant."

Andrea already knew Mag's role from the letters and tape provided by Isabelle, but she hadn't told anyone in Sonny's family. Thanks to the TV coverage, she could now tell everyone.

"Do you get Fox News? No? Yes, it *is* very confusing, but I wanted to alert you, in case you saw it. I better call Miss Adeline and Vergy. They don't have cable? I'd better call them anyway. I think this piece of news will be everywhere." Andrea hung up, called Bobby Lee, then Miss Adeline and Vergy.

Bobby Lee had already heard the news. "Are they gonna make some sideshow outta this?" he wanted to know. "They better not drag Sonny's name through the mud." Andrea didn't want to tell him it was a little late to be worrying about Sonny's reputation.

By the time Trish climbed the stairs to Andrea's sitting room in the garage apartment, Andrea had a phone at each ear. As soon as she saw Trish, Andrea put the callers on hold.

"We are moving back to Chateau Soleil," Andrea said. "Everybody. Wait until I finish these calls." She continued telling someone about having the gates unlocked and security hired, she hung up that phone. In a moment, it became clear to Trish the remaining caller was Lanier.

They talked a few more minutes, then Andrea hung up. "I'm letting everyone else go to voice mail for awhile," she said. "Lanier is sending over a bodyguard."

"A bodyguard!" exclaimed Trish. "Do you really need one?"

"Lanier seems to think so. More for protection from the press than anything else. That's why we're moving into Chateau Soleil. It has gates. You have to come too, Trish. And our children. And of course Mr. Chanel. It will be awful for a while, but not as bad as it would be if they got right up to your front door here on Habersham."

Andrea started pacing. "Another thing. Lanier's picking up Claudia and Lenora when they get in and moving them into Chateau Soleil, too. They may need protection, for all we know, and Lanier can control who they talk to so they don't blow the case against Mag. If there is a case."

"How could there not be?"

"I don't know, but he may be safe on that island of his for the time being. We'll have to wait and see."

"Jordan and Cay need to know our plans," Trish said. "I wonder if they've heard the news."

Andrea looked at the caller ID on her ringing phone and picked it up. "Oh, Claudia, I was hoping it was you! What in the name of heaven happened? Are you okay? I'm so glad you are back and safe! Bless your heart, I was so worried about you." Andrea paused to let the caller speak. "I know, Darlin'. I know you wouldn't hurt me or the children for anything. We'll talk it all over later. Lanier Poole says he is moving you and Lenora into Chateau Soleil, at least for now, to keep y'all safe from the media." Another, longer pause. "Remember don't say anything else to anyone with a microphone," Andrea said, realizing

Claudia had apparently said quite a lot already. Where was that almost invisible young woman she had known?

Below a picture of Mary Alma, a crawl was running across the bottom of the TV screen that read, "Playgirl or Prey? News special at 11." Andrea closed her eyes.

* * *

Cay was the one person on the planet spared the news blitz on the latest woman in peril. Trish reached her at last in Conyers, Georgia, at the Monastery of the Holy Spirit.

"What are you doing there? Isn't that where people go for retreats?" Trish asked.

"And bread," Cay said. "The monks make great bread. But I am in their library so I have to keep my voice down. I am looking at some of their collection. They are thinking about . . . ."

"Cay! Another time. When can you talk? I have to tell you something really important."

Cay was back on the line within five minutes, having moved to her car in the parking lot. Trish gave her a condensed version of what had gone on that morning.

"Wow! And I thought most of the hoo-ha was over," Cay said. "I've got to work, Trish, or I'm going to go broke. I've spent all my time on Andrea and her problems for weeks, and I love her dearly, but I have to get back to my life now that Andrea seems to be cleared."

Trish was a little taken aback, but she knew Cay was right. Everything had swirled around Andrea since the night of Sonny's death. It would be Thanksgiving in a week, then Christmas, and Trish hadn't given a thought to any of it. Always prepared and decorated far in advance, lately she had done exactly nothing for her own household. She told Cay they would be at Chateau Soleil, and then got on with her other calls.

Jordan's attitude was different. "I'm putting on my coat. I'll be right there." She could make arrangements for her son, Michael, to spend the night with a friend. "Don't do anything without me," Jordan shouted into the phone and hung up.

"My head is just spinning," Andrea said. "I'm not going to figure out what happened by watching TV, that's for sure. Now I really am going to ignore the phone. If we are all going back to Chateau Soleil today, we've got to pack."

"I wish I knew what Bongiovanni thought about all this," Trish said.

"Oh, I forgot to tell you. I talked with him early this morning. He said once he read over the documents and listened to the tape from Isabelle he had no choice but to give everything to his boss. The Feds have it now. I knew that was going to happen because Sonny's and Mag's projects are scattered throughout different states and other countries. With so many insurance companies involved, plus Sonny's murder, the FBI's involvement was inevitable.

"Bongiovanni said the blood sample you all found was from a person of Romany descent. They were able to identify it from the genetic marker. Jerry recognized the hit man from his profile and called him 'The Gypsy'. He'd seen stuff about him when he was on the force in Jersey." Andrea gave a little shiver. "Apparently this guy is an international killer for hire, works mostly for governments, and always manages to slip away. Creepy that he was right here in our backyard."

It wasn't long before Jordan pulled into Trish's driveway, full of questions. Andrea and Trish told her all about The Gypsy but they had to admit they knew practically nothing else except what they had seen on TV, and that had been pretty confusing. Yes, it was Lenora, in the background next to Claudia. Yes, what Claudia said on the phone to Andrea seemed to back up what they had learned from the letters and the tape. It would seem to confirm once and for all that Andrea had nothing to do with Sonny's death. And no, they had no idea why Lenora and Claudia were standing in a Miami airport hangar making statements to the media. Those questions and answers would have to wait.

Once Trish, Andrea, and their children were assembled in Trish's living room, a few packed bags in hand, Jordan guarding a wary Mr. Chanel, they were ready to leave for Andrea's house. All they needed was the bodyguard Lanier promised to send over.

"A watched pot," Trish said, and busied herself checking to be sure the appliances were off and the lamps were on timers. Hearing the rear doorbell she said, "See, what did I tell you. As soon as you make yourself busy . . . ." When she opened the back door, she found herself looking directly into the solar plexus of a very tall, very square man wearing a dark suit and a crisp white shirt with French cuffs. Looking up, she saw herself reflected in his opalescent blue Oakleys. His highly polished head radiated aggression the same way heat waves ripple above a stretch of asphalt in July.

"Oh, Mr . . . " Trish had forgotten his name. It had Lou or Louis in it. "Mr. Louis, or rather Mr. Fink, that's it, isn't it? Mr. Louis Fink?"

No response.

"I'm sorry. Did Mr. Poole send you?" Trish was feeling a little nervous.

Jordan sized up the situation and came to the rescue, followed by the two boys. "Louie the Fink?" she asked, with "the" sounding like "duh."

"Yeah, dat's me," he said, breaking into a big grin. "Howdya know?"

"Just a wild guess," Jordan said.

They settled on "Louie" and went over what would happen next, the rules of cautious behavior, and how Louie could be of help to them.

EJ and Trey had a million questions: did he know karate, had he ever killed anyone, did he carry a gun - all of which Trish tried to shush

On Louie's direction, everyone piled into his black SUV with dark tinted windows.

"This is just like the guys have in the President's motorcade," Trey whispered. "I thought dark windows like this were against the law for everybody else."

"Fasten your seat belts," Andrea said. Louie stowed their bags in the back.

As Louie headed down Trish's driveway, an old Volvo raced in toward them, stopping nearly bumper to bumper.

"Stay where you are," Louie said. "I'll handle this."

"Don't worry, Louie," Andrea said. "This is a friend of ours."

Cay backed up, and then pulled alongside the driver's window of the SUV. Louie rolled down the window and gazed down at her through his Oakleys.

"Whoa," Cay said. "Andrea? Are you in there?"

"We're all in here, Sugah. Put your car in back and get in. Couldn't stay away, huh?"

Cay got in the SUV and they once again started down Trish's drive, suppressing giggles. Andrea felt a huge weight had been lifted from her, and the LitChix shared her relief.

As they approached Chateau Soleil at six o'clock, they saw a bright aura resembling that of a used car lot on a Saturday night. TV crews were all over West Paces Ferry, their trucks with antennae raised and ready to broadcast looking like oversized insects.

"Oh, no," Andrea said.

"Cool," EJ said.

When Louie nosed the SUV into the driveway and Andrea clicked open the gate, frenzied reporters surged forward with microphones, yelling questions at the car. Several police, probably off-duty cops Lanier had put there, herded everyone back.

"Look at that guy," EJ said. "Right there. The short guy with the mustache. Isn't that . . . ?"

"I think I have reached the low point of my life," Andrea groaned. "Geraldo is in my driveway."

"There, there," Trish said. "It's always darkest . . .

"Before it gets really, really dark," Cay finished.

Chapter 36

"My, but aren't we in a pissy mood," Mary Alma said, when Mag shrugged her off. She had crept up behind him as he sat at his desk and slipped her arms around his neck, something he usually loved. But he pushed her away with a "Not now, for God's sake."

* * *

The previous evening, during a late supper in their cottage, one of Mag's employees knocked at the door and suggested, *soto voce,* that Mag should get over to his private communications center at his earliest convenience, which meant immediately. Mag kissed Mary Alma on the top of her head as she dove into an enormous seafood salad and said he wouldn't be gone long. When he failed to come back three hours later, Mary Alma, disgusted, puzzled, and a little weepy from drinking all the wine herself, fell asleep alone in the big canopied bed.

For those three hours, Mag sat riveted before four TV screens, each one pulling in news from his satellite, all plastered with Claudia's wide eyes and breathless recounting of their escape from the diabolical Mag Cramer. In the hands of hungry reporters, the billionaire businessman became more evil by the minute. Reporters sounded almost gleeful, reading wire releases announcing Global's plummeting stock prices. News that all of Global's activity had been stopped pending a full inquiry practically made them salivate.

Mag realized his assets were inaccessible, at least to him. Oh, there were a few off-shore accounts, enough for a pleasant enough life on this incredibly dull spot in the ocean, but his empire was tumbling right before his eyes on CNN.

To add insult to his already catastrophic injury, Mag knew the Gypsy, touted in every broadcast as Sonny's killer, was not his own hit man. Mag had hired a reputable killer and paid him the first half of his fee, but not only did the assassin not do the job, he also disappeared with Mag's money. Someone else must have hired The Gypsy, and how the media loved the story. Lacking a photo, the media did have sketches and news clips from past hits, and they were shown on-air endlessly. No chance Mag would ever see his down payment again. Hit men don't give refunds.

Claudia and Lenora had insured their longevity and locked Mag up on his own island with a single poorly lit press conference in Miami. No matter that Mag's hit man had not shot Sonny; Claudia's word was as good as fact. Sonny was undeniably shot by a hit man. Mag would hear how the police identified the Gypsy by the tiny drop of blood found on a magnolia tree in Sonny's backyard which revealed the man's Romany ancestry. The bullet identified the man's preferred weapon. Mag would be regaled, over and over again, with The Gypsy's history, connecting him to assassinations around the world.

The Gypsy didn't work for free, Mag knew. He didn't drop in for mere target practice. Someone hired him - someone who could pay him a very large sum of money. It gravely troubled Mag that he had no idea who that could be.

After Claudia's press conference, who would do business with him? Who would risk the bad publicity, the taint of corruption? As for his wife, Melanie had probably already contacted a lawyer, a celebrity lawyer no doubt, and was locking up everything she possibly could. The rest of his assets would probably be siphoned off by the lawyers and insurance companies. A few remaining scraps might actually get into the hands of the families of the workers whose lives had been traded for the profits of inferior construction.

And now Mary Alma's whining voice. Mag poured himself a large Scotch, straight up, and downed it in two gulps. Was this his fate, eternally stuck on this pitiful drop of sand with Mary Alma droning and drawling unceasingly in his ear? Mary Alma and a good tan were all he had to look forward to, and the prospect didn't bring him joy. Mag poured another.

* * *

Lanier Poole prided himself on being able to pull all the strings when it came to trying a case in public. He had very few of the facts, and nothing suggesting Claudia's and Lenora's attempts to hurt Sonny themselves, but he believed something was up. It had to do with his client Andrea Simmons, and Lanier was set to take center stage.

It was Lanier who arranged for the private plane to bring Lenora and Claudia to Atlanta from that grimy airport hanger in Miami, to the very same airport from which they had departed only a few days before. Their Atlanta arrival would show well on TV. He could picture it now their coming down the steps of the charter plane directly onto the tarmac. So much better for dramatic footage than the inside of some tacky, fluorescent-lit hangar in Miami. Selected members of the media received anonymous, tantalizing tips and were given plenty of time to set up their lights and position their correspondents. There was even hot coffee to make their wait in the cold a little more tolerable.

Lanier saw to it that a silver Bentley was polished and identified with a pass that permitted it to sit in wait near the runway. The Bentley would whisk the new media stars away when Lanier determined the reporters had seen enough. Although he couldn't control the weather, it turned out to be perfect: a slight breeze to muss the hair of these poor escapees, enough chill in the air to make them shiver. Lanier had no intention of letting either Claudia or Lenora say anything that could impugn their stories. A slip of the lip could jeopardize everything, a potential prosecution of Mag Cramer, even Andrea's position, which now seemed that of the falsely accused grieving widow. Not to mention the book and movie deals, of course. If there was anyone Lanier Poole wanted to be other than himself, it was John Grisham. He had no doubt about his ability to pen one courtroom drama after another with relative ease, with himself as the main character.

* * *

It would be a misstatement to say that Andrea and her entourage were waiting patiently at Chateau Solieil for Lanier to come through the gates with Claudia and Lenora. Speculation ran rampant. Andrea was in gear, making long-reaching plans. Between hands of gin rummy, which they played to distract themselves from the almost unbearable tension, she revealed the ideas she had been wrestling with during sleepless nights. It was time for her to strike out independently with her children. Andrea had looked at buildings and houses on-line, in different areas of Atlanta.

"Not live in Buckhead?" Trish said, in shock. "Andrea, how would you function anywhere else?"

"I am very resourceful, whatever you might think," Andrea replied. "I don't require twenty-four hour gourmet carry-out on every corner. And it would be good for the children to live in a more diverse neighborhood. With the lifestyle they have been living, they think underprivileged means not going skiing in Vail or to the Bahamas over spring break. There is a neat area off Georgia Avenue, where some wonderful Victorians and Craftsman cottages are located."

"You mean down by the Ted?" Cay asked. "That whole stadium area is undergoing a lot of changes, but I don't know if it's ready for you, Andrea. No offense."

"None taken. I know what y'all are thinking, and I don't blame you, but I'm turning over a new leaf, and I mean it. It's time for me to move on. Not from my good friends, of course, but from my old life. I was stuck there. I think there's a bigger purpose to my life now, and I intend to find out what it is."

"Good for you, Andrea." Jordan was beginning to like Andrea more and more. "Life is change. I say 'go for it'. Somehow I visualized you clinging to those magnolia trees by your pool saying: 'As God is my witness, I'll never shop wholesale again.'"

Andrea laughed. "One reason I would like to live in the Grant Park area is I have a plan. When I was in jail, I met all these women who shouldn't have been there. Oh, most of them did something wrong, but that's not what I mean. They never had the skills or the self-esteem to stay out of trouble in the first place. Gin." Andrea laid down her winning cards. "A lot of them were just trying to put food on the table for their kids. They were doing it the wrong way, but they didn't even know they had other choices. And they got no advice or help, except maybe from pimps and junkies."

Andrea got up from the sun room game table to refill her cup of coffee. "I realized what was needed was some kind of center where women could learn skills and get medical attention, not only for themselves but for their kids, too. A place they could get the right kind of counseling and legal help, if they needed it. All that stuff is tied together, but now they have to go to Place A if their child has an ear infection and Place B if they have a landlord problem and Place C if they have to learn computer skills to get a job. And so they go no place, because all of it is too overwhelming.

"Believe me, I could go on all night. I came up with the name 'The Women's Justice Center.' I even drew a sketch of what it should look like and how it should be organized. It has to be located near the people who will use it and near mass transit, and that brings me back to Georgia Avenue. There are already a few groups working in the area, food co-ops, that sort of thing, but think how the Justice Center could change everything. And I would be the CEO, sort of, so I would want to live nearby."

"Whoa, Nelly," Cay said. "Those are ambitious plans. It would take so many people to make something like that work."

"Which makes me just the person to do it. I know tons of people, and in case you haven't noticed, I'm very persuasive. We could start small, with a definite step-by-step growth plan. At first, we could get a group of volunteer doctors rotating in our clinic. You see? It doesn't have to be everything at once if you have a good, workable plan. And I don't have to go running around begging for money to get it started. It's only fair that dear ol' Sonny's cash from the safe should provide seed money. After that, we can apply for grants, have fund raisers. Ladies, the possibilities are endless!"

"You're taking my breath away," Trish said. "These are wonderful, amazing ideas. I am so proud of you. Mercy, Cuz."

"Well rest up, because I have volunteer jobs in mind for each of you."

Just then, Mr. Chanel launched into a round of warning barks, indicating someone was outside. Andrea pulled back one of the draperies to see reporters leaping into action, lights flaring up everywhere, and a big silver Bentley driving slowly through the gate.

Chapter 37

"Betcha didn't think I could do it," Andrea gloated, champagne bottle in hand. "No carryout, nothing catered, although I do have to say thank you to friends and family for all that they brought, and most especially to Miss Adeline for teaching me to cook a turkey." Applause erupted around the long table, a combination of folding tables smoothed over with crisp white linens. The chairs were a mix of antique Queen Anne from Andrea's dining room at Chateau Soleil and the metal folding variety found at Target.

Miss Adeline felt a little flustered by the unexpected compliment and remarked, "It warn't a real Thanksgiving turkey if you didn't kill it and clean it yourself."

"Yuk!" Tyler Louise said. "That is so gross."

Trish looked around. Here, in this shabby underheated former church building, which Andrea determined would be the starter home of her Women's Justice Center, a combination of friends and family had gathered to cook Thanksgiving dinner. They used the ancient cast iron stove that at one time had supported a soup kitchen, and it would again, if Andrea had her way. And maybe a catering service, and a nutrition clinic... and . . . . Andrea was so full of plans and ideas it was contagious.

Cay passed the sweet potato soufflé that Merla and Big had brought, and Jordan served herself some corn casserole from Serena and Bobby Lee. Old Vergy was in kind of a snooze but would revive from time to time, refill his glass, and drift off again. Andrea was the happiest she had ever been. She was among her best friends, their children and hers, Sonny's family, all ages and sorts mixed together in this spacious room. Only two days ago she closed on this property and the Craftsman cottage next door, paying with cash.

Then everyone had clicked into warp speed. It was incredible enough that Andrea had at first rounded up this far-flung group to celebrate the holiday together at Trish's, but then to move the whole operation downtown, across from a vacant bottle-strewn lot on Georgia Avenue was nothing short of amazing.

* * *

Perhaps the only thing more amazing was the presence of Claudia and Lenora. Just weeks before, they had driven through the gates of Chateau Soleil with Lanier Poole and been whisked in the back door and up the stairs, so Lanier could find out the basics before he allowed them talk to anyone, even Andrea.

After half an hour or so, a subdued Lanier came downstairs alone.

"What's going on?" Andrea had asked him.

"I believe we may have a conflict of interest," Lanier said.

"Is this the royal 'we?'" Jordan had asked. "Who are the 'we' who has the conflict?"

"Allegedly, Claudia and Lenora were in collusion with Mary Alma."

"What kind of collusion?" Trish wanted to know.

"It seems they had a plan to seriously hurt Sonny. Or perhaps just to scare him. I really don't know which. It depends on whom you talk to and when. Anyway, Mary Alma tied Andrea's scarf around his neck, which did bruise and disorient him. Lenora poisoned his drink to make him woozy, and she is the one who wrote the note luring him to the pool at 11:30. Claudia covered Sonny with the barbecue sauce after she hit him on the head with the black panther statue. Those three were responsible for everything but the shot that actually killed him. They tell me they knew nothing about the shooting and were shocked when they found out about the assassin, and I believe them."

"I want to talk to them," Andrea said, heading for the stairs.

"That might not be . . ." Lanier began to protest.

"Nonsense. This is still my house, and I am entitled to know what they did to my husband and *why*." Andrea marched up the stairs and into the bedroom where Claudia and Lenora were sequestered.

"I guess there is nothing to do but wait," Cay said. "More rummy, any one?"

"Make that more rum and you're on." Jordan tapped her empty glass.

Conversation was awkward and eventually ceased altogether, with everyone straining to hear sounds from upstairs. After a while Jordan said, "What, are they laughing?"

Cay said, "I thought I heard laughter, too."

A few minutes later the phone rang, indicating that it was on intercom. "Do we have any food down there?" Andrea asked. "We're starved."

Trish went to Andrea's kitchen to investigate. Some odds and ends were left from dinner, but not much, since Andrea had cleaned out the refrigerator and most of the cupboards when she moved in with Trish.

"I guess there is nothing to do but get takeout," Trish said. "Louie, I hate to ask, but will you go on a food run for us? I don't want any strangers driving in with deliveries. You never know who might try to get through."

Louie broke into his big grin. Trey and EJ went with him on the short trip to Pero's soon returning with pizzas and antipasto. Digging in, Jordan said, "You can't get good pizza in the South."

Cay noted, "Jordan, you always say that, but the pizza seems to get eaten."

"It's a Jersey thing. Pero's pizza is great; I just have to pretend it's not."

Over the intercom, Trish asked Andrea, "Do you want me to bring this up to y'all?"

"No, I think we are ready to come downstairs. Just save enough for us."

A few minutes later, Andrea entered the kitchen. Claudia and Lenora followed her. Immediately the questions started to fly.

"Let me say this," Andrea began. "Both have a lot to tell, but the bottom line is these women took matters into their own hands to right what they thought was a horrible injustice, to them and to other people they love. While they weren't responsible for Sonny's death, they did intend to scare the bejesus out of him, and they are really sorry about all this. They apologized profusely and I forgave them." Andrea smiled at the two ladies.

"Lanier seems to think they will be prosecuted, but he can probably get an agreement for community service. They're another example of what I'm talking about with my Women's Justice Center. Women get into some terrible situations, often because they have been betrayed by men, and we need to help them stand on their own."

Andrea looked positively evangelistic as the next idea came bubbling up, "Manicures! We will offer everyone free manicures!"

"Isn't that a little frivolous, compared to medical care and job training?" Cay asked.

"No, it isn't frivolous at all. It's about pride in oneself. The women who will come to the Center will be so lacking in self-esteem you couldn't believe it. Teaching them to love and care for themselves goes right to the heart of the matter."

Jordan beamed. "Get a manicure, save the world. I like it."

* * *

"These two are going to be my first community service volunteers, hugging Claudia and Lenora." Andrea began to applaud and the others followed suit.

"Why are we clapping?" Cay whispered to Jordan.

"I'm not sure," Jordan whispered back. "I'm clapping because they got away with it. You go, girls!"

The clapping started again at the end of the Thanksgiving meal when Isabelle came out of the kitchen carrying a tray with the pecan and pumpkin pies she and her mother had made. Mother, seated to the right of Vergy, basked in the glow of the compliments directed her way, occasionally checking the screen of her cell phone below the edge of the tablecloth to see how her bets on holiday football games were going.

"This scene is positively Dickensian," Cay said. "I think we were supposed to have learned something from all of this, but I'm not sure what."

EPILOGUE

It felt wonderful to be useful again. Isabelle always enjoyed feeling indispensable to Sonny, especially in the early days when he was new in the business, young and handsome. Oh, he had been a looker before drink and hubris bloated him and corrupted him from the inside out. Early on she had pictured herself as the heroine in a romance novel, like the scores she filled her time reading, and Sonny as her rescuer, protector, knight in shining armor.

Then she discovered Sonny was no hero at all. He lied, cheated, and caused innocent men and women to die when his shoddy projects collapsed. It was a good thing she wasn't a sentimental fool. She knew enough to plan ahead. After all, Sonny relied on her expertise to keep his books, and since she was required to keep two sets of records, she might as well keep three. Sonny never missed the regular amounts she deducted for a rainy day.

And rain it did, the day she discovered those documents and saw just how awful and intentional Sonny's cheating had been. Oh, yes, Mag Cramer was bad, but Sonny was worse, because he was her Sonny, her prince, her hero. Besides, by his own plotting, Mag was totally isolated now and unable to hurt anyone ever again. His undoing was a dividend she had not foreseen.

Isabelle loved working in the Women's Justice Center. She answered the phone, directed calls, filed, and typed on the beautiful computer Andrea bought her. Everyone expressed amazement over at how quickly Isabelle learned all sorts of computers skills. She merely smiled. As if she had been fool enough to keep three sets of books on an abacus. People were so naive. It was rather sweet.

Mother was gainfully employed, too, for the first time in many years. She made herself useful greeting people, making them feel at home, and occasionally offering betting tips on the side, which Isabelle discouraged.

Isabelle slid open her desk drawer to admire the paperclips and pens in orderly arrangements. She opened a small binder of memos and slid out several sheets of pink, scented paper. *Oh dear. Did I neglect to take care of those? Mustn't be careless.* She slipped the pages into the shredder next to her desk. A pleasant scent drifted through the office as the shredder blades whirred and sliced.

One non-computerized aid that Isabelle still used was her Rolodex. Nothing like having that actual card in front of you, so much easier to read than the computer's own address book. She hummed a little as she affectionately spun the bristling wheel. G . . . G . . . Grant, Grey . . . . The wheel flopped forward a couple of more cards and opened on the name Gypsy. *Perhaps I should remove that,* she thought smiling. *I don't imagine I'll have need of it again. On the other hand . . .* a woman betrayed will take revenge.

The End ...

Until the LitChix return in **Killer Condo**

Book Club Questions

When the LitChix attend their book club meetings, they love to discuss the questions authors provide with their books. Here are some questions about A Well-Manicured Murder that your book club might enjoy.

1. How important are your friendships with other women that you have made as an adult, as opposed to those friendships from your high school or college years? How do you keep up with these friends.

2. Of the three LitChix, Trish, Cay and Jordan, with whom do you most identify and why? Is she your favorite character? If not, who is your favorite character and why?

3. What is your reaction to Jordan's flirting. Do you think it is just playful and innocent, or is it the beginning of an import change in her life?

4. Cay is single, Trish is widowed and Jordan is unhappily married. Do you think a man is necessary to make a woman's life complete? Why?

5. Do you find that you can enjoy friendships with women who are vastly different than yourself? What are the important qualities you look for in friends?

6. Almost everything about Andrea changed when her husband was murdered. Do you think that a husband holds a woman back from even considering a significant life change?

7. Have you ever had an epiphany in your life? If so, what did you change? Was it a sustainable change? A positive one? Did others benefit from your change?

8. How significant is the Atlanta setting to the story? Did you learn anything about the city that you liked? Disliked? Did reading the book make you want to visit?

9. Were you surprised when you learned the identity of the killer? Did the last line in the epilogue make you think about a possible justification? What would you have done differently? Is killing ever justified? If so, what is your weapon of choice? How much do you charge? May I have your number?   GeorgiaAdams75@gmail.com

A Little Bit About the Authors

Patricia Melton Browning is a Florida native with a B.S from Florida State and an M.A. from the University of Florida. After moving to Atlanta, she taught history at Georgia State University. Patricia was President of the Jacksonville Junior League has held many leadership positions in civic organizations, but the title her friends won't let her forget is that of first runner-up for Miss Gum Turpentine, back in the day.

Patricia was the 2009 Atlanta Chapter President of Sisters in Crime, a national organization of mystery writers and fans, and it was she who uttered those fateful words to her friends Joann and Karen, " I'd like to write a mystery novel," which led to the LitChix and *A Well-Manicured Murder*.

Patricia lives in Atlanta with husband Philip. They have three adult children.

Joann Wasem Dunn was born in Illinois. She graduated *summa cum laude* from Bradley University in Peoria and received a *juris doctor* degree from Loyola University School of Law in Chicago.

She practiced law and taught in Chicago where she met her husband Kevin. They moved to Atlanta and later to Marietta and have two adult children. Joann responded to Patricia's musings about writing a novel by saying, "We can do that." She suffers from eternal optimism.

Joann writes in a number of genres including traditional fiction, poetry and humor. Two of her novels in the series *The Curtis Family Chronicles* were nominated by the Georgia Writer's Association for the best traditional fiction published in 2008 by a Georgia author .

Karen Purnell McColgan is a Jersey girl, born and bred. As soon as she stops saying "cawfee," she knows it is time to revisit her home turf. Karen has a B.S. and an M. Ed,. Specializing in the teaching of high risk students. In addition to teaching high school, she has been a guidance counselor, CFO of a real estate organization and has held positions in numerous community organizations. She is also a past president of the Atlanta Chapter of Sisters in Crime.

Karen has brought her eclectic knowledge and Jersey sensibility to the LitChix, not to mention her gift for one-liners .She and her husband Jim have one adult son and live in Atlanta.